guilty OF INNOCENCE

A NOVEL BY

WILLIAM C. COSTOPOULOS

Camino Books, Inc.

Philadelphia

Manufactured in the United States of America

1 2 3 4 5   03 02 01 00

Library of Congress Cataloging-in-Publication Data

Costopoulos, William C., 1944-
        Guilty of innocence / William C. Costopoulos.
           p.   cm.
        ISBN 0-940159-57-0 (alk. paper)
        I. Title.
PS3553.O76374G85 1999
813'.54—dc21   99-36755

Interior design: Jerilyn Kauffman

For information write:

Camino Books, Inc.
P.O. Box 59026
Philadelphia, PA 19102
www.caminobooks.com

Dedicated

to my beloved mother and father,
Katherine and Costos Costopoulos

ACKNOWLEDGMENTS

I want to thank David Foster, my friend and law partner for over twenty years, who helped write this book. His assistance went beyond editorial revision and rewriting. Thanks, Dave, for keeping me going.

This book could not have been written without my support staff at the office. I want to thank Tammy Weaber, who typed up the first draft; Kathryn Givler, who retyped the entire manuscript several times, and brought together our characters and plots; Susan Lichtenberger for all the corrections; Ami Gelbaugh for fixing my grammar and running the law office and my life; and Leslie Fields, my partner, for her tolerance.

I want to thank Nick Mallios, my beloved cousin, and the Lee Shore Agency for their brutal edit, which was much needed; this book may have been written without them, but it never would have been published.

I want to thank Jill, my wife, for her insights and encouragement. Thank you, Kara, Khristina, and Callista—my daughters and inspiration—for their patience and love.

CONTENTS

CHAPTER ONE

GONE

July 30, 1995.

The large moving van crept up the mile-long driveway, and though Hector Marquez had been in the moving business for fifteen years, this was no ordinary assignment. Normally, he and his men would work in broad daylight, but this move was taking place at 1 a.m. Normally, he would have one or two men with him and they could take whatever time was needed to move an entire household of furniture and belongings, but tonight he had less than two hours to get the job done. He was also told that he was to be on the Pennsylvania Turnpike heading west by 3:30 a.m., and that he was to follow the black, four-door Lexus, with the New York license plates, to wherever it was going. Hector didn't even know what the final destination was going to be.

But the attractive brunette who hired him had already paid him $5,000 in cash, and promised him an additional $10,000 when they got to where they were going. He could go all the way to Alaska for that kind of money, and he readily accepted her terms, with the understanding that what he was doing was legal, and he wouldn't get shot on the job.

She said, "It's legal."

She said, "You won't get shot."

She said, "Just make sure you have enough men to get it done on time."

She also said, "Don't ask any dumb fucking questions and do what I tell you when you get there."

Hector Marquez was a muscular Hispanic in his mid-thirties, with thick black hair and a black moustache. He had been self-employed all his life, and his veined forearms and massive back were evidence of years of heavy lifting. He had his older brother, Sylvio, with him in the cab of the truck, and four guys in the trailer who were nervous about this job, but the pay was too good to pass up.

A white board fence lined both sides of the driveway as they approached the house. Hector could tell he was in prime horse country, though all the pastures were empty at this hour. The mountain stone stable was on the left, and Hector knew from his explicit directions that the rustic home was straight ahead. He was told to back the rig up to the garage and wait until she came out.

"Hey, Hector," Sylvio said, breaking the silence, as Hector muscled his eighteen-wheeler in reverse toward the garage, "where in the hell are we?"

"I don't have any idea," Hector answered, wiping his forehead with the back of his hand. "All I know is what she told me, and here comes that crazy bitch now, so shut up."

Instantly, the electric garage door behind them started going up and Hector jumped out of the truck to get his instructions. She was tall, slender, and looked younger than her thirty-seven years, with shoulder-length, straight brown hair. Her piercing brown eyes flashed in the headlights as she ran toward Hector to get things moving. There was nothing complicated about her instructions.

"Take everything," she said.

Hector quickly ran up to the front porch and measured the huge oak front doors with his measuring tape. The front of the home was an expansive covered porch with plenty of windows overlooking the pastures and stable. The timber columns and wood railing that wrapped around the house and the four mountain stone chimneys above the cedar shake roof created a western look.

Hector then checked the back of the house for other convenient exits and noted sliding glass doors that went into the main bedroom, as well as a large, screened-in porch that accessed the living room. He could see the kitchen from the back of the house, and the adjoining dining room with its fourteen-foot sloped ceiling.

The six burly men went quickly from room to room moving ornate Victorian couches, brass beds, hand-carved mahogany bureaus, solid oak dining room furniture, Remington bronzes, western oil paintings, oriental rugs, crystal, and silver. The men ripped wires from the televisions, VCRs, stereos, and computers to save valuable time; and everything seemed to be going okay until Hector forced open one bedroom door to continue his mission.

In the corner of the bedroom, sitting on the bed, was a curly-haired girl, crying. She looked like she was ten or eleven years old, and still had on her floor-length cotton nightgown. The stuffed animals strewn on her bed, and perched on shelves in the corner, seemed to be watching her cry.

An older, gray-haired woman had her right arm around the child, trying to comfort her. She looked at Hector with pleading eyes as he burst in unannounced, but a tall, silver-haired man dressed in a double-breasted blue suit with a white collarless shirt stood between them and the door. All three occupants of that room, and Hector, froze momentarily in stunned silence.

"Wrong room, buddy," the silver-haired man said to Hector in a threatening voice.

"Call Blair Cody," yelled the old lady, "he's her father!"

"Get out of here!" the silver-haired man shouted, loud enough for every mover in the house to hear. Within seconds, Hector was confronted by the woman who had hired him, screaming in his face, ordering him to finish up, and to get his truck and men off the premises before they all got killed!

Hector wasted no time obeying *that* command, and within minutes the moving van was traveling at a high rate of speed down the driveway toward the American Truck Stop, where he was to wait for the black Lexus. Sylvio and their four helpers were only too glad to get out of there, and all five of them ran to their cars and pickup trucks when Hector dropped them off three miles before the truck plaza.

Hector double-checked the time on the dash of his truck with his wristwatch. The Lexus was late, and Hector was sick in his stomach. He had figured when he took the job that this was another domestic dispute, but he'd had no idea a kid was involved. Hector had three young children of his own at home, all sons, a loving wife, and he didn't need this shit. This was much more than he had bargained for, and he had a gnawing feeling that his involvement was far from over.

At 4:50 a.m., the Lexus pulled into the parking terminal, and soon Hector was shifting through all fifteen gears, following the car with the New York plates west on the Pennsylvania Turnpike. He could see the silver-haired man driving, and that the woman who hired him was in the passenger seat; what he could not see was the little girl, sound asleep in the back seat, under a soft blanket, out from a sedative; nor could he see the old lady back at the residence, crying uncontrollably in pain and anger, who could not call out because the phone lines had been cut.

◆ ◆ ◆

Michelle lowered the visor in the Lexus and checked her makeup and lipstick in the lighted mirror. Her milky white complexion was not as smooth as it used to be. She also hated what was happening to the corners of her eyes, but she had not been sleeping well, and she knew those little cosmetic problems could be taken care of by some minor professional procedures. She could also see in the mirror Hector's truck following close behind them, just like she told him to.

Michelle Lynn Cody, still rebounding from their bitter divorce, had been married to Blair for twelve years. She had met him when she was twenty-three years old, and at that time had dreams of becoming a professional model. She was five feet eight, and had a fine body, glamorous brown hair, and deep-set, piercing brown eyes that were forever inviting. Her dreams had never materialized, and she blamed it on her lack of connections and not being at the right place at the right time. For the past several years, she had blamed it on a marriage that had taken her out of the mainstream of professional life, and having a daughter didn't help.

Pregnancy had blemished her once-flawless body, and the scarring on her abdomen was a constant reminder. It's not that she minded being a mother, she just didn't really love it, and it certainly didn't fit in with her plans.

Michelle had met Blair at a victory party at the Penn Harris Hotel in downtown Harrisburg — Pennsylvania's capital city — in the fall of 1981. Her Republican boss, Senator Stewart Greenfield, had just been re-elected to the Pennsylvania Senate after a close race, and everybody was wining and dining in regal fashion. Over four hundred people at this black-tie affair were enjoying the best of chilled champagne in long-stemmed crystal glasses, and hors d'oeuvres — caviar, Swedish meatballs, brie, oriental skinless chicken, and stuffed mushrooms — artistically laid out on pink, lace-covered tables, in the glow of candles in silver candelabra.

Michelle was first assistant to the senator's executive secretary, and though she didn't like being an assistant to anyone, it was a good state job with full benefits. Her father, Thomas Fitzgerald Keating, the influential chairman of the state's Republican Committee, had gotten her the job with one phone call to the good senator's office. Blair was attending the party because he had been a major contributor to Greenfield's campaign. When Michelle was introduced to him by her boss, she felt an instant attraction.

But that was fourteen years ago. Now, the divorce was final and Michelle was going to do what she wanted.

"You know you're beautiful, honey," John said, as he too checked the rearview mirror to make sure that Hector was still with them. John Morgan, fifty-five, a tall, thin man, clean-shaven, with manicured nails and soft hands, was soon to be Michelle's new husband.

John and Michelle had met less than two years ago at the Taj Mahal Casino in Atlantic City, New Jersey, where they were both playing the slot machines while Blair was in the poker room enjoying a high-stakes seven-card-stud game. John immediately liked what he saw, and when he told her that he was an editor for *Vogue* magazine, she told him that she was a professional model. John certainly dressed the part that night in his conventional black tuxedo, with starched white shirt, black tie, and black patent-leather shoes. Michelle also looked like the model she said she was, in a white satin chemise and matching spike-heeled shoes.

"Honey," John said, again breaking the silence, "what's Blair going to do when he gets home tonight and realizes what happened?"

Michelle didn't answer and continued to stare straight ahead. Billowing smoke could be seen on the distant horizon from Pittsburgh's steel mills. Huge trucks whizzed by them going in the opposite direction on the Pennsylvania Turnpike.

Michelle hadn't said one word since they left the house earlier that morning. She knew that this had been her last time in the house she once called home, but it didn't bother her. Over the last twelve years she had come to resent the secluded ranch, her marriage, and what she considered to be the life that was forced on her. Being back at that house, however, brought back repressed memories and rekindled her bitterness.

When the divorce had been finalized between Michelle and Blair, the property settlement wasn't satisfactory to her. Tonight's effort at the house evened things out; and even though custody and visitation of Courtney Louise was all Blair Cody ever cared about, it was going to be a long, long time before that issue was resolved.

Unless, of course, Blair came up with a revised property settlement.

Blair had spent enough money on her, adorning her with fur coats, diamonds, and a four-door, pearl-burgundy Jaguar; but the money he spent on her, and her generous personal expense account, was really no sacrifice on Blair's part because he had a lot of money. He had made it practicing law, and though he was highly regarded as a top-notch criminal defense lawyer, he had hit a home run with a $12 million personal injury verdict.

Their sex life, even after Courtney was born, had been heated enough.

It's just that after Courtney was born, things changed between them. Blair went crazy over Courtney Louise from the day she was born, and Michelle constantly accused him of loving Courtney more than her. Blair also had a hard time dealing with Michelle's modeling aspirations.

Then there was that awful incident in Lawton, Oklahoma, when Blair's father was killed.

Michelle was convinced that John Morgan was her ticket. He boasted about his wealth — he referred to it as "old money." Generous and thoughtless in his spending, he sported a flawless diamond ring, drove a $50,000 car, and bought Michelle whatever suited her fancy.

He also cared about her career. He constantly reassured her that her looks were stunning enough to make it. *Vogue, Cosmopolitan,* and especially the European print media were looking for the more "mature" look in women because that's what all the controlling, rich baby boomers wanted.

John said he was married once, and childless, but divorced because the spark wasn't there. Even if Courtney never loved him as much as her dad, John would at least be a good father, and was certain that he could love Courtney.

"Is Courtney still out?" John asked, again checking his rearview mirror to see if Hector was keeping up with John's seventy-five-mile-an-hour pace as the two vehicles rolled by the Pittsburgh exit, deadheading toward Ohio.

"Yes," Michelle answered, glancing over her shoulder to the back seat.

"What did you give her, honey?" John asked.

"One of those quaaludes you gave me," Michelle answered in a matter-of-fact tone.

"Those things work well," John said.

"Yes," Michelle answered, staring straight ahead.

CHAPTER TWO

TROUBLE

Blair Cody decided to work the five-year-old gelding early that morning. The horse was a pretty little chestnut appaloosa, with a white blaze and four white socks, sired by Impressive Prince. By noon the sun would be scorching the sand floor in Rocky's large, oval riding pen outside of Lexington, Virginia. It was already eighty degrees and humid.

With his mirrored sunglasses sparkling in the sun, Blair anxiously tightened his saddle and mounted Impressive James. Rocky B. Jones, who trained the fiesty appaloosa as a reining horse, watched from the perimeter.

Blair walked the relaxed gelding into the center of the pen, stopped, and did four quick spins to the left. Blair paused, gently pulled the reins to his right pocket, and the gelding blurred four spins to the right. On cue, the horse picked up its right lead and ran several fast circles to the right, shifted gears to a slow right circle, switched leads, and repeated the circle pattern to the left.

The horse switched again, and now going to the right but not closing the circle, ran the alley and did a perfect twenty-five-foot sliding stop.

"Perfect!" Rocky yelled.

Blair then rolled the spirited gelding back to the left, and going back over his tracks, rounded the top of the pen and did another sliding stop, creating a cloud of stone, dust, and sand.

"Perfect!" Rocky yelled again, excited. "Back him up, Cody."

Blair had made the five-hour drive to Rocky's training center to find a solid horse for his kid. Courtney Louise, though only eleven years old, could ride the hair off a reining horse. Last year, Courtney had made the top ten in the national rankings and was the youngest rider in history to do so.

Blair had been bringing Courtney to Rocky's training facility since she was two years old, and they were both very proud of her. Rocky's ranch, known as Jones'N On Horses, was a complex of indoor and outdoor arenas and metal barns with cupolas.

"That little gelding's going to work," Rocky said to Blair as Blair approached him, leading the horse to the fence where Rocky was sitting.

"This bronc better not hurt my kid," Blair answered, smiling.

"This horse will test her, Blair, but you and I both know that's what she wants," Rocky said.

"How much, Rocky?" Blair asked.

"That's one hell of a horse, Blair," Rocky said as his horse-trader mode kicked in. "Impressive James is going to make your kid a star!"

"How much, Rocky?" Blair asked, knowing the ritual.

"$15,000," Rocky answered without batting an eye.

"$10,000," Blair responded, having been down this road many times.

"$12,500," Rocky countered, "but only because I love you, buddy."

"Sold," Blair said, closing the deal, knowing the horse was worth every penny that Rocky was asking. Blair also knew that a vet check for soundness wasn't necessary.

Rocky was a leather-necked, sixty-year-old horse trainer who chewed tobacco, chain-smoked, drank too much Seagram's whiskey, and had been divorced three times. He was also a gambling man—laying everything on the line in the reining pen—and for the past three decades had set the standard for the reining horse industry by never playing it safe. His health defiantly withstood it all as he became the first trainer in the National Reining Horse Association (NRHA) to reach the million-dollar mark in winnings.

Blair liked and trusted Rocky. They had met nine years ago in Oklahoma City at the NRHA National Finals for three-year-old reining horses. Blair introduced himself and asked Rocky if he was willing to take on another customer. Rocky said yes, and three weeks later Blair showed up at his facility in Lexington, Virginia, with his two-year-old kid.

Rocky never saw Courtney without jeans, roper boots, jingling spurs, and a baseball cap down over her eyes; and never without her dad. She was a skinny little girl who loved horses, drove a red motorized scooter from the barn to the show pens, and played baseball in the summer with the boys her age. The brown-eyed kid thought she was a tough little cowgirl, which she was, and her Shirley Temple curls were so naturally tight that they jumped on her head like springs when she ran.

But, tough or not, she was still Blair's little girl, and he insisted that she hold his hand whenever they walked anywhere; and up until last year, Courtney had played with Barbie dolls, dress-up, and make-believe, and had had her picture taken while sitting on Santa Claus' lap.

"I'm telling you, Blair, that gelding you're taking home is going to work for Courtney. He's one of my better ones," Rocky said as he and Blair sipped fresh coffee in Rocky's office, which overlooked his indoor riding ring. Rocky's desk had steerhorn legs, as did all the chairs and couches, which were covered in cowhide. It gave you the feeling that you were among a herd of cattle, and that was fine if you liked cattle. Everywhere in his office were statues of bronze reining horses doing their slide, hard-won trophies of the last thirty years. His walls were covered with ribbons and winner's photos.

"Thanks, Rocky," Blair replied. "I can't wait to get him home and surprise her."

Outside, Impressive James was tied to Blair's four-horse trailer, which was hooked up to his customized dually, a rig that had more lights than most circus wagons. Impressive James was already washed and brushed down, and would soon be traveling north to his new home in Pennsylvania.

"Rocky, do you mind if I use your phone?" Blair asked. Blair wanted to call home to make sure everything was all right, and to let his mother and Courtney know that he would be home before dinner. His mother hadn't driven since his father's death, and Courtney was home alone with her grandmother. Because it was Sunday, the ranch hands weren't around.

"No problem, Blair," Rocky answered.

Blair dialed his home number. There was no answer.

Blair had been gone for over twenty-four hours. When he called last night to check on them, everything was okay. The situation at home for the past year had been difficult, but was getting better with each passing day. Michelle had left him and Courtney in January without any warning or explanation.

Because Blair had given Michelle everything she wanted, or so he thought, the divorce was an uncontested paper ceremony that ended twelve years of marriage. Her mega-firm lawyers had wanted a $2 million cash settlement in exchange for signing off on the house and possessions. They had also agreed in writing that Blair would get Courtney, and that Michelle would have unrestricted visitation.

Courtney had not seen or heard from her mother in three months, and Blair didn't know where she was, or even care.

Blair repeatedly called home from his car phone. There was no answer.

He called again, and again, and again. Still no answer.

Blair's heart began to race. He was no stranger to anxiety since his father's death. The familiar surge of guilt and anger would never go away. He convinced himself that the phone was off the hook as his rig rolled north on Route 81.

It was almost dark when he turned into his driveway. The sun was just beginning to set on the horizon, casting a fiery glow in the distant sky. As Blair passed his barn, four quarter horses and a yearling ran along the fence row following his rig, and Impressive James whinnied from within the trailer. All seemed quiet enough on the home front when Blair finally pulled into the turnaround in front of the house.

Blair glanced at the garage door that was still wide open. Then, before he got to the front door, his mother came onto the porch, crying. "Don't go in!" she sobbed.

"What's wrong, Mother?" Blair asked, terrified. "Where's Courtney, Mother?"

"Blair, Blair," his mother cried hysterically, a cry he had heard before.

"Courtney is gone, Blair! Courtney is gone!"

◆ ◆ ◆

Early the next morning.

Blair walked past the receptionist without saying a word. Several businessmen were already waiting in the lobby for Keating to discuss important business, dressed in dark, pin-striped suits, with their briefcases placed neatly on the floor beside their shiny shoes. The young girl at the front desk frantically buzzed her boss to warn him of the unannounced visit, and Blair could hear her apologizing to her boss, "Your ex-son-in-law is headed your way. I tried to stop him, but he wouldn't listen."

Blair walked in on Thomas Fitzgerald Keating, who was sitting behind his ornate mahogany desk in his tufted leather chair. Michelle's father was Pennsylvania's GOP chairman, the former lieutenant governor of the commonwealth, and had amassed an incredible power base over the years. Keating's influence encompassed the governor's office, the state legislature, Philadelphia government, the business community, the courts, and the banking industry. In a newspaper summary of power players in the Commonwealth of Pennsylvania, his name appeared at the top of the list.

Photos in Keating's office, on the twenty-first floor of Liberty Place—a building considerably taller than City Hall—showed him with a variety of well-known faces: former President Eisenhower, Supreme Court Justice David Cappy, Governor Maxwell Foster, and United States Senators Bob Wambaugh and Jesse Arnette. Philadelphia District Attorney Ed Riggins was Keating's best friend. Over the years, Keating had made a lot of friends as lieutenant governor of Pennsylvania and as comptroller of the GOP coffers.

Today, however, the only picture that got Blair's attention, as he was sitting across from his father-in-law, was the picture on Keating's desk of Courtney with her mother.

"Where is she?" Cody asked, trying to keep his composure.

"Blair," Keating answered, puffing on his Cohiba cigar, pushing his chair back from the desk, "like I told you last night on the phone, I don't have any idea where Courtney, or Michelle, is. She certainly didn't tell me about Sunday's doings. I haven't heard from Michelle in weeks, and you didn't have to drive here this morning from Harrisburg for me to tell you the same thing I told you last night."

"Where was she before Sunday?" Blair asked.

"She was living in New York City, Blair," Keating answered, "but that isn't going to help you because after your call last night, I called her there and the phone has been disconnected."

"Give me the New York address and I'll check for a forwarding one," Blair suggested, determined. He didn't believe for one second that Keating was as innocent as he claimed.

"I . . . I'm not going to do that, Blair," Keating responded, annoyed, "because I don't want to get in the middle of this. I just don't want to get involved. Michelle is still my daughter, and this divorce has already caused me a lot of embarrassment."

Blair stood up and walked to the corner window of Keating's office, and looked down onto Chestnut Street. Below, the early-morning traffic was just beginning to back up. The City of Brotherly Love didn't feel too brotherly as Blair thought about his painful situation.

Blair knew that Keating, at age sixty-five, was a tough-fisted power broker who cared about one thing, and one thing only: his power base, the perception of his power base, and not even *his* family was going to get in the way of that, let alone Blair's.

Blair and Keating had never gotten along. Keating told Blair on too many occasions that Blair's attitude about life, his defense of criminals, and his damn horses were in wanton and reckless disregard of how the world worked.

Blair, at forty-two, had a rugged look, with straight black hair that was long in the back and short on the sides. He was clean-shaven and stood six feet tall, with an athlete's build, though he had never participated in organized sports. He went to college at Texas A&M and back then rode broncs. While in law school, at Stanford University in California, he roped calves on weekends. Maybe his love for horses and rodeos had to do with growing up on a small farm outside of Lawton, Oklahoma . . . most likely, however, it had to do with his outlook on life, his attitude.

"Mr. Keating," Blair said, without turning around, still looking out the window, "you know I'm going to find Michelle."

"You'd better use the civil process," Keating replied, threatening.

"Like Michelle did on Sunday?" Blair shot back sarcastically, controlling his voice, but feeling the anger.

"Blair," Keating continued, now on the defensive, "don't do anything foolish."

"All I want is Courtney back," Blair answered, now looking straight at Keating, "and I'm going to find her."

There was nothing more to say.

Blair, his hands in his pockets, walked aimlessly up Chestnut Street to his car. A steady rain began to drench the streets, forming small streams in the gutters. The people walking by hastened toward their destinations, and umbrellas were being sold on the corners. It was the first storm after several weeks of blistering heat, and steam rose from the asphalt and concrete sidewalks.

CHAPTER THREE

WEST

The black Lexus and Hector's truck were parked side by side in the crowded McDonald's parking lot on the outskirts of Denver, Colorado. Outside, several cars were backed up at the take-out window.

Inside, the fast-food restaurant was bustling with noisy people clamoring for their food. In the far corner, by the McDonald's playland patio, at a small table on four plastic chairs, sat John, Michelle, Courtney, and Hector.

John Morgan and Michelle had taken turns driving straight through for the past thirty-six hours, stopping only for gas and something to eat. Courtney had slept in the back seat for over twelve hours, and when she woke up, she lay there, pretending to still be asleep.

"Eat some of your fries and Chicken McNuggets, honey," Michelle said to Courtney. Courtney just sat there, staring down at the food as she picked at it. She was still sick in her stomach from the "aspirin" her mother gave her, but Courtney wouldn't tell her mother that she wasn't feeling well.

"How are you holding up, Hector?" John asked, chewing his chicken sandwich.

Hector just shook his head.

"We had to do it this way, Hector," Michelle said. "I'm her mother, and she needs to be with me."

"Her dad," John added, "is capable of anything, if you know what I mean."

Courtney didn't like anybody talking about her dad. She overheard her mom and John talking about him in the car. Her mom said that he would come looking for them, and that Hector could be a problem.

She also overheard John say something about California, and how his contacts were good ones. He told her mom it would be a great place for her to take some acting classes, which could only help her career. Something was also said about magazines.

"Can I ride with Hector?" Courtney asked, without looking up.

"Why, honey?" Michelle asked sweetly.

"I'm tired of riding in the back seat, and I'll be able to see better," Courtney answered, still looking down at her food.

"It's okay with me," Michelle replied. "What do you think, John?"

"We're going to have to get some rest," John said as he finished up his Big Mac and Coke.

Hector nodded.

"We'll check into the next motel we see," John continued, "and we'll roll out about midnight tonight. I don't see any problem with Courtney riding with Hector."

◆ ◆ ◆

Courtney sat in the cab of Hector's truck, a big Mac cab-over with chrome wheels and fuel tank, and a chrome California antenna secured to the mirror, pulling a forty-eight-foot trailer.

She was staring straight ahead into the darkness as his eighteen-wheeler crawled through the Rocky Mountains of the West. At this hour there was no sightseeing, only darkness, and the tail-lights of the Lexus in front of them. Hector had to shift down from his fifteen gears more than once to climb some of the steep grades. His diesel engine roared, and black smoke billowed out of the two chrome exhaust pipes that looked like periscopes above the cab's roof.

"Do you have any kids, Hector?" Courtney asked, still staring ahead, breaking the silence.

"Yeah," Hector answered. "I have three little boys at home. One is your age, and the other two are younger."

Then, just like that, Courtney went back into her silent world. She was dressed in new green Esprit shorts, with a matching jacket, and new white Reeboks. She continued to stare out the window, wondering if she could trust him.

"I have a pillow and blanket if you want to lie down," Hector said.

"No thank you," Courtney answered politely. "I'm not sleepy."

"I've got some candy in the glove box," Hector said, pointing to it.

Courtney opened the glove box and took out a bag of M&M's.

"Thanks," she said.

There were a million questions that Courtney had as they got onto an expressway. She saw a sign along the highway that read *Utah*. She wanted to trust Hector, but couldn't be sure. He was trying to be friendly, and seemed like a nice man.

"Where are we going?" Courtney asked innocently.

"I don't have any idea, Courtney," Hector answered. "I wish I did. I don't have any idea whatsoever. Do . . . do you have any idea?"

"No," Courtney answered.

"How did your mom know that your dad wouldn't be home?" Hector asked.

"She left me and Dad a long time ago," Courtney began, and

continued, "I didn't even know where she was. She called once in a while to talk to me, but not very often. She called Saturday afternoon . . . I think it was Saturday afternoon. When did you and Mom come to the house?" Courtney asked.

"Early Sunday morning, Courtney, about 1 a.m." Hector answered.

"Then it was Saturday afternoon because she asked me where Dad was. I told her he went to Rocky's to look at a horse for me and wouldn't be back until Sunday night. Grandma Cody was watching me," Courtney said, thinking it through.

Hector just shook his head as he drove. Courtney sensed that Hector was upset. She wanted to ask him something, a favor, but she hardly knew him. Maybe he would tell her mother.

"I didn't know you were going to be there," Hector said apologetically.

Courtney did not respond. She thought about it, and thought about it some more, then glanced over at Hector several times when she didn't think he was watching. She finally concluded that she had nothing to lose.

"Will you call my dad, Hector?" Courtney asked, looking straight ahead, with a lot of reservations about the question that meant most to her.

Hector didn't answer at first. Courtney watched him closely, and held her breath.

"I . . . I don't know, Courtney," Hector answered. "I could get in a lot of trouble."

"My dad won't hurt you," Courtney said.

"Your mom said he would shoot us," Hector answered.

Courtney didn't say any more after that about calling her dad. In the quiet lull that followed, Courtney dozed off into a deep sleep on the goosedown pillow and blanket Hector gave her.

◆ ◆ ◆

It was 6 a.m. Courtney was still sound asleep in Hector's cab. The Salt Lake City Auto Truck Plaza, off of Route 80 in Utah, was busy at the diesel islands with huge eighteen-wheelers fueling up for their long trips east and west, north and south. Kenworths, Macs, Peterbilts, Freightliners—conventionals and cab-overs—with their boxed trailers, tankers, lowboys, and flatbeds loaded with heavy construction equipment, steel coils, and chained logs, were either lined up or neatly parked side by side on the acres of blacktop. The fuel smog hovered like an isolated cloud on an otherwise perfect western morning.

Big truckers, almost uniformly dressed in their blue jeans and black t-shirts, with cowboy and Harley Davidson hats, belts, and chained wallets, were standing around chatting among themselves. They were like old friends, though most of them didn't know each other and would never see each other again.

Inside, the restaurant was crowded and noisy, and the waitresses and kitchen help were as loud as their customers. John and Michelle were in a corner booth by themselves, and looked as out of place as their Lexus did in the parking lot. John was figuring out on a napkin how much support money they would be getting from Blair if all went as planned. John's calculations, based on what Michelle told him, came to almost $5,000 a month. A big bite of Michelle's $2 million settlement had been taken when she paid for their new home near Beverly Hills; and the additional money would help maintain their current lifestyle.

Michelle had told Hector to take some milk and vanilla-frosted doughnuts to Courtney, but not to wake her up.

After Hector gassed up and parked his rig in formation, he locked the cab and ran in for a quick shower. As he was leaving the terminal to go back to his truck, with his bag of doughnuts and milk in hand, he noticed Courtney among truckers at a bank of phones along a wall by the bathrooms. She was easy to notice among the crowd in her bright green Esprit outfit, and because of her size.

Hector stopped suddenly, staring in her direction, thought for a moment, then quickly moved on, hoping she would get away with it. Courtney was calling her dad. She had to ask one of the truckers beside her for some help making the long-distance call, and even had to ask for a quarter. Her helper, a big, burly, red-bearded trucker wearing a black leather baseball cap, dug in his tight jeans for change.

◆ ◆ ◆

On the very first ring, Blair grabbed the phone. For the past three days, he had contacted the police, but to no avail. The desk sergeant told him, "This is a domestic matter to be dealt with in the civil courts." Blair then called every friend and relative of Michelle's that he could think of, but they knew nothing, they said. He also hired a longtime friend of his, a private investigator, Pat Greely, who specialized in missing persons. And finally, he paced and waited for Courtney to call.

"Hello," Blair said, hoping.

"Dad!" Courtney said, whispering, then broke down and cried.

"Where are you, Court?" Blair asked hurriedly, his heart racing with excitement.

"I . . . I don't know, Dad . . . at a truck stop . . . I don't know where," Courtney answered, still crying softly.

"Court, are you okay?"

"I'm okay . . . but I want to come home."

"Are you still with your mom?"

"Yes."

"Do you know where you're going?" Blair asked.

"No."

"I'm going to come get you, as soon as I can find you, Court, but you're going to have to help me."

"I will, Dad."

"Is anybody with you?"

"Not right now."

"I mean with your mom, with you. Is anybody else with you and your mom?"

"Some guy named John, I don't know his last name. I think he's mom's boyfriend."

"Does John have white hair?"

"Sort of."

"Anybody else?"

"Hector."

"Hector? Who's Hector?"

"He's the guy driving the truck with the furniture. I've been riding with him."

"Courtney, do what I tell you."

"Okay, Dad."

"The next time you get a chance to call me, and I'm going to wait right here next to the phone, call me with the license plate number of the car you're in, and the truck. Do you understand, Court?"

"Yes . . . Dad . . . I have to go now . . . I just saw Mom and John walk out the door . . . I love you, Dad."

Before Blair could say "I love you" back, Courtney hung up the phone.

For several seconds Blair held the dead phone to his ear, listening to the dial tone. As he slowly hung up the phone, he felt some relief, some excitement, but guilt and pain overwhelmed him. He still didn't know where Courtney was, or where she was going, or who John was, or who Hector was, or when he would hear from Courtney again.

Blair had barely slept since Courtney disappeared; he couldn't eat and had lost weight; between the four-day growth on his face and the stress in his eyes, he looked like he had aged ten years. He was overwhelmed by the raging guilt, feelings of helplessness, and anger. Why did he leave Courtney overnight with his defenseless mother when he knew something like this was possible? What was Courtney being put through? Was she really all right?

Blair retreated into a world of silence, a world familiar to him since he had watched his father die, a world of visible darkness, a world of relentless, gnawing anxiety. For the past several nights, he had lain awake in Courtney's bed—her furniture hadn't been taken, her stuffed toys weren't moved, even her clothes were untouched—and there were times in the darkness of that room when Blair swore he heard Courtney calling him, like she always did when she needed him; but Blair couldn't get to her, or reach her, or find her, though he could distinctly hear her, louder and louder. Then Blair would sit up, wondering if it was a dream, or whether he was awake and losing his mind.

Yet, throughout the depths of his depression, Blair vowed to himself that he was going to wait it out, no matter what it took, or how long, not only for his sake, but for Courtney's as well. Blair was consumed with thoughts of getting her back, and how that would happen.

Blair also had thoughts of revenge.

Chapter Four

LEADS

Blair received the second call from Courtney six hours later. She whispered the two license plate numbers, and though she didn't know where she was, she had seen a sign to Las Vegas.

"Good job, Court," Blair said. "Are you okay?"

"I have to go, Dad," Courtney answered, and the phone went dead.

Finally, Blair had something to work with. The leads Courtney gave him may not have been enough to get him to her, but they were enough to get him to the person or persons who could.

Blair immediately put his home phone on call forwarding. He alerted Ami at his office to stand by for Courtney's call, just in case it came while he made the twenty-minute drive from his home. He explained what was going on to his mother, and asked her to watch the house.

Blair arrived at his law offices on the fourth floor of Strawberry Square, in downtown Harrisburg, across from the state capitol building and the federal courthouse. His offices were professionally decorated, in dark, somber colors, with solid walnut furnishings. Brass chandeliers illuminated the foyer and reception area. The library was the conference room, dominated by a huge, oval, polished walnut table, surrounded by twelve tapestry-covered chairs. Blair's personal office included a wall of barrister cases with antique law books, and an antique partner's desk. At one time, his office was his second home.

"Ami," Blair said as he got off the elevator, "get me Pat Greely on the phone right away."

"Sure," Ami answered, and immediately began dialing.

"Put Courtney through if she calls, and no one else," Blair added as he headed for his office.

Ami nodded her head.

Blair asked Pat Greely to drop everything and get to his office immediately. Pat Greely was a former central intelligence agent with the federal government, recently retired, and at fifty years old, looked the part with his gaunt face, reading glasses, receding hairline, pinstriped suit, and wingtips; he was so ordinary-looking that he could disappear in any crowd, which was perfect for the life of a private investigator who specialized in missing persons. Pat was also Blair's good friend, and had been for years.

Blair, still unshaven, dressed in blue jeans and ostrich boots, with a white t-shirt under his buckskin sport coat, met Greely in the conference room to brief him. Blair told Greely what had happened to Courtney, and about her phone calls.

"It won't take me long to trace these tags," Greely said encouragingly. "I still have my connections, you know."

"Thanks, Pat," Blair said, "and I want you to call me with the information as soon as you get it. . . . I also want you to find out everything you can about the owners of those two vehicles. I want to know where they live, what they do for a living, whether they are married, whether they have children, where their children go to school, anything that will help me run them down, or get word to them, immediately."

"I get the picture," Greely said, shaking his head.

"I know you do."

"When is Courtney going to call again?" Greely asked.

"I don't have a clue," Blair answered, "but I can't wait any longer to get moving on this thing. I'm going crazy waiting around. I'm going fucking crazy!"

"I understand," Greely said.

"Thanks, Pat."

"Hey, Blair," Greely added.

"What?"

"Don't do anything foolish."

Blair stayed at the office until dark. He asked Ami to wait at the office until he got home in case Courtney called again. For hours the phone at the house was silent, and in the sparsely furnished dining room, he and his mother talked things through.

He knew that his mother was heartsick. She told him repeatedly that she wished she could have locked Courtney's door and called the police before the silver-haired man took them hostage. She said she could still see that man standing over her and Courtney in his fancy suit, and helping Michelle carry the child out to their car.

Her anguish only added to Blair's as he held his mother's trembling hand while she wept. He tried to convince her that she was not responsible for Courtney's abduction, not in any way. He assured her that everything was going to be all right, and that Courtney would be coming home soon.

Hours later, after midnight—well after Mrs. Cody was asleep— the phone rang. Blair answered it on the first ring, and Pat Greely reeled off the facts like a computer printout.

Pat told Blair that the New York license plate belonged to a black, four-door Lexus LX, leased six months ago to a man named John Morgan. Morgan was a contributing editor for *Vogue* magazine, with business offices on Madison Avenue in New York. Two weeks ago, he quit without any advance notice. Morgan was fifty-five years old, never married, had no children, and had lived at 64 Prince Street, SoHo.

"The Pennsylvania license plate number Courtney gave you, Blair, must be wrong," Pat continued. "I checked it out, and the number given just doesn't exist. I intend to run every combination of numbers, but you know that's going to take a long time.

"Now, back to this guy Morgan. He's either a deadbeat, or he's having real money problems. He's behind on the car lease three months, and on the apartment six months."

"Any criminal record on John Morgan?" Blair asked.

"Yes, one count of possession of child pornography. It was five years ago and he got probation," Pat answered.

"Child pornography!" Blair gasped.

"Yeah," Pat replied, "but I called a prosecutor friend of mine in Manhattan, and he ran it at his office for me. He said it didn't look like that big of a deal. The judge didn't order counseling or anything, and the fine was only $500."

"I don't like it," Blair said.

"I knew you wouldn't," Pat conceded.

"I'll take it from here," Blair added, and thanked Pat again.

◆　◆　◆

They had traveled over three thousand miles in six days and five nights. They had slept in a Motel 6 outside of Denver, and in a Holiday Inn west of Vegas, frequently napping in their vehicles at roadside rests. To save time, they ate at fast-food restaurants or truck stops, and usually got their food to go.

Courtney, since she hooked up with Hector at the McDonald's days ago, refused to ride with Michelle and John.

Michelle didn't care who Courtney rode with because she had other things on her mind. She knew Blair was going to do whatever he had to do to get Courtney back. She just needed some time to get situated, and was willing, although she wasn't crazy about the idea, to marry John to create the appearance of a stable family environment. She knew that's what the custody courts would be interested in. Michelle wanted the estimated $5,000 a month in child support, or a heftier cash settlement.

"It really looked terrible when you left your daughter," Michelle's father had told her the last time they talked. Though Michelle was thousands of miles away, she could still hear her father's gruff voice echoing in her head.

Her father also told her that he had made some calls about John. He warned her that John had no money or assets, and lived from paycheck to paycheck. He added that a prenuptial agreement would be in her best interest, and that John should have no problem with it if he was marrying her because he loved her. John said he loved her and wanted to marry her, but he would not sign any prenuptial agreement.

John insisted that he had plenty of money, but most of it was tied up in off-shore investments. "To beat the IRS," he said. He told Michelle that her father, of course, could not trace it.

John was tall, thin, took care of himself, and dressed in expensive, casual clothes. His nails were always manicured, and he kept his silver hair professionally styled, often colored blond. He also had a charming personality, and unlike Blair, laughed easily, loved dancing, loved parties, and kept up with the times. Michelle also enjoyed the recreational use of cocaine that he introduced to her. They kept it private, and she enjoyed it more than she was willing to admit to herself. Even on their way to California, they kept a small vial hidden under the dash, which came in handy when they got sleepy.

She was a little bothered, however, because their sex life was not that great. She assumed John's frequent "inability"—she would never use the word impotence—was due to his age, or maybe the cocaine use. It got to the point that it wasn't worth the effort, the stress, or the anxiety it caused.

John would never talk about it.

Michelle told herself that for the modeling career she always dreamed about, there would have to be some small sacrifices. She also believed that John could help her realize her dreams. He did get her that photo shoot at *Vogue*, something she would never have been able to get on her own. The resulting portfolio was fantastic. Maybe they could get something done with it, now that they were minutes away from the movie capital of the world, where beautiful people were loved and appreciated.

"There it is," John said, as they crested a hill overlooking Hollywood. Michelle was excited about this moment, and playfully put on her Oakley wrap-around sunglasses.

Michelle looked across the majestic, panoramic view with a horizon line of seven miles. The infamous Los Angeles haze wasn't there, and she looked at the great stretch of homes and hills that seemed to go on forever. It was far different from the remote farm in Pennsylvania, or the crowded streets and high-rises that blocked the sun in New York. Even the sun seemed more brilliant here, and Michelle couldn't wait to put on her bikini and walk the beaches of the Pacific coast.

But first, they would go straight to their new home.

A realtor in Pennsylvania, a friend of Michelle's father, had contacted a realtor in Hollywood who found the house and handled the closing. Michelle had viewed several videos mailed to them by the energetic salesman from California, and she fell in love with the sprawling, rose-colored, stucco ranch house located high in the Hollywood Hills. The video captured the view of the valley from the burgundy-tiled terrace; and the kidney-shaped swimming pool in the back yard, with a separate cabana, was the perfect party setting for her.

The interior of their new home was in shades of white and cream, with black and white Spanish-tiled floors, arched doorways, floor-to-ceiling windows, and French doors. Michelle wasn't sure that the furniture they were bringing was going to work, but if it didn't, there was plenty of time to shop and decorate. Besides, she had given Blair the parting shot she felt he deserved by taking as many of his possessions as she could.

And Courtney.

The lot to their new home and the black, macadamized driveway were small. Michelle could see that Hector was having a difficult time backing his eighteen-wheeler to the front door, where he was to unload. The California realtor, whom John called on the car phone when they were two hours from the house, made arrangements to have three laborers to help move in the furniture and belongings. John had already said that he wasn't lifting anything, and that he wasn't going to help.

The realtor also had the utilities turned on in advance, and the phones hooked up. The central air conditioning was hard at work as the outside temperature rose above one hundred degrees.

The furniture, piece by piece, was carefully unloaded by Hector and three guys he didn't know (they didn't even exchange first names); and the unloading of Hector's trailer took far, far more time than it had taken to load it one week before. It was not only a slower operation, but Michelle changed her mind, over and over again, as to what should go where. Hector said nothing, and showed no emotion, but the California boys were awfully impatient and took repeated breaks.

Michelle got suspicious when Courtney went to the master bedroom and shut the door. She put her ear up against the door, and could hear Courtney whispering.

"Dad," Courtney said, "we're here."

"I love you, Dad," she added after a slight pause.

"I got the address off the mailbox," Courtney continued, still whispering. "It's ... "

Michelle rushed in, grabbed the phone from Courtney's hand, and hit her across the face with the receiver. Courtney fell back, covering up her bleeding mouth with both hands, crying in pain and screaming, "Don't ... don't ... please don't, Mom."

Michelle slammed the phone down and continued to slap Courtney in the face with her open hand.

Out of the corner of her eye, Michelle saw a crazed Hector running toward her. Courtney was sitting on the floor, with her knees up and her hands over her face, trying to protect herself. Hector grabbed Michelle by the arm and easily pulled her from the crying child, causing Michelle to slam up against the bedroom wall.

"What in the hell is going on?" John yelled as he ran into the room. He could see Courtney in the corner crying, and Michelle getting off the floor, and Hector standing between them. He could also see danger in Hector's eyes.

"That son-of-a-bitch grabbed my arm!" Michelle yelled. "He hurt my arm, and attacked me!"

Hector said nothing, but stared at Michelle, then at John.

John said nothing.

"I'm going to sue you, you son-of-a-bitch!" Michelle continued, screaming. "This is none of your fucking business!"

Hector went over and helped Courtney up. He took her hands from her face to look at her wounds, then shook his head in disgust. Hector then took Courtney into the bathroom to wash the blood from her face.

Michelle, holding her bruised arm, continued to scream at Hector, "You fucking bastard, look what you did to my arm!"

Hector, behind the closed bathroom door, held onto Courtney as she hugged him, and when she slowly pulled away, he took his hand and tenderly brushed the tears from her face. Courtney was trying so hard to stop crying, she was having trouble catching her breath. Hector noticed the deep gash in the corner of her mouth, and sponged the blood with tissue paper and cool water, realizing that she would need stitches.

"Courtney," Hector whispered, "what's your dad's phone number?"

"717-555-7158," Courtney answered, whispering back through her tears and hugging Hector.

Hector, looking at Courtney, repeated her dad's number slowly and distinctly.

Courtney nodded, and hugged Hector again. He could feel her body trembling with fear and hurt.

Courtney then ran to her bedroom, still crying.

Hector said nothing to anyone after that, and with his speechless helpers from California, finished unloading the trailer in less than an hour. The rest of the trailer's contents—furniture, lamps, paintings, bronzes, and boxes—were set on the floor throughout the house, helter-skelter, wherever there was available space. Michelle and John stayed out of their way, leaving the decorating for another day.

When Hector nodded "we're finished" to the helpers, they left in their pickup truck without saying goodbye. Hector then went to the kitchen to wait. He sat at the breakfast bar with no intention of leaving until he got paid what he was promised. Michelle and John let him sit for a while, and after realizing that he wasn't leaving, entered the kitchen together, leaving Courtney in her room.

"I'll send you a check," Michelle said to Hector angrily, wanting him to leave.

"You will pay me now, or I'm not leaving," Hector said, seething.

"I'll call the police," Michelle threatened. "Look what you did to my arm!"

"Call the police," Hector said, daring her. "Maybe we'll show them the cut on Courtney's face that needs stitches."

"Pay him," John said, looking at Michelle, realizing that Hector wasn't bluffing, and could cause problems.

Throwing on the counter a tightly wrapped wad of $100 bills that totaled $10,000, Michelle stormed out of the kitchen.

Courtney was waiting in the darkness by Hector's truck. As he slowly pulled out of the driveway, his headlights scanned her standing on the edge of the lawn, waving goodbye, trying to smile.

CHAPTER FIVE

ABUSE

Jagged lightning flashed on the horizon, followed by rumbling thunder as torrents of rain poured from the black sky. The streams and creeks of central Pennsylvania were already overflowing, rushing to the slow-rolling Susquehanna River, and by morning, flash flood warnings would be the local news of the day.

A bolt of lightning struck an oak tree along the fence row of Blair Cody's barn, splitting the tree in two, and the cracking sound could be heard for miles. The top branch of the tree crashed down and broke three sections of white-board fence.

It was after 2 a.m. Hours ago, Blair's phone call from Courtney was cut short, but he had heard her cry for help.

Wearing a t-shirt and jeans, drenched from head to toe, water running down from his face, Blair continued to ride into the driving rain, circling the chestnut horse wide open. The floodlights lit up the riding ring on the hill, casting eerie shadows on the house. Pools of water had already formed in the ring, a treacherous surface for the speed they were going, but Impressive James splashed through them without slowing down.

A compact digital phone was securely attached to Blair's belt, in case Courtney called again.

Blair was fighting his fury, running from his thoughts, and from what he imagined was going on with Courtney. Blair could still hear that awful blow, and her cry echoing in his head, and the harder he tried to deal with it—not forget it, but deal with it—the more enraged, the angrier, the more out of control he became.

Blair's emotional turmoil was driving him crazy.

If only he hadn't gone to Rocky's that weekend.

If only he could have caught them.

If only he knew where Courtney was.

Blair did not get in until 4 a.m., cold and exhausted. He had worked a young stud colt, as well as Courtney's gelding, and fed his stock of five before walking back to the house. The hot shower felt good, and helped to relax him.

Outside, the first light of dawn came late in the morning because of the continuing rain. The lightning and thunder had stopped hours ago, and the rain hitting the roof had a comforting rhythm. Blair's dreamless sleep was much needed, but was broken when the phone rang again.

Blair instinctively grabbed the phone on the first ring, almost knocking over the lamp on the bedside table.

"Hello," he said, instantly wide awake.

"Is this Mr. Cody?" a strange voice asked.

"Yes," Blair answered, "who is this?"

"Mr. Cody, my name is Hector, and I'm calling about your daughter."

Blair knew exactly who Hector was, not only from Courtney, but from his mother as well. His heart was racing; he braced himself for more bad news.

"I'm listening, Hector."

"Mr. Cody, I know where Courtney is."

"How much?" Blair responded, wasting no time.

"No, no, Mr. Cody, you don't understand. I don't want any money. I told Courtney I'd call you. She's at 719 Valley View Road, Hollywood, California."

"Please, Hector, tell me . . . how is she?" Blair asked, saying a silent prayer, having already written down the address on a piece of paper by the phone.

"Her mother hit her tonight when she tried to call you, and cut her mouth. She's going to be okay, but Courtney really wants to come home."

"She's going to come home, Hector, you can count on that," Blair said with conviction. "Are you sure she's okay?"

"She's okay," Hector said again, "but I have to go now."

There was nothing more that needed to be said. Hector had kept his promise to Courtney, and one of Blair's prayers had been answered. Blair now knew where Courtney was and he was going to bring her home, back to her room, back to her toys, her horses, and her dad.

◆ ◆ ◆

The Boeing 707 skipped on the concrete runway, its tires squealing as it smoothed out for a perfect landing at the bustling Los Angeles International Airport. Air traffic control had cleared the landing, and within minutes United Airlines flight 672 would be at Gate 7, on time.

The midday arrival originating in Baltimore, Maryland, was the earliest possible flight that Blair could get. Ami had driven Blair to BWI and dropped him off, making the drive that normally took two hours in less than an hour and a half. Blair was clean-shaven, and dressed comfortably in jeans and a white, button-down oxford shirt, carrying a blue blazer and leather carry-on bag; he had no luggage, because he wasn't planning on staying. He told Ami, before he slammed the door and ran into the terminal, to wait for his call, and to call Greely to let him know what was going on.

Upon landing in LA, Blair joined the throng of people heading for the escalators to baggage claim and car rental. He picked up the keys to the rental car that was waiting, received directions to Hollywood Hills from the girl at the desk, and headed for 719 Valley View Road. Blair had in his jacket pocket two envelopes: one contained the written custody agreement, and the other contained two open-ended tickets to Pennsylvania for himself and Courtney.

His intention was simple; he was going to get Courtney and take her home.

◆　◆　◆

Blair pulled into the driveway, looked for the black Lexus, didn't see it, and slowly got out of his car, looking all around. He double-checked the address Hector had given him with the address on the mailbox. The evening was still, the neighborhood quiet, and Blair walked straight to the front door and knocked.

At first, no one answered, and Blair knocked harder the second time.

Then the door opened. Blair immediately recognized the tall, thin man with silver hair. His mother's description of him was perfect.

"Where's Courtney?" Blair asked. There was no mistaking the tone in his voice. Blair was there to get Courtney.

"She's not here," John answered nervously. "Who, who are you?" he asked, feigning ignorance, obviously stunned, trying to buy time.

"You know who the fuck I am, Morgan," Blair answered angrily. "Where's my daughter?" he asked again, already out of patience.

"She's with her mother," John answered, quickly adding, "I don't know where they went and I'm not sure when they're getting back."

Blair looked right past John, and assumed everything was a lie.

He pushed John out of his way and searched the house, room by room. He recognized Courtney's from the furnishings, and quickly jotted down a note before continuing his search through the rest of the house.

Blair also recognized the master bedroom because of the king-size brass bed that he and Michelle once shared. A picture of John and Michelle, embracing, was on the nightstand; Blair opened the top drawer to check something out.

It was still there—the black, holstered, Walther's PPK—a nine-millimeter, semi-automatic handgun. Blair quickly popped the clip to see if it was still loaded, which it was, then shut the drawer, leaving the handgun in its place.

John never left the foyer. He knew that neither Courtney nor Michelle was in the house. Michelle had taken Courtney shopping for more suitable bedroom furniture and clothing. He didn't expect them back for several hours.

After he was satisfied that Courtney wasn't there, Blair told John that he wasn't leaving but would wait outside.

John said nothing, not wanting a confrontation; but as soon as Blair went out the door, he ran for the phone to call Michelle on the cellular that she carried at all times.

"Michelle!" John said excitedly. "He's here!"

"Who's there, John?" Michelle asked impatiently, as she was heading home from Rodeo Drive.

"Blair!"

"Oh, really," Michelle responded, controlling her voice because Courtney was paying close attention.

"Yeah, really," John answered, annoyed at Michelle's nonchalance, "and the son-of-a-bitch pushed right past me, and went through the whole fucking house like he owned it."

"Where is he now?" Michelle asked, having more difficulty controlling her voice.

"I don't know," John answered, "but I think he's waiting in his car outside. I know and you know he's not leaving."

"I'll call you back," Michelle said, hanging up. She turned off the next ramp to look for a motel. Finding a motel was going to be easy. Figuring out what to tell Courtney was not. Getting rid of Blair was going to be impossible.

Michelle knew that she hadn't seen the last of Blair when she left Pennsylvania with Courtney. But she wasn't expecting him this soon. She had told no one where she was moving, and they had just arrived yesterday, three thousand miles from the isolated farm. Michelle instinctively kept checking her rearview mirror, wondering how Blair had found her.

Michelle could tell that Courtney had paid close attention to the phone call. She told her that a pipe had broken at the house and there was no water, and for that reason the two of them were going to check into a very nice motel, maybe with a swimming pool and room service.

Courtney had said nothing since the car phone rang, and asked no questions when Michelle abruptly pulled off at the next exit. The gash in the corner of Courtney's mouth was becoming a scar, but Michelle was irritated that their shopping spree had done nothing to make up for it.

Ahead, the magnificent Regent Beverly Wilshire Hotel stood among the palm trees like a palace. The cascading water fountains in front of the grand hotel were creating miniature rainbows, and uniformed valets greeted the guests as they stepped from their cars and stretch limousines. Michelle was hoping to catch a glimpse of a movie star, and loved the glitz and the glitter of the entranceway; this was what she was meant for. Even Courtney was in awe, having never seen anything like it before.

After they checked in, a young, fresh-faced bellhop showed them to their room on the second floor, overlooking the pool. It was an easy tip for the bellhop because there was no luggage, only shopping bags.

Michelle asked the bellhop to send up a babysitter. A heavy-set, matronly woman who appeared to be in her fifties showed up within fifteen minutes, and Michelle instructed her to watch Courtney and keep her off the phone.

Before taking off "to run some errands," Michelle told the babysitter that they could order room service.

◆ ◆ ◆

It was after midnight.

The lights at 719 Valley View Road were out.

Two marked police cars slid up behind Blair Cody's vehicle, which was still parked in the driveway. Blair watched from his rearview mirror as they pulled in. He sat up and felt his jacket pocket to make sure the envelope with the custody agreement was still there.

"Mr. Cody," one officer ordered from his bullhorn, "please step out of your car, and keep your hands where we can see them."

Blair did exactly as he was told.

Four police officers, two from each car, approached Blair with extreme caution. They did not have their guns drawn, but their holsters were unsnapped, with their hands on their guns, ready for action. They were taught at the academy, and learned from fellow officers, that nothing was more dangerous than responding to a domestic call, or approaching a car. This time they had both.

The first officer to reach Blair asked him if he was armed; Blair shook his head.

"What are you doing here?" the officer asked.

"I'm here to take my daughter home," Blair answered, sensing a volatile situation. "The written custody agreement is in my pocket," he added, but made no quick movement.

"Well, Mr. Cody," the lead officer said, "we're not here to resolve a custody dispute. We're here to arrest you, based on a sworn affidavit by one Michelle Lynn Cody, for simple assault and battery on her person. The affidavit swears and affirms that you struck her more than once, intending to do bodily harm. It further alleges that you threatened to kill her."

"When did I do that?" Blair asked, incredulous.

"Earlier this evening," the officer answered, and added, "She showed the desk sergeant the bruises on her arm to prove it."

Blair had been married to Michelle for twelve years, and dated her for a year before they were married. He had never laid a hand on her in his life, nor even thought about it, let alone threatened to kill her. Blair had been a lawyer for eighteen years and knew that he wasn't going to try this case on the street with four police officers as his jury. The system didn't work that way.

Blair shook his head in dismay, and without saying another word, got in the back seat of one of the police cruisers to be taken in for processing. At the police station across town, he was finger-printed, photographed, and booked for the two reported crimes of domestic violence.

The committing magistrate, before releasing Blair from police custody, ordered that he have no contact with Michelle Lynn Cody, and that he stay away from her residence. "Or else," the magistrate said, "your bail will be revoked," as he handed Blair a form setting the preliminary hearing date for the end of August, which was two weeks away.

That night, after posting bail, Blair stayed at a modest hotel within blocks of the Regent Beverly Wilshire Hotel, intending to get other accommodations in the morning.

Blair had no intention of leaving California in the meantime, not without Courtney he didn't.

CHAPTER SIX

NO DEAL

Magistrate Ross, wearing a black robe open in the front, banged the gavel on his desk loudly, calling the hearing to order. He already had impatient litigants waiting in his reception room since the Cody hearing was late getting started.

It was 9 a.m., Magisterial District 32.

Blair, dressed in a conservative suit, sat in the sparsely furnished hearing room. He was anxious for the slow wheels of justice to get rolling. His good friend and lawyer, Kimberly Wells, sat to his right.

Blair and Kimberly had gone to Stanford Law School together, and kept in touch over the years. After graduation, Blair moved to Pennsylvania to clerk for the Pennsylvania Supreme Court for a year. Kimberly settled in Los Angeles and went into the family firm that her great-uncle and father had founded fifty years ago. Kimberly was highly respected in the legal community, based on years of success in the courtroom.

"Magisterial District Court 32 is now in session," Ross said ceremoniously, and continued, "Let the record reflect that the defendant is present with his counsel, Ms. Kimberly Wells, that the District Attorney's Office of Los Angeles is represented by Mr. William M. Reed, and that now is the time and place for the preliminary hearing in the case of the State of California versus Blair Lee Cody.

"Mr. Cody," Ross said, looking straight at Blair, "you have been charged with assault and battery on the person of one Michelle Lynn Cody on or about August 7, 1995. And further, you are charged with threatening to take her life. How do you plead to those two charges, Mr. Cody?"

Kimberly stood up and answered for Blair, "Not guilty."

"Mr. Reed," Ross said, looking at Reed, who was sitting beside Michelle at the prosecution table, "call your first witness."

"Yes, Your Honor," Reed answered, looking at Michelle, pointing to the witness stand.

Blair watched Michelle being sworn in. The woman he had loved years ago was a total stranger to him. Their past together seemed so long ago, in another world, and the recent events—Courtney's disappearance in the middle of the night and his arrest—were so unreal.

For the previous two weeks, he had awakened in a strange hotel room, with nothing to do, nowhere to go, and no Courtney. His ranch, his familiar surroundings, and the life he knew were miles away. He killed time buying clothing and other necessities, worked out at the hotel gym every day, and made calls to his office. He called Pat Greely and his mother to let them know what was going on. Last week, he spent three days in Oregon with Eddie Turner, who was a reining horse enthusiast like himself, and helped Eddie work his young horses; it wasn't the same without Courtney.

"Please state your full name for the record," Reed asked, breaking Blair's reverie.

"Michelle Lynn Cody," Michelle answered.

"Ms. Cody," Reed continued, "would you please tell Judge Ross the events which led to your charging Mr. Blair Cody with assault and battery, and with threatening to take your life."

"Yes," Michelle answered.

Michelle then shifted her chair, and facing Judge Ross, proceeded to tell a story with a lot of truth, except for the events that led to her criminal charges. She told him that she and Blair had been married for twelve years, that she was the mother of Courtney Louise Cody, age eleven, that because of irreconcilable differences she and Blair were divorced under the laws of the Commonwealth of Pennsylvania, and that since then she had become romantically involved with another man.

Then, Michelle's rehearsed drama unfolded with complete disregard for the truth.

Michelle testified tearfully that Blair had physically abused her throughout their marriage. She said that she kept it in the closet for Courtney's sake, and because she was embarrassed. She said she took Courtney three weeks ago because she felt the child could be subjected to Blair's violent behavior. She told Judge Ross that Blair had killed a man five years ago in Oklahoma, but quickly passed over the circumstances surrounding the death.

"Two weeks ago, Your Honor," Michelle continued, uninterrupted by Reed or Kimberly, "Blair came to my new home in Hollywood at 719 Valley View Road. My fiancé, John Morgan, was home. Courtney was asleep in her room. I opened the door and was shocked to see him, and before I could close the door, he grabbed my arm so hard that I started to cry. He was screaming that he was going to kill me. I was terrified. John had to help me shut and lock the door. I finally snuck out the back with Courtney, took her to the Regent Beverly Wilshire Hotel, then went to the police station to file this complaint."

"Did you leave Pennsylvania, Ms. Cody," Reed asked, "and move to California to get away from Mr. Cody's violent, assaultive behavior?"

"Yes," Michelle answered.

"Did Mr. Cody threaten to kill you?" Reed asked.

"Yes."

"Do you believe that Mr. Cody meant it?" Reed asked, summing up.

"I not only believe that Blair meant it, I also believe that he's going to do it. I just don't know when, or where, or how," Michelle answered.

Blair watched as Michelle wiped the tears from her face with a tissue, then sat quietly on the witness stand with her hands folded neatly on her lap, looking down, glancing furtively toward Reed to see how she had done.

Blair, who had tried cases in courtrooms for almost twenty years, felt that Michelle was effective. He knew what a tangled web was being spun in that courtroom. Blair knew that his innocence meant nothing.

As Michelle waited patiently on the witness stand, Blair conferred with Kimberly. He spoke in a whisper, giving her key questions to challenge the rehearsed lies. Blair knew Michelle better than anyone, but would leave the cross-examination to Kimberly.

"Ms. Cody," Kimberly began, "during the twelve years you were married to Blair, did anyone ever witness his abuse toward you?"

"No," Michelle answered, "Blair always made sure nobody was around."

"Including Courtney?" Kimberly asked.

"That's right."

"Did you ever complain to anyone, or did anyone ever see any bruises?"

"No."

"Yet, Ms. Cody," Kimberly asked sarcastically, "is it your testimony that this time you have a witness?"

"That's right."

"That witness is your fiancé, John Morgan?"

"That's correct."

"John Morgan saw the assault and battery on your person?"

"Right."

"John Morgan heard Blair threaten to kill you?"

"Right."

"Is John Morgan here today?"

"No."

"Courtney was asleep?"

"Right."

"Did you tell Courtney what happened to you?"

"No."

"Did she ask you what happened to your arm?"

"I wish you would keep our child out of this," Michelle answered defensively.

"Where is Courtney?" Kimberly asked, and Blair sat up, wanting to know.

"Objection," Reed interjected. "I don't think that is relevant to the purpose of this hearing."

"Sustained," Ross ruled.

It was obvious to Blair that Reed had a friend in Magistrate Ross. Reed was controlling Kimberly's cross-examination of Michelle. Reed nailed Kimberly every time she got close to exposing Michelle, or even upsetting her.

And every time Reed yelled "objection" and Ross ruled "sustained," Michelle gave a slight, triumphant smile, looking directly at Kimberly to rub it in. Blair had seen that smile on Michelle's face many times before. It would appear whenever Michelle was pleased with herself.

Blair followed Michelle's gaze to the back of the courtroom. Two men, holding their briefcases, nodded to Michelle approvingly.

Kimberly stayed focused, and doggedly pursued her line of questioning. She argued that Michelle's case rested with Michelle's credibility. Kimberly pointed out that John Morgan, Michelle's only witness, wasn't there, and that the two of them took Courtney in the middle of the night contrary to the written custody agreement.

"Isn't it a fact, Ms. Cody," Kimberly asked, ending her flurry of barbed questions, "that you brought these false criminal charges to negotiate Courtney's custody?"

Michelle glared at Kimberly, and after pausing, answered, "No, Ms. Wells, I did not."

"Keep in mind," Ross interjected, breaking the tension, "that this is a preliminary hearing, not a determination of guilt or innocence, and that my responsibility is simply to determine whether the state of California has proved a prima facie case. Anything else, counselors?"

"No, Your Honor," Reed answered.

"No, Your Honor," Kimberly answered.

"Very well," Judge Ross said, "I hereby find that the state of California has met its burden and I am binding this case over for trial."

"And now, counselors," Ross added, standing up, banging his gavel loudly on his bench, "this hearing is over. Bail will continue. The next criminal term begins the second week of December."

Ross quickly left the bench and went into his chambers. Michelle walked over and shook Reed's hand.

David Wallace and James Johnson got up from their pews in the back, approached Blair, and handed him two blue-backed Orders of Court, captioned "Temporary Protection from Abuse" and "Temporary Custody."

Michelle was granted temporary custody of Courtney because of the "exigent and dangerous circumstances." The final PFA (protection from abuse) and custody hearings were scheduled by Judge Franklin Hester for September 25.

Blair didn't say a word as he read over the court orders. He knew the slow wheels of justice had just come to a screeching halt. He was sick about the fact that he could not see Courtney and suddenly felt "dangerous" to those around him.

Reed gave a quick good-bye to everybody and got out of there.

The two lawyers from LA's largest law firm introduced themselves to Blair and Kimberly. There was no hand-shaking, no pleasant amenities.

Michelle watched from the back of the courtroom, but was close enough to hear everything.

Her private lawyers were dressed in pin-striped suits, solid white shirts, and powder-blue ties that matched the handkerchiefs in their breast pockets. They looked almost like twins.

James Johnson wasted no time getting down to the business at hand—legal business, dirty legal business—suggesting that they all have a private meeting in the magistrate's small conference room across the hall.

Kimberly looked at Blair, who nodded okay.

The conference room consisted of a round pine table and four chairs. The beige-painted walls had no pictures, and the brown tweed carpeting was worn.

With two neatly stacked piles of blue-backed paperwork in front of him, Johnson sat directly across from Kimberly. Wallace and Michelle sat on each side of Johnson. Blair stood off to the side with his arms folded, leaning against the closed door.

"Ms. Wells," Johnson began in a formal tone, "we have a proposal here that can end this criminal prosecution for your client today. We have already discussed this proposal with Mr. Reed, who realizes that if Michelle does not testify, he will have no witnesses. As you know, Mr. Reed is LA's first assistant district attorney and has the authority to dismiss this case."

"Go on," Kimberly said.

"It's a rather simple agreement we are suggesting," Johnson continued. "Mr. Cody is to give Michelle Cody full custody of Courtney. He will have liberal visitation during the school year and two weeks during the summer. We have already prepared the agreements for execution, which will be reduced to a court order."

"Oh, really," Kimberly said, raising her eyebrows. Blair knew she was not intimidated. Her looks were deceiving to those who did not know her. She was attractive, with deep-set green eyes and naturally curly auburn hair, which she kept bobbed. Her good looks and refined femininity never got in her way when it was time to work; maybe it distracted others, but not her.

"Yes," Johnson responded, "or else . . . "

"Or else what?" Kimberly interrupted abruptly.

"Or else we are going to let the criminal justice system take its course, Ms. Wells," Johnson continued. "Mr. Cody is charged with assault and battery and threatening to kill Mrs. Cody. Magistrate Ross has now bound these serious charges over for court action. We have served Mr. Cody with two court orders signed by Judge Hester. Until you straighten all this out, Ms. Wells, Mr. Cody won't see his daughter for at least six months, maybe a year."

"Is that right?" Kimberly asked defiantly.

"That's right," Johnson answered, "and I suggest that you speak with your client now before we go any further."

"I'll be happy to, gentlemen," Kimberly answered, glaring at Johnson.

"That won't be necessary," Blair interjected.

Everybody in the room looked up toward Blair.

"My answer to your proposal," Blair said, controlling his tone, "is that you all go fuck yourselves. And tell Reed that goes for him too because he's got no business in this. I'm not giving Michelle a damn thing and I'm taking Courtney home."

Johnson and Wallace froze.

Michelle was no longer smiling.

Kimberly was.

◆ ◆ ◆

Courtney still had in her pocket the crumpled note she found under her pillow. She never did believe her mom about a pipe breaking in the house that night, leaving no water. After making sure her bedroom door was closed, she pulled out the note and read it again, as she sat on her bed:

Courtney, I was here to take you home. Love, Dad.

The note made her cry again. She prayed every night that he would find her. She knew he was around somewhere, but didn't know where, or what was taking so long. She had called home the other day when her mother had gone shopping, and Grandma Cody told her everything. Grandma said Dad came to get her, and Mom had him arrested for hurting her arm—which made no sense, because Courtney knew what happened. Grandma also said that Dad was still out there, and not coming home without her.

Michelle had already taken her to the Melrose Middle School to register her for the sixth grade. It was a pretty school, all red brick, with a lot of archways, long hallways, a big cafeteria, a library, modern classrooms, computer labs, and the biggest gymnasium she had ever seen; outside there was a football field, baseball diamonds, and tennis courts, with palm trees, flower beds, and grass everywhere.

But Courtney didn't want to go to that school. She didn't have any friends there, didn't know anybody, and back home she would still have been in elementary school. She'd been looking forward to Mrs. Simon's classroom, because she knew Mrs. Simon was a fun teacher. Her school at home was about to start.

Her mom also knew that she was running for a reining horse title in the youth class, and that she was to go with her dad to the Reining Extravaganza Classic in North Carolina. She really kicked butt there last year, and was the hands-down favorite this year if her old horse behaved. Courtney wondered if her dad had gotten Impressive James from Rocky; she really liked that horse.

Last night, Courtney overheard her mom and John arguing, screaming and yelling. She heard something about Dad's hearing today, then heard a door slam, and couldn't hear any more after that.

Why was her mother doing this to her?

Courtney looked at her dad's note, which she was still holding in her hand. She folded it carefully and put it in her pocket. Courtney lay down and buried her face in her pillow.

CHAPTER SEVEN

DOCTOR

Their reserved table at Spago's was in a quiet corner, and Kimberly and Melanie arrived early together to talk things over before Blair got there. Both were dressed casually. Kimberly wore a dark blue sundress with matching flats; Melanie wore black slacks and a brocade vest.

They had met in court years ago when Kimberly was defending a child who ran away from home. Melanie Castille, a respected psychiatrist among the local judiciary, was court-appointed to evaluate her client. She concluded that the eight-year-old had multiple personalities, causing her to run, and therefore should not be punished.

You would never know that Melanie was forty years old. Her raven hair was straight and short, a serious look. Her flawless complexion, rarely exposed to the sun, accented her dark chestnut eyes. An hour on the treadmill several days a week, though she hated the regimen, kept her trim.

Twenty years ago, Melanie had been asked to participate in the Rose Bowl parade in Pasadena, California, and she had laughed at the idea of being on a flowery float, waving to throngs of people along the sidewalks on New Year's Day. "Absolutely not" was her answer; it just wasn't her style.

The tuxedoed waiter, a young man with a black moustache and black hair slicked over to the side, introduced himself as Joseph. He poured a glass of Chablis for his two attractive customers, placing the bottle in a sterling silver ice bucket by their table. The white linen cloth over the table was accented with an oil lamp burning softly, and a single fresh rose. Kimberly asked Joseph to keep an eye out for Mr. Cody, who was scheduled to arrive in twenty minutes.

"Tell me about your friend," Melanie prompted.

"Cody's a neat guy, Melanie, and a tough guy," Kimberly answered. "We went to law school together, and while everybody was out playing golf or tennis, he was roping calves. Cody was a loner, kept his distance, and a hard read. He's a brilliant trial lawyer but hasn't done it for a while. I had a crush on him in law school."

"Who didn't you have a crush on in law school?" Melanie asked, kidding. Melanie loved teasing her longtime friend. Twice a week they played tennis at the exclusive West Hills Country Club, with frequent lunches at different upscale, trendy cafés.

"Cody was different, Melanie. I really had a crush on him, and when you see him, you'll know why," Kimberly answered, teasing back.

"Go on, tell me more," Melanie said. "Why is he out here, and how can I help?"

Kimberly told Melanie how Courtney was shipped to Hollywood in an eighteen-wheeler, about Courtney's call to Blair which ended suddenly, and how Hector tipped him off. Kimberly talked about the preliminary hearing and scoffed at Michelle's story, "unless John Morgan was a World Wrestling Federation titan in disguise, and then it would have been a knock-down, drag-out fight to the bitter end, with Blair leaving with Courtney."

Melanie listened closely to Kimberly's account, enjoying her animation as she clenched her fist, jabbing the air, strangling her opponent. Kimberly looked like she was going nuts in the quiet dignity of Spago's formal dining room, and Melanie smiled at several patrons who were looking in their direction. Kimberly was about to tell Melanie how frustrating the preliminary hearing was when she spotted Joseph across the room, leading Blair to their table.

Blair nodded his head politely when Kimberly introduced them. Melanie could see why Kimberly had a crush on him in law school. It wasn't just his rugged good looks. His blue eyes were penetrating, his smile was sincere with a genuine warmth. There was also a sensitivity about him that Melanie liked.

Kimberly winked at Melanie.

Blair, dressed in jeans, with a blue blazer over a white shirt with pearlized buttons, was happy to see them as he sat down beside Kimberly. He thanked them for the invitation, telling them that he had been dining alone for the past three weeks. He ordered a manhattan on the rocks.

The dinner was excellent, and they all enjoyed each other's company. For the first time in four weeks, it was a calm respite for Blair. But as the coffee was being served with dessert, Blair needed to discuss why they were there.

He had balked at the idea of seeing a psychiatrist, for any reason, but Kimberly hinted that Melanie could be a perfect witness in the upcoming court battles. She guaranteed him that "Mother Michelle" would have her own psychiatrist, or psychiatrists, say whatever had to be said in Judge Hester's courtroom. She had impressed upon Blair that Melanie was a good friend.

More importantly, Kimberly added, she was eminently qualified. Melanie was a board member of all the important associations at the national and state levels. She had authored several books — *What to Tell Your Children About Divorce*, *The Early Dynamics of Life*, and *Caught Between Fighting Parents* — all of which became desk manuals for family practitioners.

"Kimberly tells me that you're an excellent child psychiatrist," Blair said, looking at Melanie.

"Thank you, Blair," Melanie responded.

"Well, my immediate crisis is this," Blair continued, his tone and mood changing to pained frustration. "I have to get to Courtney. I just have to. It's been weeks and I haven't been able to talk to her, to let her know that I love her and that I'm here to take her home, which is where she belongs and wants to be.

"I just want to grab her and run," Blair added, gulping down the last of his second manhattan. "I'm willing to risk jail and disbarment, but I don't want her to witness an ugly confrontation. I don't want to snatch her from school, or grab her from a playground, or stick her in the middle of endless legal proceedings. I just can't disrupt her life any more than it has been."

"When are your hearings?" Melanie asked.

"In a month," Kimberly answered. "His PFA and custody hearings are scheduled for September 25. His criminal trial is mid-December."

Blair grimaced, "I can't wait that long."

Melanie and Kimberly looked at each other across the table. They didn't know what Blair's intentions were, but they sensed they had nothing to do with courts, hearings, continuances, or appeals. Only Blair knew the answer to that.

"What are you going to do?" Melanie asked, concerned about Blair's obvious frustration.

"Let's just say," Blair answered, "that I'm taking Courtney home. Whether it's now or later. But for right now, Melanie, this is what I would like to do, and here's where you can help me."

"I'm listening," Melanie said.

"In a couple of days, right after Labor Day, Courtney is to start the sixth grade at the Melrose Middle School. Michelle has already enrolled her."

"You already know that?" Melanie asked.

"Yes," Blair answered, continuing, "and here's what I have in mind. That school has a counselor-psychologist with offices in the main administration building, and I would like you to make arrangements for me to meet with Courtney, privately, in the counselor's office on her first day."

"I know the school psychologist at Melrose personally," Melanie said. "His name is Paul Johns, and he's a good friend of mine, and a good psychologist. He would do me a favor, even break the rules, but how do I know that you're not going to take the opportunity to take off with Courtney?

"I hardly know you, Blair," Melanie added, "and that would cost Mr. Johns his job, and embarrass me."

"Well, you don't," Blair answered matter-of-factly, "but if that were my intention, I wouldn't need you. I know exactly where Courtney's school is, how it's laid out, when the recesses are, and the route to and from her home. My reason for this approach, with your help, is to try to work within the system. Not because I trust the system, I don't, but to minimize the emotional damage already being done to my daughter."

Melanie continued to study Blair closely in the dim light of their corner table, with only a candle flickering between them. Kimberly was right when she said Blair was a hard read, and Melanie didn't know what to think. Yet he seemed so sincere, so genuine, and everything he was saying made sense; he didn't need her if he wanted to grab Courtney and run. He could do that anytime he wanted to.

But why should she take the risk?

For Kimberly, because they were friends?

For him? She didn't even know Blair Cody.

Blair added that he wanted Melanie to talk to Courtney, too. Not the first day, he said, which was his. Soon, maybe at the school without Mr. Johns, just the two of them. That way Melanie could help him decide what was in Courtney's best interest. Blair promised Melanie, and Kimberly, that he would listen to what they had to say on how to get Courtney home.

"I want to think about this, Blair, at least overnight," Melanie said, already deep in thought.

"I understand."

"I'll call you tomorrow," Melanie added.

"Kimberly has my number, Melanie," Blair said, waving Joseph over to pay the bill.

"I've got his number, all right," Kimberly said jokingly, breaking the serious mood.

◆ ◆ ◆

John Morgan chopped the white, powdery substance on top of the bedroom bureau with a single-edge razor blade, skillfully shaping and forming two thick, white lines. He then snorted them through a short piece of plastic straw into each nostril. The sting in his nose went rushing to his brain and heart, causing the immediate euphoria that he desperately needed, and craved, more and more with each passing day.

He pulled the blinds back to let the sunlight in before unlocking the bedroom door. He walked out onto the bedroom balcony and looked out across the valley, the sun warming his face.

No longer would he work for some magazine in New York editing articles. He had given twenty-eight years to that company and all he had to show for it was some furniture and a car that he couldn't make payments on. He would even have lost his apartment if it hadn't been for Michelle.

Things were different now, more peaceful, more beautiful, and he was looking forward to living the life of a free spirit. He had never been married before, never really wanted to be. Free spirits didn't get married, but it was a small price to pay for the good life he now had. Michelle's incessant narcissism needed constant stroking, and that kid of hers was a pain in the ass, but he could handle them both. If all he had to do was run around Hollywood with her damn portfolio and get her into some acting classes, what was the big deal?

He knew what Michelle was doing by insisting on a quick wedding that would take place before the custody hearing. Her big-shot lawyers must have told her that a stable home environment was essential to their case, as opposed to living out of wedlock with her boyfriend. He knew that her father, who hired them in the first place, wanted a prenuptial agreement, and John's name removed from the deed to their house.

Not so fast, old man, John thought. *Maybe I don't have any money, Pops, but your daughter doesn't know that.*

He wasn't going to let Michelle use him for this custody thing, then dump his ass penniless a year from now, if their marriage lasted that long. There wasn't going to be a prenuptial agreement, and he wasn't taking his name off the deed. If Michelle, or her fucking lawyers, or that greedy father of hers got too pushy, then he was going to tell all.

How Michelle had committed perjury at the preliminary hearing. How Blair never laid a hand on her, or even saw her since he got here. All John needed to prove it was that Spanish, or Mexican, or whatever the fuck he was, truck driver to put everybody in their place. Oh yes, wouldn't they all love that?

In addition, his sweet little Michelle was dipping more and more into his cocaine reserve. Recreational use my ass. Michelle was stringing out lines of cocaine and popping quaaludes every day. She probably had enough shit in her purse to land her in jail for a long time. Wouldn't Reed and her father, those assholes, just love to hear about that?

A prenuptial agreement, huh? My name off the deed? I don't think so, he thought, turning back toward the bedroom bureau. He hastened to the mirror and razor blade to cut another line.

CHAPTER EIGHT

SCHOOLYARD

Yellow buses were pulling in between the white-painted lines on the black-topped parking lot. Many students of this upscale middle school were within walking distance of their exclusive homes, and were walking in groups, carrying their bookbags. Others were being dropped off at the front door by their parents in Jaguars and BMWs.

It was the first day of school at Melrose.

The black Lexus, driven by John Morgan, arrived at the entrance as the bell started ringing. Courtney got out of the car, dressed in designer jeans and Reebok sneakers, and slowly walked to the front doors, where she was directed to the gymnasium to receive her classroom assignment. The gymnasium was packed with students waiting in line for their class schedules, and after a thirty-minute wait, Courtney was told to report to her classroom on the second floor.

Her homeroom had at least thirty-five kids in it, the biggest class that Courtney had ever been in. Courtney didn't care how big it was, or that she didn't know anybody, because she wasn't planning on staying there. Mrs. Cooper seemed nice enough, but Courtney hated it when she was introduced to everyone as "our newest addition from Pennsylvania."

To be polite, Courtney returned the smiles and shy hellos of her classmates. It wasn't that anybody was being unfriendly, but she had no intention of getting to know them.

At mid-morning, somebody walked into the room and handed her teacher a note as she addressed the class. Courtney was surprised and embarrassed when Mrs. Cooper called her to the front and whispered that she was to go to room 110, which was the guidance counselor's office.

With her new sneakers squeaking on the polished linoleum floor, Courtney wondered what was going on as she walked the long hallway to the office. She was sure she hadn't done anything wrong, and figured it was because she was new. A hall monitor stopped her and asked her where she was going, then assisted her with directions.

A friendly man at the front desk said his name was Paul Johns and that he was her guidance counselor. Courtney thought he looked a lot like her principal back home, because of his paunchy build, hairy arms, and graying beard that was much whiter than his dark, thinning hair. Mr. Johns told Courtney that someone was in his office waiting to see her; he then pointed to the door with his name on it.

Courtney walked into the office, alone, but no one was there. The empty room felt eerie and her heart began to pound. She heard the door close behind her, and in that still moment, without seeing him, or hearing him, she knew her dad had found her.

"How's my kid?" Blair said, standing behind her, and Courtney spun around, throwing herself into his arms, holding him tightly, not wanting to let go, fearing that he would disappear like he did in her horrible dreams. Tears ran down Courtney's cheeks, but she did not cry out loud because people in the outer office might hear her.

Blair held her tight, closing his eyes, restraining his own tears. "Everything is going to be okay, Courtney," Blair said, still holding her.

"Take me home, Dad," Courtney said, not letting go.

"I will, honey," Blair answered, assuring her as she pulled away so they could talk.

"Then let's go," Courtney said, pulling his hand toward the door as if there were nothing more to talk about.

Blair laughed, and wanted to cry. He was so happy to see that she was all right. Her answer to their problem was so simplistic, so impetuous, so pure—he wanted to take her home, that's where she belonged, that's where she wanted to go, right now, let's go.

He was her father, for God's sake.

She was his kid.

Blair looked more than once at the open window in Johns' office. It had nothing to do with Mr. Johns, or Melanie, and certainly not himself; he just couldn't do it to Courtney, though Courtney would not understand for years to come.

Courtney needed Blair's strength at this point in her life to do the right thing.

Blair held Courtney's hand tightly and tried to explain that the two of them, together, had to see this thing through. He told Courtney about the upcoming custody hearing that he had to go through, and how Dr. Melanie Castille would be talking to her, but that was okay because she was a friend.

Blair promised Courtney that he would not leave Hollywood, and that he would see her often. They would meet a block away from the school every morning, by the pond, where the ducks were. Maybe they would even have lunch there. He was sure Mr. Johns would go along with it if Dr. Castille asked him.

Courtney did not understand, but trusted her dad, and listened to everything he was saying. She asked her dad about the hearing Grandma Cody told her about, the one involving her mother's arm, and really didn't understand why her mom was blaming her dad when everybody knew that Hector did it.

"Is that how you got the little scar on the corner of your lip?" Blair asked Courtney, touching the small but noticeable cut.

Courtney nodded yes.

"I can hardly see it," Blair said, lying, venom pouring in his stomach.

"I can see it," Courtney insisted, "and I'll always be able to see it."

"Hector called me, you know," Blair confided, thinking he was telling Courtney a secret, knowing she loved secrets betwccn them.

"I know," Courtney said with a little smile. "Hector told me he was going to call you. We became friends."

Blair loved it when Courtney smiled and knew that he was going to get a big one before he left. He took Courtney by the hand and walked her to Mr. Johns' desk, asked her to close her eyes, and when she opened them she saw on the desk a color photo of Impressive James doing a beautiful sliding stop. Courtney hugged her dad lovingly, giving him that big smile, and promised him that she would hang in there until they went home.

Blair stuck a twenty-dollar bill in Courtney's pocket, and the two of them went out to talk to Melanie and Mr. Johns, who were waiting nervously in the outer office. Blair could not have been more appreciative.

Melanie, dressed in a cool, flowery sundress, told Courtney that she was a friend of her dad's and that she was going to do what she could to get them together as often as possible, starting right away.

"Thank you," murmured Courtney.

◆　◆　◆

Melanie studied Blair as they sat across from each other in her comfortable office, in cloth, wing-backed armchairs with a low coffee table between them. Melanie never put a desk between herself and her clients, believing that was a barrier to essential communications.

Melanie had devoted her life to child psychiatry and had seen, time and time again, children of fractured families become pawns in a game of love and hate, bitter revenge, and unmerciful spite. Innocent children taken hostage for money and property was a common ploy. Blair's account of the recent events was another shocking example.

Melanie had read everything in Blair's file. She read the divorce pleadings and the property agreement. The custody stipulation was underlined in red, making it clear that Blair was to have custody. The recent petition to modify custody alleged "Blair Cody, the natural father, is potentially dangerous."

Blair seemed much better, more relaxed, since his morning reunion with Courtney. Melanie liked Blair a lot, but questioned her trusting instincts about him. Maybe he was dangerous, capable of hurting, or killing, for that matter. She had read about, and counseled with, the gentlest of human beings who turned out to be cold-blooded murderers.

"I really appreciate what you did for me, Melanie," Blair said.

"I know you do, Blair, and I'm glad I could help," Melanie answered.

You just can't tell, she thought to herself.

She certainly didn't doubt his love for Courtney.

Why else would Blair have grabbed the first flight across America when he learned of Courtney's whereabouts? He didn't go home for weeks, living in motels, just waiting to see her. Blair told Melanie that he had found a small apartment downtown somewhere, sparsely furnished, expensive, but the month-to-month lease sold him. Blair said he wasn't leaving Hollywood without his daughter. To Melanie, all of that spoke of love from the heart.

Melanie knew about a different kind of love, once. She had married a young, handsome doctor with storybook credentials. Dr. Robert Castille was bright, graduated valedictorian, came from a strong family background, with a promising career. He came from money, big money, and their wedding reception on top of City Towers was a gala event with two orchestras. Five years later, they owned their high-rise condominium overlooking the Pacific Ocean. Their careers were flourishing—she was a psychiatrist and recognized author; he was a surgeon, soon to be chief of staff at the Sinai Memorial Hospital. She thought their home life was filled with passion and romance.

Then Melanie found out.

She came home early from work and walked in on Robert with his pal Tom, in their bedroom—naked, clutched in each other's arms. It wasn't just the infidelity, or the shock of Robert's sexual preference, either one of which would have been enough to end the marriage; but Melanie felt professionally violated, as if she should have known, or sensed it, because she was a psychiatrist.

That life experience made her distrusting.

Melanie stayed single, and avoided the fast-paced Hollywood nightlife.

"I read your file, Blair," Melanie said, wanting Blair to talk, to find out more about him.

"It's pretty standard stuff, but tough to deal with," Blair answered.

"How have you been holding up?" Melanie asked.

"The past couple of weeks have been rough," Blair answered. "This morning helped, and if I can do this lunch thing, it'll make it easier for both of us."

"I think that can be arranged," Melanie said optimistically.

"Thanks, Melanie."

"What else?" Melanie asked, sensing that Blair had an agenda.

"I'm going to want you to talk to Courtney, to help me. Maybe you can testify at the upcoming hearings if you believe she's better off with me."

"I'll talk to her, Blair, anytime you want."

"I brought a check, payable to you, in the amount of $10,000 for your time. If it goes over that, just let me know."

"We'll talk about that, Blair," Melanie answered, "but if you don't mind, I'd like to talk about you a little bit. Right now, you know more about me than I do you."

"What do you want to know?" Blair asked.

There were a lot of things Melanie wanted to know. She didn't think his file was "pretty standard stuff." The file gave all the legal history, but Melanie was more interested in his personal history. He was very bright, and by all accounts a brilliant lawyer. The old newspaper clippings and magazine articles that Kimberly gave her portrayed Blair as a dynamic litigator—"someone to be reckoned with, serious," according to the *Philadelphia Inquirer*. Yet Blair hadn't tried a case in over five years and seldom went into his office.

Kimberly had already told Melanie about the death of Blair's father. The newspaper report of that incident, replete with photos, was big news in Oklahoma and had made the wire service. The front page of the *Oklahoma Star* featured a gruesome photo of the dead assailant, his face blown away, lying in a pool of blood. From that point on, Blair had refused all media interviews and disappeared from public life.

Melanie was interested in that episode. Blair wanted her to be an expert witness for Courtney, to testify in a court of law, to subject herself to skilled cross-examination. Melanie wasn't going to put her credibility on the line without knowing who she was vouching for. Blair was going to answer her questions, and being a lawyer, he would understand.

"You read the petitions, Blair?" Melanie asked.

"I read them."

"They allege you're dangerous," she pointed out.

"They allege a lot of things," Blair retorted.

"Did you assault Michelle?" Melanie asked.

"No," Blair answered.

"Did you ever assault her, abuse her physically?" Melanie probed.

"I never laid a hand on her, never," Blair fired back.

"Did you threaten to kill her?" Melanie asked, not letting up.

"No, I didn't threaten to kill her," Blair answered, shaking his head in obvious disgust.

"Are you dangerous, Blair?" Melanie asked, and with that question she watched Blair closely for a reaction, something, anything.

Blair gave Melanie a funny look that told her nothing. He peered hard at her, but his eyes were vacant, and his breathing seemed to stop. Kimberly was right when she said that Blair was a difficult read. Melanie didn't know if Blair didn't like the question, was thinking about the answer, or didn't know the answer.

"I could be asked, Blair, on the witness stand, whether in my professional opinion, with a reasonable degree of medical certainty, you are *not* dangerous," Melanie added, to encourage an answer from him.

"Let me try answering your question this way, Melanie," Blair said, starting out slowly, leaning forward. "Danger, by definition, means able or likely to do harm. I believe, I know, that I am capable of doing harm, and therefore able. I am not likely to do harm ... unless ... unless ... "

"Unless what, Blair?"

"Unless the situation warrants it," Blair answered, telling her nothing.

"For example?" Melanie asked. It was like pulling teeth, but she was determined not to let him evade her.

"For example, Melanie," Blair said, as if the answer to her question were obvious, "I know that you and Kimberly have talked. You know exactly what happened with my father five years ago. I don't want to relive that with you, other than to say that I've lived with it, day and night, for five years, and there have been emotional consequences."

"Please, Blair, go on," Melanie asked, getting to the heart of her concern.

Blair stood up and walked over to the bay window. He looked out across the vast ocean; directly below, waves crashed into jagged rocks, cascading spray into the red evening sky. Blair watched the force and power of the white-capped ocean, saying nothing.

The incident with his father happened five years ago, Christmas 1990.

Blair remembered, and would never forget, that fateful night.

He and Michelle had taken Courtney, who was then six, to Lawton, Oklahoma, to spend Christmas with his parents. The small farmhouse Blair grew up in was decorated with a fresh-cut spruce tree, complete with an array of blinking lights, and an angel on top. Gifts of all sizes, shapes, and wrappings were waiting to be opened, and for days the kitchen smelled like cookies and bread in the oven.

Marshall Cody had worked at the grocery store the day before Christmas. Blair drove down to help him close up like he had as a boy throughout grade school and high school. Blair was in the back stocking shelves for his dad when he heard a confrontation coming from the front of the store. He saw a man with a bandanna across his mouth, holding a handgun to his father's head, demanding the money in the register.

Fearing any movement on his part would cause his father's death, Blair froze at his vantage point. Seemingly in slow motion, he watched Marshall hand over the money. He watched the assailant pocket it. He watched the gun go off in rapid fire, killing his father. Then, Blair went crazy.

He jumped the assailant from behind, knocking him down, causing the handgun to fall to the floor. Blair won the race for the gun, and after that, everything became a blur. When the police and ambulance arrived, the man was dead. He was flat on his back with his face blown off. The autopsy report confirmed that the handgun was placed deep into the gunman's mouth when the trigger was pulled. The bandanna had been wedged into his throat.

The district attorney of Blair's home county refused to prosecute after spending twenty minutes reviewing the file.

"Guilt plagues me," Blair finally answered, breaking the silence. He turned and looked at Melanie.

"Because you killed a man?" Melanie asked cautiously.

"No, Melanie, not because I killed him," Blair answered firmly. "Because I waited, because I hesitated, and that delay on my part cost my father his life. *That*, Melanie, is the source of my guilt. Not because I killed him. I'm glad I killed that motherfucker," Blair answered, as the anger and pain in his heart surfaced.

"Do you remember the actual killings," Melanie asked, still treading lightly, "or did you block them out?"

"I remember them both," Blair answered, reliving that moment. "I remember him killing my father, and I remember putting the gun in his mouth and pulling the trigger. In my dreams, I push the barrel in deeper, deeper into his throat. No, Melanie, my guilt isn't because I killed a man. It's because I waited."

Moments later, from where he was standing, Blair told Melanie that her question was unfair because it had nothing to do with being a good father. It had nothing to do with what was in Courtney's best interest, or with what Courtney wanted.

Blair repeated for Melanie that the "ability to be dangerous" was not the same as "likely to do harm," as if that was supposed to satisfy her intellectual or professional curiosity.

It didn't.

"Blair, what I have to know is this," Melanie asked. "Is Michelle in any kind of danger from you? For any reason?"

"I came out here to take Courtney home, Melanie. That's why I'm here."

"You didn't answer my question," Melanie sighed in frustration.

"Yes, Melanie, I did," Blair answered.

CHAPTER NINE

HONEYMOON

Las Vegas, Nevada.

Towering gold Roman statues, flanked by an enormous Phoenix, and lion heads with water gushing from their mouths into tiled pools adorned the majestic entrance and lobby. It was the perfect setting for John and Michelle, who were checking in for a two-night stay.

The grand Caesar's Palace was buzzing with action: high rollers shooting them up at the craps tables, yelling and cheering when their prayed-for sevens rolled facing up, moaning in pain when the dreaded elevens burned them to a crisp. Across the aisle, the black-jack tables were filled to capacity with people desperately waiting for an empty seat. The baccarat players were not as noisy, and many of them were dressed in formal attire. The throngs of people, however, were at the fast-paced slot machines, jamming the one-armed bandits with quarters and silver dollars as fast as they could pull the levers; occasionally, bells would ring announcing a winner, adding to the frenzy and excitement.

Michelle, who was watching the action from the lobby, would soon hear other bells.

Their wedding was scheduled by the minister for 2 p.m. the next

day, and they were told not to be late because another was scheduled at 2:15.

John and Michelle had already driven by the cute, little mountain stone chapel and paid the nondenominational minister.
Michelle could have picked any denomination she wanted from his
book, but decided to keep it neutral. The package included beautiful, fresh flower arrangements. She decided to pass on the rice, but
opted for a white Mercedes limousine that would take them to and
from Caesar's Palace. The ceremony, the minister said, would be
exactly like the one movie stars insisted on.

Michelle would have preferred a lavish wedding with friends, relatives, and musicians. She loved dancing to the spontaneous sound of
jazz. Not that long ago, while a student at Penn State, she had taken
classes in modern dance. Even as a child, she had taken ballet and tap.

Michelle often wished that she had followed her dream. She was
meant to be a professional dancer, performing in theaters everywhere. Why she ever listened to her father, and took a job as an
executive secretary to Senator Greenfield, she would never know.
Maybe it wasn't too late to start over.

That evening Michelle wore a black, full-length Christian Dior
gown, with side slits showing her long, shapely legs. Her diamond
necklace and matching earrings sparkled against her skin. She
wore her long, dark brown hair in a simple twist.

John wore his tuxedo, with black bow tie, the same suit he was
wearing when they met at the Taj Mahal in Atlantic City two years
ago. Michelle noticed it was a little tighter, but the cummerbund
took care of that.

Downstairs, the two of them, side by side, played the dollar slot
machines; at one point, Michelle hit for $1,200, but by the time
they went to dinner at the famous Pompeia restaurant the winnings
were gone, plus $2,000 more.

"How do you like the coke I brought along?" John asked
Michelle while the two of them sipped Kahlua before the ten
o'clock show in the Grand Ballroom.

"I like it, John," Michelle answered, "but unless I keep doing it, I get irritable."

"Well, the answer to that is simple enough," John said, smiling.

"What's that?" Michelle asked innocently.

"Keep doing it," John answered, laughing out loud at his recommendation.

"Sounds good to me," Michelle said, reaching under the table for the vial, and then excused herself to go to the restroom.

The Diana Ross show had been sold out, but their reserved table in the front couldn't have been better. They were right at the foot of the stage, and when Diana Ross walked down the steps to sing among the cheering crowd, Michelle could have reached out and touched her. The back-up group, three beautiful, harmonizing girls and a weird-looking guy with braids all over his head, was fantastic. Michelle fantasized that she was up there with them.

Throughout the show, Michelle and John took turns going to the restrooms with the vial.

The strong cocaine kept them up all night, talking and wired, and they went right from their suite to their wedding. More white powder lines for each of them, taken discreetly in the back of the limo, took care of their exhaustion.

The minister, dressed in black with a white collar, stood at the altar facing Michelle and John. Michelle was dressed in a cream lace wedding gown with a shoulder-length veil. John wore his only tuxedo.

Michelle and John held hands as the minister read from his book that they were "to have and to hold, for better or worse, in sickness and in health, for richer or poorer, forsaking all others, till death do us part."

Earlier that morning, and for the past two weeks, Michelle and John had argued plenty about the "richer or poorer" part of their vows. John refused to sign any prenuptial agreement. He told her that he didn't care what her father wanted. He said that he had read the carefully worded contract whereby he was to have nothing in the event of divorce or her death.

Then, John reminded her that she needed him. "Don't forget, honey, that I am your only witness."

Michelle seethed.

John wasn't bringing any assets into the marriage. He wasn't taking his name off the deed or signing away his rights.

Michelle, on her father's advice, without telling John, transferred her cash assets before the wedding into a trust account for Courtney. Courtney wasn't going to get anything until her mother's death, and until then, it was all Michelle's.

Michelle and John looked into each other's eyes when the minister pronounced them man and wife, and then kissed to confirm their vows.

Michelle was doing what she had to do. The custody hearing was fast approaching and she needed to win. She would deal with John later.

Outside, the white limousine waited with its motor softly running to return the newlyweds — now Mr. and Mrs. John Morgan — to Caesar's Palace for their honeymoon.

◆ ◆ ◆

From where Blair was standing along the tree line by the pond, he could see Courtney walking briskly toward their private meeting place. Courtney waved when she spotted him and ran up a dirt embankment into his waiting arms. The two of them had been meeting there, and having lunch together, every day at noon for the past week.

Today, Blair had packed her a peanut butter sandwich, chocolate milk, pickles, potato chips, and chocolate chip cookies, plus a bag of Skittles. Blair also had his own peanut butter sandwich because he didn't want Courtney eating alone. They used their laps for tables, and found two comfortable, flat rocks in the shade overlooking the pond, which was not so quiet because of the quacking ducks that were always waiting for leftovers.

Blair knew that Mr. Johns, at Melanie's request, had gone out of his way, violating every policy of Melrose so the two of them could spend time together.

"How's my kid doing?" Blair asked, handing her the peanut butter sandwich, just the two of them, sitting on their rocks in the shade.

"Mom and John went away, Dad," Courtney answered. "Mom told me they were going to Las Vegas."

"For what?"

"I don't know, Dad," Courtney answered, throwing crumbs to the ducks.

"Who's watching you?" Blair asked.

"Some lady. Her name's Mrs. Fickes. She's okay, I guess . . . she's kinda old."

"What are you going to do after school with Mrs. Fickes?" Blair asked, making small talk.

"Nothing, watch TV," Courtney answered, watching the ducks swarm to the few crumbs in the pond.

"What about your homework?" Blair asked, enjoying Courtney's fascination with the ducks.

"I'll do my homework, Dad," Courtney replied, sounding like her old self.

"What else?" Blair queried.

"Maybe I'll go down to Kristen's," Courtney answered, then added, "Oh yeah, and Mom said she was taking me to see a doctor when she got back. I think it's about going to court."

"Are you feeling okay?" Blair asked, now concerned.

"Yeah, I'm not sick or anything. I'm sure it's about going to court. When is the custody hearing?"

Blair told Courtney that the hearing was two weeks away. He told her not to worry about it, that everything was being taken care of by him. "In the meantime," he added, "we'll have lunch here every day, but I wish you would eat more of your sandwich instead of giving it all to the ducks."

"Oh, Dad," Courtney replied, giving him that loving smile.

Blair took Courtney by the hand, kissed her tenderly on the cheek, and scooted her back to school. His deal with Melanie and Mr. Johns was for her not to be late. It broke his heart to see her walking alone.

Blair was worried sick about Courtney. Her anger toward her mother was growing like a cancerous tumor with each passing day. Hopefully, the upcoming custody hearing would put their lives back on track.

CHAPTER TEN

DANGEROUS

Judge Franklin Hester sat in his chambers on the fourth floor of
the Los Angeles courthouse, smoking his pipe, tapping it occasionally into a glass ashtray on his desk. The cherry blend filled the air,
but it was much too early for Kimberly to be enjoying the sweet
smell of fresh tobacco. Kimberly sat across from Judge Hester,
waiting patiently for the pretrial conference to begin.

To her left sat David Wallace and Jim Johnson. First Assistant
District Attorney Reed sat behind all of them on a leather love
seat facing the pontifical judge. Directly in front of Reed was a
chess board at the appropriate height for play, with hand-cast,
oversized pewter pieces. Judge Hester had other accessories
throughout his office that suggested intelligence and learning—
leather-bound classics, an enormous dictionary on an easel, a globe
of the world, and historic lithographs of courtroom scenes—but
Kimberly wasn't buying it.

Kimberly was also concerned about Hester's neutrality. The law
firm of McNett, Wallace & Johnson had been a major contributor

to his campaign five years ago. In addition, David Wallace and the judge played golf regularly at the prestigious Beverly Hills Country Club. The only reason Wallace was in chambers, Kimberly thought, was to send his golfing buddy a message.

Jim Johnson was another story in Kimberly's book. He was a good trial lawyer, but truth never seemed to get between him and his money. Kimberly had read his experts' reports, prepared by Drs. Meeshok and Goldstein, and was appalled at their conclusion that Courtney was better off with her mother. She believed that Courtney belonged with her father and agonized at the thought of losing his case.

To Kimberly, Blair was a rare find. She had known him since law school, and even then he lived by his own code. He was a mass of contradictions: a down-in-the-dirt cowboy, a fierce litigator, a millionaire, a common man, a true friend, loved by many, hated by few. Blair was always a gentleman and it was not a facade. You could trust him. The most telling thing about him, however, was his love for Courtney.

Franklin Hester, at age sixty-three, had been on the bench five years. His drinking and smoking made him a perfect candidate for a heart attack. He was overweight, but kept much of it concealed with tight-fitting vests and oversized suits. He was never seen without his reading glasses perched on the tip of his nose, or hanging from his neck on a gaudy gold chain.

Judge Hester did not have his robe on for the conference, but wore his gray suit jacket to maintain a semblance of formality in his august chamber. He refused to see lawyers in his office unless they were appropriately dressed, and his receptionist was told that meant coats and ties for men, and business suits for women.

Judge Hester took himself seriously, and he expected everybody else to do the same in his chambers, in the courtroom, and on the street. Married for forty years, with three sons, he made it a point to tell everybody who came before him on domestic matters that good marriages were the fabric of society, and that broken marriages unraveled society in a shameful way.

"Mr. Reed," Hester began, looking past everybody to see him on the love seat, "what are you doing here for what seems to be a standard PFA hearing? Don't you have an election coming up?"

"Never too busy for a just result, Your Honor," Reed answered, smiling politely, with his right hand on the thick file by his side.

"Must be an important case," Hester added.

"Yes, Your Honor," Reed said, "I have a related matter, so I'm just going to observe."

Kimberly could not understand why the number-one prosecutor in LA was sitting in on a custody case. His presence made no sense, and she smelled politics mixed in with Hester's cherry blend tobacco.

Johnson, grinding his bleached teeth, was going to be handling the hearings for Michelle. Every brown hair on his head was in perfect position, parted neatly to the side. The white silk handkerchief in his suit pocket was starched and pressed.

"Well, counsel," Hester said, "I suggest that we do the PFA first."

"Your Honor," Kimberly said, speaking for the first time in chambers, "I have no objection to the PFA going first. I am objecting, however, to plaintiff's counsel calling John Morgan regarding Blair's fitness as a father, and what is in Courtney's best interest. Such testimony would be baseless and irrelevant."

"His testimony is extremely relevant, Your Honor," Johnson fired back arrogantly, "to prove the dangerous propensity of Mr. Cody. The man poses a risk to the life of my client, Courtney's mother, and one who is capable of taking the life of a child's mother cannot be deemed to be a fit father."

"I agree with that," Reed chimed in, though nobody asked him.

"I do too," Wallace volunteered.

Kimberly felt like she was being triple-teamed, which she was. Reed was a criminal prosecutor and had nothing to do with custody determinations. Wallace wasn't trying the case. She could see the political markers being called. This was not going well.

Judge Hester relit his pipe, and as the aromatic smoke surrounded him, he thought pensively about the issue before him. He then ruled that he was letting John Morgan's testimony in at the custody proceeding "because I agree with petitioner's counsel that the alleged dangerous propensity of the natural father is admissible to prove his fitness."

"Anything else before we get started?" Judge Hester asked impatiently.

"No, Your Honor," Johnson, Wallace, and Reed said simultaneously.

"Ms. Wells?"

"No, Your Honor," Kimberly answered.

◆ ◆ ◆

Blair sat in the defendant's chair, his hands clenched in front of him. From there he would observe the proceedings that would forever affect his life. He had been in many courtrooms over the years, but never as an accused criminal.

Ceiling bullet lights illuminated the bench. The rest of the courtroom's lighting was toned down, giving Judge Hester, now robed and in his throne, a majestic glow. On the wall behind the bench was a life-size, brass Lady of Justice, blindfolded, holding her empty scales, with the inscription "Truth is the Mother of Justice."

A podium in the well of the courtroom faced the elevated bench for lawyers to present their arguments and examine witnesses. The chrome and black microphone attached to the witness stand waited ominously for witnesses to tell all. There was no jury in Judge Hester's courtroom because he would determine the facts and make all the rulings.

"May it please the court," Jim Johnson began, standing at the podium, adjusting his tie and puffing up his handkerchief, "let the record reflect that today is September 25, 1995, the date set for the

PFA and custody hearing in this matter, and the petitioner is ready to proceed."

"Very well," Judge Hester said, peering at the parties over his reading glasses, "call your first witness, Mr. Johnson."

Blair watched Michelle take her second walk to the witness stand. She was wearing a new Armani suit, with a single strand of pearls around her neck and matching earrings. He showed no emotion as his ex-wife glanced at him while adjusting the microphone to tell her tale.

"Mrs. Morgan," Johnson began, "would you please tell Judge Hester the events which led to your charging Mr. Blair Cody with assault and battery, and with threatening to take your life."

"Certainly," Michelle answered.

Michelle then shifted her chair, and facing Blair, repeated verbatim what she had told Judge Ross a month before. Kimberly followed along in the transcript, flipping the pages as Michelle droned on for an hour.

"Did you leave Pennsylvania, Mrs. Morgan," Johnson asked, summing up, "and move to California to get away from Mr. Cody's violent, assaultive behavior?"

"Yes," Michelle answered.

"Did Mr. Cody threaten to kill you?"

"Yes," Michelle answered.

"Do you believe that he meant it?"

"I not only believe that Blair meant it, I also believe that he's going to do it. I just don't know when, where, or how," Michelle answered, and then broke down and cried.

Unbelievable, Blair thought to himself. Listening to her lies was hard to take. He watched Johnson take his transcript from the podium and return to the prosecution's table. His partner, Wallace, nodded approvingly.

As Johnson sat down, Kimberly stood up and approached Michelle. She cleverly read her questions from the transcript, looking up at Michelle for her memorized answers. At the conclusion of her cross-examination, Kimberly asked Judge Hester's stenographer to do the following:

"I am now handing you the transcript of the preliminary hearing taken before District Justice Ross, and ask that you compare this transcript with the testimony given today. Take whatever time you need and tell Judge Hester whether they are identical."

"Objection!" Johnson shouted, standing up at his table. "That tactic by Ms. Wells is totally inappropriate. I don't know what she's trying to prove with this grandstanding."

"I'll tell you what I'm trying to prove, Your Honor," Kimberly answered angrily, looking back from the podium at Johnson. "Comparing Mrs. Morgan's testimony today with the preliminary hearing transcript will demonstrate that her testimony today has been memorized and rehearsed. Truthful testimony does not have to be memorized or rehearsed."

"Objection, Your Honor!" Johnson shouted, again with disdain, brushing his misplaced hair away from his eye. "Ms. Wells is now arguing her case."

"I'm stating my offer," Kimberly retorted resentfully.

"Hold it, hold it," Judge Hester said, putting both hands up in the air, signaling time out. "I understand the offer, and the objection, and I am sustaining the objection."

Kimberly lost that ruling but not her composure. Knowing that she had made her point, she approached the stenographer for the transcript and noticed Michelle glaring at her from the witness stand.

"I have no further questions of Mrs. Morgan, Your Honor; we can all read," Kimberly said sarcastically, and went back to her table.

Blair appreciated Kimberly. She was a talented lawyer and a loyal friend.

John Morgan was dressed in a conservative, two-piece, single-breasted blue suit. Blair had already given John the once-over, and he was looking forward to watching Kimberly dismantle the asshole.

The nude pictures that had been found in John's possession were of children—girls and boys ranging from six to thirteen years old in provocative positions—for which he had paid a hefty price to a black-market dealer. Blair knew that he certainly hadn't told Michelle, or her lawyers, about his predilections.

Morgan, after taking the oath, took the witness stand and faced the judge, giving him a polite smile.

"Please state your full name for the record," Johnson said.

"John Edward Morgan," John responded as he cleared his throat.

"What is your present address?"

"719 Valley View Road, Hollywood."

"And how are you related to Michelle Morgan?"

"She is my wife."

"When were you two married?"

"We were married in a church about two weeks ago, but we were living together as husband and wife for almost a year," John answered, looking at Michelle.

"Were you present on the date of this alleged incident, August 7, 1995, involving Blair Cody and Michelle?"

"I was."

"Mr. Morgan," Johnson asked, "would you please tell Judge Hester what happened on that day between Mr. Blair Cody and Michelle."

John Morgan, again clearing his throat, and with his hands still folded neatly on his lap, leaned forward and spoke softly into the microphone. Blair, who had heard a lot of stories from the witness stand throughout his career, was paying close attention to this one. The thought of that despicable pervert being Courtney's replacement father was a bitter pill for Blair to swallow.

"We had just moved into our new home," Morgan began, "and Courtney was sound asleep in her bedroom. It was mid-evening, and we were still unpacking odds and ends. Then I heard this loud, very loud, knocking at the door. Michelle was closer to the door than I was, so she opened it. I could see that it was him."

At that point in his testimony, Morgan pointed his finger at Blair to identify the assailant.

Blair sat expressionless, but the knot in his stomach got tighter.

"I couldn't believe it!" Morgan continued, looking at Judge Hester, who was taking notes at a furious pace. "I had no idea how he had found our new house so quickly, though we intended to notify him of Courtney's whereabouts through proper channels. I could see Michelle trying to close the door on him, and I ran from the kitchen to help her. She was screaming in pain and crying because he had grabbed her arm and wouldn't let go. He screamed, 'I'm going to kill you, bitch. I'm going to kill you.' With my help, Your Honor," John added, "we got the door shut in his face, and locked it."

"So you witnessed the events which gave rise to these charges?" Johnson asked.

"Yes."

"You heard Mr. Cody threaten to kill her?"

"Twice," John answered, holding up two fingers.

"I have no further questions, Mr. Morgan. Thank you," Johnson said, flipping his file closed.

◆ ◆ ◆

Blair waited with Kimberly in the small witness room during the fifteen-minute break. The air in the room was stuffy with stale cigarette smoke. The silence between them was occasionally broken by the sound of footsteps in the hallway.

So far, there had been no surprises. Michelle repeated her testimony, John backed her up, and a PFA order was going to be issued. Blair's concern, however, was the impact of their testimony on the custody issue.

"Blair," Kimberly said, "we both know Hester is going to grant the restraining order."

"I don't care about that," Blair answered.

"How do you want me to handle Morgan?" Kimberly asked.

"He doesn't have a clue that we know about his conviction," Blair answered, and added, "Hold off on that aspect of your cross until the custody phase."

"I agree," Kimberly said, nodding. "You know I'm looking forward to nailing him."

◆ ◆ ◆

Blair watched John carefully as Kimberly questioned him about Hector. John didn't know that Blair was unable to find him, but it was obvious that Kimberly's questioning was getting to him. She had John fumbling for words, shifting in his chair, and sweating.

"All I'm saying," John finally said, "is Mr. Cody assaulted Michelle and threatened to kill her. I was there and saw it. I heard it. Hector wasn't there and Courtney was sleeping. That's all I'm saying."

Pat Greely had been running license plate numbers for weeks with no luck. All he had to work with were the numbers Courtney had given them, and the first name Hector. That left Kimberly with no witnesses except Blair.

Blair could tell that Morgan was badly shaken, and focused on his gritting teeth and heavy breathing. Blair's courtroom instincts were surfacing. "Kimberly," he whispered, "ask him if he's on any kind of drugs. Johnson's going to object, but the added heat will do them both good."

Kimberly smiled.

"Mr. Morgan," Kimberly asked, standing at the defense table, "are you on any kind of medication or mind-altering drugs that may be affecting your memory and judgment?"

"Objection, Your Honor!" Johnson shouted. "Ms. Wells is on a fishing expedition!"

Blair was right. They had hit a nerve.

"Sustained," Judge Hester ruled, which stopped Kimberly's line of questioning.

Blair signaled to Kimberly to end it there, and Johnson immediately rested his case.

"Are you calling any witnesses, Ms. Wells?" Hester asked, leaning forward.

"No, Your Honor, we are not. We rest, too."

"Then this record is now closed," Hester said, looking at his young stenographer, a tall, thin woman.

Reading from the legal pad in front of him, Judge Hester issued his order: "Blair Cody is hereby restrained from appearing at, entering, or trespassing at petitioner's residence, 719 Valley View Road, Hollywood, California. He is also enjoined from coming within striking distance of Michelle Morgan.

"Mr. Cody," Judge Hester added, "if you violate this order, you will be arrested and taken directly to jail."

The tipstaff banged the gavel.

Judge Hester, robe flowing, abruptly left the bench.

John Morgan moved from the gallery to the well of the courtroom and shook Johnson's hand, thanking him.

Michelle was staring at Blair to get his reaction, but got none.

Blair told Kimberly that she had done a nice job, and that he would see her first thing in the morning.

◆　◆　◆

That night, Courtney went to bed early.

Her mother told her that tomorrow would be another long day, and that she would be talking to the judge. Yes, she would be waiting in the library again. No, she could not stay up and watch TV. "There are some things that John and I have to discuss, honey," Michelle said as she turned Courtney's bedroom light out.

Courtney did not like waiting in the spooky library of McNett, Wallace & Johnson. There was nothing to do. She felt like Alice in Wonderland among enormous bookshelves, row after row, with pictureless books. The library table was the biggest one she had ever seen.

Mr. Johnson had told her that a young law clerk would be driving her to the courthouse, and a judge would be asking her questions.

Courtney couldn't sleep, and couldn't help hearing the argument in the kitchen. Her mother was yelling. John was swearing. Some of it made sense to her; a lot of it didn't.

"Tell me!" her mother yelled. "Were you on that shit this morning?"

"What do you care? I told you I wasn't. If I was, so fucking what! I commit perjury for your ass, and that's not good enough!"

"You looked drugged up on the witness stand after the break, for Christ's sake! You're lucky Hester stopped the questioning!"

"And you're lucky, honey, that I didn't tell the truth!"

"You're in this for the extra money, John!" Michelle screamed. "It wasn't because you love me. I know exactly what in the hell you're doing!"

"You're in this for the money, too, Michelle. I don't see any love between you and Courtney. Why don't you just ask Blair for a cash settlement and give her to him?"

"Now that would look like hell, wouldn't it?"

"How did Blair find out about Hector?" John asked, changing the subject.

"I don't have any idea," Michelle answered.

"Well, I do," John said. "I checked our phone bill, which just came in the mail, and that little shit Courtney called her father. She told him everything, you can bet your ass on that! Who knows what in the fuck she's going to tell the judge tomorrow," John added.

"Quit worrying, the psychiatrists will take care of Courtney," Michelle retorted.

All Courtney heard after that was their bedroom door slamming. She was trembling, and wished that her dad could be there.

CHAPTER ELEVEN

CUSTODY

The only sound disturbing the quiet courtroom was the antique English clock above the doors. Even the stenographer and tipstaff were motionless as they waited for Judge Hester to begin the proceedings. Drs. Meeshok and Goldstein, Johnson's experts, were in the back of the courtroom. Dr. Melanie Castille sat with Blair and Kimberly.

Melanie had spent weeks preparing for this custody fight, knowing that a friendly settlement was impossible. She conferred with Mr. Johns and Courtney's teachers, interviewed Courtney at the school, and counseled her father. The efforts she made to discuss the matter with Michelle or her lawyers were spurned.

"Ms. Wells," Judge Hester began, which triggered the stenographer's mechanical mode, "I have given serious consideration to your prehearing motion questioning the jurisdiction of this court under the Uniform Child Custody Act. Your challenge has a great deal of merit, but I am denying your motion. I am maintaining jurisdiction because of the unique circumstances of this case. The child has been living here for some time, is now enrolled in school here, and in my view, to send this matter back to Pennsylvania for resolution would be too disruptive. Your exception to this ruling is noted.

"Mr. Johnson," Judge Hester ordered, looking at him, "call your first witness."

Melanie was anxious to hear Michelle's testimony. It was hard for her to remain objective, based on what Courtney told her and her growing feelings toward Blair. As Michelle took the witness stand in her beige Liz Claiborne suit, she looked like the perfect mother. She was wearing very little makeup, low heels, and a single strand of pearls; in addition, her brown hair was loosely curled and simply styled.

As Michelle testified on direct examination for over an hour, she occasionally wept, and seemed distraught over Courtney's anguish. She told Judge Hester that Courtney was her only child, and that it was in Courtney's best interest to be with her mother. "I love Courtney," Michelle said, "and I have always been a loving mother."

Michelle testified that she could offer Courtney a more stable home environment than Blair. She was now a remarried woman, which would provide the child with a two-parent household. Blair, on the other hand, was single, with only his eighty-year-old mother to help him.

Courtney's new home was more suitable, Michelle said as she showed Judge Hester a large, glossy photo of their new ranch house, which illustrated its residential locale. She said Blair's home was an isolated farm in Pennsylvania, a mile from the main road, where there were no other children. Michelle's new home was within walking distance of playgrounds and the Melrose Middle School, where Courtney had already formed new friendships and was doing well.

"Anything else?" Johnson asked.

"Yes," Michelle answered quickly, obviously prepared for the question. "Blair Cody is dangerous. Though he has never exhibited any violence toward Courtney that I know of, he is capable of anything. Five years ago, he killed a man in the state of Oklahoma by putting a handgun in his mouth and pulling the trigger. I know the killing was ruled justifiable by the coroner's jury and the district attorney, but that doesn't change the fact that Blair is unpredictable. I know that I'm afraid of him, and believe that if given the opportunity, he would kill me."

"I have no further questions, Mrs. Morgan," Johnson said, ending on that chilling note.

Melanie watched Michelle on the witness stand with some fascination. More than once Melanie caught Michelle looking at her. *The woman,* Melanie thought, *is a pathological liar.* Either that, or everything Courtney and Blair had told her was a lie.

Kimberly, sitting beside Blair at their table, began her cross-examination softly. Melanie admired Kimberly, who could skillfully pull the truth from anyone. Melanie had seen her work in the courtroom time and time again, and knew Michelle was in for it. Kimberly would set the pace, but leave the tone to the witness, once the preliminaries were out of the way.

One preliminary was the written custody agreement previously entered into. Yes, her lawyers had drawn up the agreement and explained it to her. Yes, she understood it, but, Michelle fired back, "a daughter should be with her mother."

That was the wrong thing to say to Kimberly. "A daughter should be with her mother, is that what you said?" Kimberly asked, sounding intrigued.

"That's right," Michelle answered.

"But isn't it a fact that you left Courtney without telling her, and then refused to call her for six months while you lived in New York with John?" Kimberly asked.

"That doesn't mean I stopped loving her, Ms. Wells," Michelle answered, annoyed.

"Answer the question, Mrs. Morgan," Kimberly said.

"Ask it again."

"Isn't it a fact that you left Courtney without telling her, and then refused to call her for six months while you lived in New York with John?" Kimberly repeated, not letting up.

"It was less than six months."

"How much less?"

"I don't know."

"Do you know when Courtney's birthday is?"

"Of course, Ms. Wells, I gave birth to her," Michelle answered, rolling her eyes.

"Courtney is eleven years old?"

"That's right. She'll be twelve in January."

"Did you call her, or send her anything, on her last birthday?"

"No."

"Did you forget?" Kimberly asked sarcastically.

"No, Ms. Wells, I didn't *forget*. It's just that, at that time in my life, I was going through some changes," Michelle answered, glaring at Kimberly.

Melanie watched the exchange with interest. Kimberly's questioning was getting to Michelle, who may have looked like the perfect mother, but was coming off as a self-centered bitch. And Kimberly's tone was so personal, it made Melanie wonder if Blair had intentionally hired a female to represent him.

Melanie could feel the resentment from Michelle as Kimberly went after her, backing her into a corner, exposing her true side. The mother Courtney described was finally making an appearance.

"Whose idea was it to take Courtney from her home in the middle of the night, drug her, and bring her to California?" Kimberly asked.

"I didn't drug her," Michelle answered angrily. "The child was tired and fell asleep before we took her out of the house."

"All right then, whose idea was it to take Courtney from her home in the middle of the night and bring her to California?" Kimberly asked, rephrasing the question.

"It was my decision. I am her mother and know what's best for her," Michelle answered defensively.

"Blair doesn't?"

"Blair thinks he knows everything."

"You are happily married now?" Kimberly asked.

"That's right."

"For two weeks?"

"That's right."

Kimberly ended it there; her timing was perfect. She returned to where Blair was sitting and left Michelle hanging. After several minutes, Kimberly finally told the court that she had no further questions.

Michelle was obviously furious, on the verge of uncontrollable, and Johnson got her off the witness stand immediately. He whispered to her, and Melanie watched her collect herself, but not without a final venomous look in Blair's direction.

Dr. Meeshok, in his mid-fifties, looked a lot like a distinguished Elmer Fudd: very short, pudgy, bald, a little slovenly with his loose-fitting tie and old, brown, wing-tipped shoes. It took him forever to get settled in the witness chair, but he quickly rattled off his credentials for Judge Hester without referring to his neatly printed résumé. He was a member of the American College of Forensic Psychiatry, the American Association of Family Conciliation, the American Psychiatric Association, and the California Psychiatric Association. He was certified by the state of California as a licensed psychiatrist.

Dr. Meeshok testified that he was a forensic expert in competency, psychic trauma, personal injury, and family law. He specialized in incest, criminal responsibility, traumatic reactions, custody evaluations, and child abuse.

"Your Honor," Johnson said after the doctor recited his qualifications, "I offer Dr. Meeshok to this court as an expert child psychiatrist."

"Ms. Wells," Judge Hester said, "do you wish to cross-examine on credentials?"

"No, Your Honor," Kimberly answered, "but I would like to point out to the court that Dr. Meeshok seems to be an expert in everything under the sun."

"Objection!" Johnson shouted, standing up, irate.

"Sustained," Judge Hester ruled, smiling.

True to his reputation, Dr. Meeshok testified that after reviewing the file and all documentation, and interviewing the mother, the stepfather, and the child, it was his professional opinion that Courtney Louise Cody should stay with her mother. "My paramount concern," Dr. Meeshok bellowed, "is what's in the child's best interest."

Melanie had been a player in courtrooms for years. The likes of Meeshok were not uncommon, and his testimony didn't surprise her, but Melanie was outraged at his baseless testimony. She knew from past experience that he could be bought to say whatever had to be said in any kind of case.

"Dr. Meeshok," Kimberly asked impatiently, "how much time did you spend with the child whose life you may be permanently affecting?"

"With the child or the case, counselor?" Meeshok asked shrewdly.

"With the child, doctor."

"Maybe an hour."

"Maybe less?"

"Maybe, I wasn't checking my watch."

Kimberly went after Meeshok with a vengeance. She brought out that his brief interview with Courtney was at Johnson's law office—in the presence of Dr. Goldstein, Mr. Johnson, Mr. Wallace, and her mother. He admitted that Courtney wanted to live with her father, and that she wanted to go home with him immediately. It was like pulling teeth, but Meeshok finally confessed that Courtney hated being in California, hated John, didn't trust him, and felt that all her friends were in Pennsylvania.

"Why wasn't any of this in your written report?" Kimberly asked with indignation.

"I didn't consider it relevant, counselor," Meeshok answered matter-of-factly.

"You didn't consider it relevant?" Kimberly asked, looking amazed.

"That's right," Meeshok answered, holding firm.

"Didn't you have an opportunity to review Courtney's test results and records, which indicate an exceptional IQ?" Kimberly asked, tossing his report on the table.

"I did, counselor," Meeshok answered defensively, "but she is still a child. She is eleven years old and has the mind of an eleven-year-old. She doesn't have any idea what she wants, and certainly doesn't know what is in her best interest. That's why her input is irrelevant."

"Irrelevant?" Kimberly asked incredulously, looking at the judge.

"That's right," Meeshok answered.

"Have you talked to Blair Cody?" Kimberly asked.

"No."

"We made him available to you."

"I said no."

"Would you consider his input irrelevant?" Kimberly asked point-blank.

"I am not here to say that he is a fit, or unfit, father. I'm just telling you that in my opinion the child belongs with her mother," Meeshok answered, with perspiration visible on his forehead.

"Doctor, whose input was relevant to that determination?" Kimberly asked, determined to expose this expert for what he was.

"Mine," Meeshok answered arrogantly.

◆ ◆ ◆

Courtney walked around the huge conference room table for something to do. The library that nobody seemed to use was getting to her. She was also becoming more curious by the minute about what was going on.

It was almost noon.

Her mother had told her that she would be talking to the judge sometime today. Her mother had said that yesterday, too; and last evening, when Courtney asked what was going on, her mother wouldn't talk about it. Courtney didn't know whether her mother was telling her the truth about anything. She didn't even know if she was going to be talking to a judge at all. Yesterday? Today? Tomorrow? Ever?

Courtney had grown tired of the bag full of books and crayons that she had brought with her that morning. Even school was better than waiting around for two days with nothing to do. It wouldn't be so bad if she had somebody to talk to.

Maybe she could call Grandma Cody in Pennsylvania. Grandma would tell her what was going on. Grandma Cody told her everything.

◆　◆　◆

Melanie recognized Dr. Goldstein, frequently used by the District Attorney's Office of Los Angeles in criminal cases to refute claims of insanity. The tall, soft-spoken man with his chiseled face and dyed auburn hair sometimes seemed unreal. Melanie didn't know that Dr. Goldstein was also a child psychiatrist.

Until today.

I guess anything goes in custody cases, Melanie thought.

Dr. Goldstein, in his rote voice, echoed Dr. Meeshok's opinion and conclusion. He said it was in the best interest of the child to stay with her mother. After all, Michelle was a married woman with a stable home, and was willing to promote and encourage the relationship between the child and her father. He said the child was doing well in school. In addition, Goldstein added, he was concerned about the dangerous propensities of the natural father, based on the father's history as recounted by the mother.

Over objection, Dr. Goldstein testified that he believed Blair would be capable of killing Michelle if he were adequately provoked. The killing in Oklahoma clinched it for him.

"Thank you," Johnson said, concluding his direct examination.

Kimberly, having been thoroughly prepared by Melanie, challenged Dr. Goldstein's credentials in this case. He admitted that this was his first time as a child psychiatrist in a court of law. Furthermore, his exposure to the child was less than an hour.

Goldstein acknowledged that the child was emphatic about where she wanted to live. Goldstein testified that the child was bright, according to the test results in her school file, and seemed to know what she wanted.

"But she's still a child," Goldstein added, "and I agree with Dr. Meeshok."

Portrayed as an important influence in Courtney's new family, and the loving stepfather, John was again called to the stand. He was the only witness left for Michelle, and Jim Johnson had to call him.

John testified that he loved Courtney very much and was looking forward to being there for her. He said he personally checked out the school district because her education was important to him. He said that it was important for the three of them—Michelle, Courtney, and himself—as a family to join a denominational church.

Johnson kept it short.

Kimberly, who had been waiting for Morgan's direct examination to end, was prepared.

"Mr. Morgan, you testified that you love Courtney?" Kimberly asked, without tipping her hand.

"Yes," John answered politely.

"Do you love *all* children?"

"I'm not sure what you mean."

"Maybe Ms. Wells could clear that last question up for Mr. Morgan," Johnson interjected.

"Certainly," Kimberly agreed. "Mr. Morgan, isn't it a fact that you were convicted of possessing child pornography in the state of New York in 1988?" she asked, staring right at him.

The question shocked him and everybody else in the courtroom. Melanie loved it.

Johnson was too stunned to object. Michelle was visibly surprised and upset. Drs. Meeshok and Goldstein looked at each other with concern. Judge Hester sat forward for Morgan's answer.

"I . . . I was a victim of circumstances," John answered, obviously shaken.

"Would you please explain that answer, Mr. Morgan?" Kimberly asked, moving in for the kill.

"I was set up. It was entrapment," John answered.

"Who entrapped you?"

"The guy who sold it to me."

"Did you think you were buying landscape photography, or what?" Kimberly asked with a slight laugh.

"I just bought it to get rid of him. He kept persisting," John answered, turning red.

"How many pictures of nude children did you have when you were arrested, Mr. Morgan?"

"I don't remember."

"Would you dispute the police inventory report of over one hundred?"

"I don't remember."

"Would you agree that the pictures of these children were sexually provocative, and that the children ranged in age from six to thirteen?"

"I don't remember. I really didn't look at them."

"Did you plead guilty in a court of law to intentionally, willfully, and knowingly possessing child pornography for sexual gratification?"

"My lawyer told me to."

"Did you tell Drs. Meeshok and Goldstein about this proclivity of yours to help them in their assessment of what's in Courtney's best interest?"

"No."

"Did you tell your wife, Courtney's mother?"

"No."

Kimberly turned around and looked at Melanie, eye to eye.

Melanie nodded. She knew that Morgan was dying a slow death in the electric chair, and Kimberly was providing the current.

Johnson sat expressionless.

Judge Hester, for the first time in two days, seemed concerned about his judicial assignment and responsibility.

◆ ◆ ◆

Jim Johnson called his young paralegal, Sue, to tell Courtney about the night session. Johnson suggested that she take her someplace for dinner, and then wait at the office for his call.

Sue walked down the hallway to the library, entered quietly, and scanned the vast open area.

Courtney was not in her chair.

Her bag of books and crayons was missing.

She did not answer when Sue called out her name.

Courtney was gone.

Sue immediately checked the lunch room, the bathrooms, the offices, the elevators, stairwells, and hallways. She could not get through to tell Johnson because the courthouse switchboard was closed. She was afraid to leave the building just in case Courtney came back or Johnson called. Frantic, she dialed the police.

CHAPTER TWELVE

EMPEROR

Blair, waiting for the evening session to begin, looked up at the Lady of Justice looming on the granite wall. *"Truth is the Mother of Justice,"* Blair thought to himself, *and this courtroom hasn't seen it in two days.*

The poetic hypocrisy was laughable.

Michelle had portrayed him as a stalking killer. Meeshok and Goldstein were bullshit. A child pornographer said he loved Courtney.

Jesus! Blair thought, shaking his head.

He hoped that Hester wasn't in the petitioner's bag, but he wasn't sure. His relationship with the Wallace firm, and deference to Reed, bothered him every time the judge ruled in Michelle's favor.

"I call at this time Dr. Melanie Castille," Kimberly said, bringing Blair back to the present moment.

Melanie had the credentials, and laid them out for Judge Hester without fanfare.

She had courtroom presence, dressed in a black business suit, with a high-collared white blouse.

She had credibility. For the past fifteen years she had devoted her life to the emotional well-being of children.

Testifying with poise, Melanie impressed upon Judge Hester that Courtney was intellectually brilliant. She went on to emphasize the fact that Courtney was strong emotionally and psychologically, and that she was also sensitive. She said that Courtney was old enough and bright enough to know where she wanted to live, who she wanted to live with, and what was in her best interest.

"Courtney Cody belongs with her father," Melanie said unequivocally.

"She told you that?" Kimberly asked.

"Yes, and it's important to note that the child not only wants to go with her father, but indicated that she belongs with him."

"What did she say about her mother?"

"She said that her mother doesn't want her. Courtney also doesn't trust John Morgan, and is uncomfortable around him when her mother isn't home," Melanie answered.

Blair knew that Michelle resented Melanie with a passion. She hated being told from the witness stand, especially by another woman, that she was an unfit mother. Melanie testified that Michelle had been preoccupied with herself for some time, if not always, and had abandoned her child when she ran off to New York with John Morgan.

Having sat through two days of baseless rhetoric from Drs. Meeshok and Goldstein, Blair was convinced that neither of them appreciated or cared about Courtney, or about the role he played in her life. Blair saw Melanie as a lifeline in the raging waters. Maybe, he thought, she could save him.

"Blair Cody, Your Honor," Melanie asserted, "is a rare individual. I can tell you that he loves Courtney more than anything in the world and is an excellent father. He has devoted his life to this child, and will forever assure her protection, her education, and her moral upbringing. He is in a position to do so. It is my professional opinion that it is in Courtney's best interest to be with her father."

Dr. Castille looked directly at Blair as Kimberly questioned her. As Melanie spoke, Blair was touched by her belief in him as a father and a person. It had been a long time since anybody had said anything nice about him publicly.

Jim Johnson, a skilled cross-examiner, had met his match in Melanie Castille. Blair enjoyed watching Melanie nail him on every question. Her answers destroyed his theory that a daughter should be with her mother, assuming both parents were fit, because Melanie would not concede that Michelle was a fit mother.

"Do you agree, Dr. Castille," Johnson asked, "that children often change their minds about matters of importance to them?"

"Yes, as do adults."

"When did you talk to Courtney last?"

"Six days ago."

"Are you sure, Dr. Castille," Johnson asked, standing up at the table beside Michelle, suggesting with his question that the circumstances had changed, "that since you talked to Courtney, she hasn't already changed her mind about who she wants to live with?"

Melanie seemed to freeze on the witness stand. Blair watched her expression change suddenly, as if Johnson no longer existed. Judge Hester, at that last question, also stopped paying attention and looked to the back of the courtroom.

"We're going to find out right now," Melanie answered, and Blair tracked her gaze.

Courtney had quietly opened the ornate oak doors and was walking toward him. She opened the gate to the well of the courtroom, and ran into his arms.

Michelle jumped up and yelled, "Courtney, what do you think you're doing!" She moved toward Courtney, who had already reached her father.

Blair, startling everyone, instinctively got between Courtney and her mother, scaring the hell out of Michelle.

Judge Hester sat dumbfounded for a moment. He then pushed the emergency button to alert the sheriff's office, but they were gone for the day.

John Morgan was paralyzed.

Kimberly was not prepared for this chaos.

Melanie had the best seat in the house, next to Judge Hester.

Michelle slowly and carefully, very carefully, backed away from Blair.

Judge Hester wiped his forehead with the back of his hand and ordered a recess, directing the lawyers to his chambers.

"Only the lawyers," he said, but Courtney was to be included.

In chambers, Judge Hester politely offered Courtney a soda to get things started.

"No thank you," she said, fidgeting.

Courtney sat on the love seat by the chess board. She was overwhelmed by the surroundings and wished that her dad were with her.

Judge Hester took off his robe and sat in the cushioned chair beside her. The lawyers in the office and the stenographer made Courtney feel uncomfortable.

"I heard that you got a little scared when they turned the lights out in the library," Judge Hester said in a friendly tone.

"A little bit. It wasn't dark or anything, but I thought that I might get locked in," Courtney answered, plenty nervous. She had made up her mind that she was going to tell Judge Hester that she wanted to go home with her dad. Her mother's lawyers already knew that. She didn't understand what was taking so long. Everybody, it seemed, asked her what she wanted. Nobody, it seemed, listened or did anything about it.

"Did you walk down here?" Hester asked.

"Yes," Courtney answered.

"How did you know where to come?" the judge continued.

"Sue told me earlier that it was just down the street, so I asked some lady outside where the courthouse was, and she showed me. It only took me a couple minutes," Courtney answered proudly.

"Sue?"

"Mr. Johnson's secretary."

"How's everything going for you, Courtney?" Hester asked, clearing his throat.

"I want to go home with my dad," Courtney said emphatically. She finally got it out, and was hoping the meeting was over. There was nothing more to say. It was time to go.

"Did he tell you to say that?" Hester asked, frowning.

"No," Courtney answered, not looking away. Courtney did not like the suggestion that her father had put her up to this. Her mom's lawyers had tried the same thing. She was very clear, again, about her wishes.

"Your mother loves you too," Hester offered.

Courtney did not respond, and there was an awkward silence that was quickly broken by the judge.

"I hear you're a good little horse rider. What do they call it . . . reining, or something like that?" Hester asked, changing the subject.

"Yes," Courtney answered, without adding anything more.

"Is reining some sort of horse event?" Hester continued, making small talk.

"Uh-huh," Courtney answered. Everybody knew what reining was, she thought. You walk your horse into a riding pen, run a pattern which always includes spins and sliding stops, and walk out. The best rider wins. Courtney loved talking about reining and horses, but that's not what she had come to talk about.

"Are your horses in Pennsylvania?" Hester pursued, not getting the point.

Courtney nodded.

"Is that why you want to go home?" Hester asked finally.

"No," Courtney answered without hesitation. *So that's what he was leading up to,* she thought. "I just want to go home with my dad, sir, because that's where I belong," Courtney repeated, and wondered how many more times she was going to have to say it. Judge Hester glared at Wallace.

"I don't want to live out here with Mom and John," Courtney continued, without being asked.

"Why not, Courtney?" Judge Hester probed.

"I don't want to live here," Courtney answered, frustrated.

The judge again looked at Wallace, who avoided his darting glare.

Finally, Hester stood up, thanking Courtney for talking to him, and extended his hand. Courtney shook his hand politcly before she got up to go. When she got to the door, Courtney turned around and faced Judge Hester.

"Sir," she said, "my dad didn't grab my mom's arm. Hector did."

◆ ◆ ◆

Kimberly told Blair everything that had gone on in chambers.

He was really proud of his little girl. He thought it took a lot of courage to walk into the courtroom like that. Talking to a judge, surrounded by lawyers, was no easy task either.

Blair hoped Hester was troubled by the turn of events in his courtroom. Courtney's dramatic appearance and innocence should have muddied his predisposition to award custody to Michelle.

"Maybe," Blair whispered to Kimberly before he took the witness stand, "Courtney has turned this around."

Blair's testimony was concise and to the point, without embellishment.

Judge Hester asked Blair one question during his testimony. Neither Kimberly nor Johnson had brought it up.

"Mr. Cody," the judge began, leaning forward, peering over his reading glasses, "do you know who Hector is?"

"Your Honor," Blair answered truthfully, "I spoke to him once. I understand that he drove the moving van, and I have not been able to find him."

"Does anybody else have any further questions of Mr. Cody?"

Hester asked, looking across the courtroom, bringing the hearing to a close.

"No, Your Honor," Johnson answered.

"No, Your Honor," Kimberly repeated.

"Well, here's what I am going to do," Hester said, adjusting his glasses.

Blair, still in the witness chair, held his breath. He believed the judge was about to render his verdict.

"I am going to take this matter under advisement," Hester continued, "and issue my final order in the near future. In the meantime, the father, Blair Lee Cody, shall have immediate visitation rights, which will include every weekend. All visitation shall be exercised within the jurisdictional confines of this court, which is the state of California, except that the father may take his daughter to Raleigh, North Carolina, on the weekend of October 13, 1995, for the reining horse competition."

Everybody sat motionless.

Blair had won a partial victory.

He was still stuck in California until Hester made up his mind. But tonight, since it was Friday, Courtney was going with him.

◆ ◆ ◆

Courtney told Blair the apartment was awesome. She would be sleeping on an air mattress that he bought on his way home from the courthouse. He also bought her casual clothes and personal articles at the Wal-Mart. Neither of them wanted to go to her mother's to pick up her stuff.

That night, they talked, and Blair explained everything. Though disappointed, Courtney said she understood, and was glad to have the weekend with him. She said she couldn't wait to fly to Raleigh to hook up with Impressive James, and run around on her scooter with her friends.

Blair laughed when Courtney told him how she had snuck out of Johnson's law offices. Grandma Cody had said that it was okay.

At 1 a.m., she fell sound asleep on her new bed in the living room.

After tucking her in, Blair was startled when the phone rang in his bedroom. He was happy to hear from Melanie, and the late hour meant nothing to either of them.

"How's Courtney?" Melanie asked.

"She's great," Blair answered.

"Courtney really is something else. I absolutely loved it when she walked into the courtroom," Melanie said, laughing.

"You? I couldn't believe it either, but then again, that's Courtney," Blair responded happily.

"You should have seen the look on Michelle's face," Melanie said mischievously.

"I didn't have a chance."

"You got pretty close when you got up," Melanie teased.

"Yeah, I know."

"I didn't know what in the hell you were going to do," Melanie said, obviously digging for an answer.

"Neither did I, Melanie," Blair admitted.

"I couldn't believe it. I was holding my breath."

"Melanie?" Blair said, suddenly getting serious.

"Yes?"

"I really appreciate what you've done. I can't tell you how much your help has meant to me," Blair said, with a hint of something more.

"Blair, I meant everything I said on that witness stand about you. I think you know it was more than a professional opinion," Melanie added, keeping it going.

"How about, when I get back from Raleigh, we go to dinner?" Blair asked, already knowing the answer.

CHAPTER THIRTEEN

POLITICS

William Reed was reviewing the latest polls for the upcoming, hotly contested election. He was way ahead—and very likely the next district attorney of Los Angeles County—based on telephone surveys, door-to-door solicitations by committee people, and endless fundraisers and speaking engagements. His advisors told him, "Don't screw up, and the office is yours."

Expensive billboards of Reed looking down upon the passing motorists dotted the major highways. They depicted him standing at his desk with the American flag in the background. His clean-shaven face and receding hairline spoke of maturity. He looked tall and able to deliver on his slogan, "Tough on Criminals."

His TV ads were blitzing the airways. "I am the experienced candidate, the proven prosecutor," Reed proclaimed, either on the courthouse steps or walking the corridors in the profession-ally choreographed footage. The voice-over at the end of the thirty-second spot told the viewing audience that Reed, LA County's first assistant district attorney, had been trying the people's cases for twenty-five years, and was proud to be their servant of justice.

A consummate politician, Reed intentionally avoided all cases that were controversial. He refused to prosecute two police officers in his county who were allegedly taking bribes from businessmen in the Asian community in exchange for added protection. The LA police department was not behind the prosecution, and the community was staying out of it.

An aide to the Republican governor of California was busted for distributing small amounts of cocaine to friends and associates while at a party in the governor's mansion. Reed wanted nothing to do with that, and gave it to an assistant.

Reed also refused to try any case in front of a jury that could result in an acquittal. If the prosecution's case wasn't airtight, with multiple credible eyewitnesses and a confession, Reed would hand it off to a young deputy. In the past ten years, he had won forty cases in a row, and was proud of that impressive record.

And Reed never wanted to be bothered with petty cases. The file on his desk captioned *California v. Blair Cody* fell into that category. He was only handling the Cody case because his party boss, Doc Bunt, had asked him to.

Bunt held the keys to the party war chest, and his coffers had been fattened up with a major contribution from Pennsylvania. Reed didn't know who this guy Keating was until Doc told him he was Michelle's father and the chairman of the Pennsylvania State Republican Committee. The prosecution of a simple case by Reed, one that was open and shut, was a small price to pay to keep Doc happy.

The aggressive campaign was keeping Reed busy. His platform was law and order, victim compensation, and returning the streets to upright citizens. Spousal abuse worked its way into his brochures. It was an old platform that always worked.

The trendiest aspect of Reed's campaign was to get tough on juveniles. He knew that during the last decade, the number of minors committing murder, rape, robbery, and assault had increased by a stunning 93 percent. His press conferences were spiked with sound bites that youthful offenders would be treated as adults and face the wrath of the law. Reed was in touch with the public outrage over young delinquents getting away with crimes that ranged from vandalism to homicide.

Indeed, the California legislature was equally outraged at the lawbreaking youth of America, calling them "parasitic," "animalistic," "depraved," and "super-predators." That same year California's lawmakers passed the Juvenile Criminal Act, which placed *any* juvenile charged with a violent crime in the adult criminal system.

Then, two weeks before the November election, a perfect political opportunity presented itself. Three young African Americans, captured on video, entered a small Italian bakery on the outskirts of Los Angeles and demanded the elderly proprietor's money; after he gave it to them, one of the boys, aged thirteen, waved a semi-automatic handgun in his face, and for no reason, shot him in the chest three times. The three young assailants—the others were twelve and sixteen—were quickly apprehended because of the concealed camera that caught them live and in color, with sound. That footage was immediately picked up by the media and became the lead story throughout California.

Reed knew to move fast, and called a statewide press conference, which he held on the courthouse steps. It was a major media event, and a political coup. Television crews were there from all the major networks, with towering antennas on their trucks positioned for immediate, live broadcast. All of LA's radio stations had their microphones strategically positioned on Reed's podium, and the print media were there in flocks with their pens, pads, and tape recorders in hand.

"This senseless crime," Reed began, eyeing the crowd of reporters and onlookers, "which you have witnessed yourself on film, was committed by three juveniles. Regardless of their ages, their unprovoked act took the life of Roberto Giovanni, a hard-working immigrant baker, and I promise you that these young assailants will be charged as adults, tried as adults, and if convicted, punished as adults. I intend to put them in jail for the rest of their natural lives."

"Mr. Reed," a reporter from the local NBC affiliate asked, with his crew's cameras rolling, "are the young men in custody?"

"Yes, they were arrested and are in lock-down as we speak."

"Do you see any racial overtones, Mr. Reed?" another reporter asked, jamming a microphone into his face.

"Absolutely not," Reed fired back, prepared for the question. "This was not a racial crime. This is not a racial prosecution. The bullets that took the life of Mr. Giovanni were color-blind. My position on violent juvenile offenders is a matter of public record."

"In fact, cracking down on delinquents has been your slogan," a friendly reporter chimed in.

"Exactly!" Reed responded, pointing at the reporter.

The live news coverage captured the attention of the Los Angeles community in a big way.

After the conference, Reed and his entourage of campaign advisors met in his office to assess the political impact. Everybody was excited about the maximum exposure they had gotten during prime air time. There was no way Reed's Democratic opponent could come back after this. Reed played his advantage as the first assistant district attorney flawlessly.

"Are you going to try this case, Mr. Bill?" Doc Bunt asked.

"You're assuming, Doc, that I'm going to be elected in two weeks."

"You're going to be elected in two weeks, Bill, because you've played it like I told you," Bunt answered confidently. "We've got plenty of money to finish up strong with our TV ads. The murder of Giovanni couldn't have happened at a better time," Bunt added.

"I'm giving this one to an assistant, and I can guarantee everybody here that Giovanni isn't going to complain," Reed joked.

Everybody in his office—Bunt and his most trusted committee people—laughed.

Two weeks later, William Reed was elected in a landslide victory as the new district attorney of Los Angeles County.

◆ ◆ ◆

He would not be sworn in until after January 1.

Cardboard boxes filled with files and framed photos were stacked in a corner. Reed's desk was uncluttered. All of the stress of the campaign was behind him.

Reed reluctantly took Kimberly's call, knowing that her timing was intentional. He also knew what she wanted.

She wanted him to dismiss the charges against Blair. This was a simple domestic dispute and there was no reason to keep dragging it on. The heart of the matter was the custody of Courtney, and Judge Hester had heard all the testimony, including Michelle's allegations of abuse. In fact, according to Kimberly, Judge Hester was still considering the matter, which meant that he was on the fence.

Reed refused.

He was adamant about trying the case. Though Kimberly didn't know it, Reed had promised Bunt that he would personally handle it. In addition, the word from Wallace was to take it to trial. They had to have a criminal conviction. Courtney's abrupt appearance and testimony had jeopardized Michelle's custody case. That's what Judge Hester had told Wallace at the country club.

"Bill, you know these allegations are bullshit," Kimberly said angrily.

"That's for a jury to determine," Reed answered.

"You're not talking to the cameras now, Bill, so cut the crap and tell me why you're really prosecuting this case," Kimberly asked, exasperated.

"I've already told you. I can't help you. I'm against spousal abuse. I'll see you in court next week, unless you want a continuance," Reed said sternly.

"I don't want a continuance, Bill," Kimberly answered.

◆ ◆ ◆

One week later, Blair was back in court.

The giant Christmas tree outside the courthouse was decorated for the joyous holidays. Red and white tinsel was wrapped around light poles, which made them look like candy canes. A Santa Claus stood on the corner, ringing a black bell with a nearby hanging pot, raising money for the Salvation Army. A Christmas carol could be heard in the distance, coming from a retailer's store.

Inside, a jury was in the box about to hear opening arguments from Reed and Kimberly. The nine men and three women were selected from a panel after being questioned by the judge about their ability to be fair and impartial. No one on the panel knew anything about the case.

Judge Clarence Morrisey, an African American, was assigned to this routine case. He was a tall, thin man of forty-nine, who had never been reversed by the appellate courts.

Blair watched and listened carefully to Reed's opening statement. He had heard from Kimberly that Reed was a heavyweight, but he would decide for himself.

"Ladies and gentlemen," Reed began without the benefit of a podium or notes, "I represent the people of the state of California, and will prove to you beyond a reasonable doubt that the defendant in this case, Blair Lee Cody, assaulted his ex-wife in a fit of rage, caused her bodily harm, and threatened to take her life. Such threats are not taken lightly by the District Attorney's Office of Los Angeles County. Too often, they are carried out in domestic cases. We will show you the defendant's motive for carrying out such a threat. We will prove to you that Blair Cody is a dangerous man capable of keeping such a promise."

Reed's opening, Blair thought, was very effective. He suspected that Reed was playing to the tune of Michelle's father. There was no other explanation for this aggressive prosecution of him by their number-one prosecutor.

Kimberly's opening was also well done. She not only stressed that the assault hadn't happened, but explained to the jury that behind these allegations was strategic posturing to obscure the wishes of Courtney Louise, age eleven, who wanted to go home with her father.

There was a time when Blair would have enjoyed trying a case like this, against the likes of Reed. Prosecutors whose primary concern was to win for themselves, without any regard for the truth, had to be dealt with. Knocking them on their ass in the courtroom was the only way to deal with guys like that.

Reed's first witness, his opening act, added drama and theater to the quiet courtroom. He called the 911 operator, who authenticated the taped call from Michelle on the night in question. Reed then played the tape for the jury, who wore headsets as the reel-to-reel tape slowly turned. The rest of the courtroom listened over a speaker.

Not knowing what was on the tape, Blair put his headset on and adjusted the volume.

"This is 911, may I help you?"

"This is an emergency."

"Go on."

"My name is Michelle Cody and I have been assaulted. My life has been threatened and I don't know what to do."

"Where are you located?"

"I'm at a pay phone. My daughter is waiting in a hotel room."

"Do you know who did this to you?"

"Yes, my ex-husband, Blair Cody. He came out here unexpectedly from Pennsylvania, and he's trying to take my daughter. He threatened to kill me, and I am terribly frightened because I believe that he's going to do it. Please, please help me."

Blair shook his head. *That lying bitch,* he thought.

"Where is he now?"

"I don't know."

"What's your location?"

"I'm outside the Regent Beverly Wilshire Hotel. Where is the nearest police station? I have my car and can go there for protection."

"Go straight to Boas Street. That's in the Fourth Precinct. It's only ten blocks away. I will radio them and tell them you are on your way."

Everybody in the courtroom could hear Michelle quickly hang up, and the eerie dial tone. Reed let the dial tone play for almost five seconds, and then there was dead silence in the courtroom.

Reed had the jury's attention.

Reed had Blair's attention! Michelle actually sounded terrified and credible. Already, Blair didn't like the way things were going. He felt like a stalking killer, and if he felt that way, then the jury saw him that way.

Michelle then took the witness stand, and for the third time told her story. Her feigned fright on the night in question was still ringing in the jury's ears when she recounted her horror. Michelle's lies were a lot more polished than they had been at the preliminary hearing. Her delivery was a lot more emotional and detailed than it had been before Judge Hester. Reed was a skilled prosecutor and had prepared his witness well, especially the part about how Michelle feared for her life.

John Morgan didn't do badly either. The main reason for his adequate performance on the witness stand, however, was due to Judge Morrisey's pretrial ruling that Morgan's conviction for possessing child pornography was not relevant, and therefore not admissible. It was an important ruling for Reed, and a tactical victory that got Morgan off the hook.

Reed got another pretrial ruling from Judge Morrisey that was a major coup. The judge agreed to allow Dr. Goldstein's opinion testimony regarding Blair Cody.

Blair was having a hard time controlling his frustration. He knew how sidebar rulings turn cases. He also knew that innocence is not a defense.

Dr. Goldstein testified that "certain people are dangerous." He said that "dangerous proclivities are genetic, and cultivated by life's experiences." It was Dr. Goldstein's expert opinion that Blair

Lee Cody fell into that category, and over objection, he testified that he believed Blair would be capable of killing Michelle if he were adequately provoked. In part, his opinion was based on the fact that Blair had killed a person in Oklahoma.

Reed was on a roll. He had Blair right where he wanted him, defending genetics and history.

Reed finished up by calling the uniformed police officers who testified, agreeing with each other, that Blair was "lying in wait" outside Michelle's home on the night in question, after midnight.

◆ ◆ ◆

Again, Blair refused to allow Courtney to testify. He believed the emotional damage to her would be too great, and Melanie Castille was in agreement. Kimberly could only go along with their wishes.

Hector was still nowhere to be found.

That left Kimberly with one witness: Blair.

Blair said what he had to say, that it didn't happen. He testified that he did not strike Michelle, that he did not threaten to kill her, and that he was outside the home on the night in question to take Courtney home pursuant to his written agreement. He testified that during his twelve-year marriage to Michelle, he had never abused her.

"Mr. Cody, your daughter means everything to you, doesn't she?" Reed asked, and the exchange between the two combative lawyers began.

"That's right," Blair answered.

"How far would you be willing to go to get Courtney back, Mr. Cody?"

"The answer to that question, Mr. Reed, depends on the circumstances," Blair answered matter-of-factly.

"Did you decide what the circumstances were in Oklahoma?" Reed asked accusingly.

"I did," Blair answered, without batting an eye.

"How did you get that handgun into the victim's mouth before pulling the trigger and blowing his head off?" Reed asked, shocking the jury.

"Objection, Your Honor!" Kimberly shouted, standing up.

"I'll answer that question, Mr. Reed," Blair stated. Reed stood in the well of the courtroom, unprepared for Blair's challenge.

Judge Morrisey quickly summoned Reed and Kimberly to sidebar. Outside the presence of the jury, in whispers but on the record, Reed insisted that his question was relevant to show how dangerous Blair could be if adequately provoked. "I'm not suggesting Mr. Cody wasn't legally justified in the Oklahoma killing, Your Honor," Reed said, "only that if adequately provoked he can be dangerous." Kimberly objected on the grounds that the question was irrelevant as to whether Blair struck Michelle or threatened her. She also argued that the question was so inflammatory that a mistrial was in order.

Judge Morrisey was troubled by the question and ruled in Kimberly's favor, but denied her mistrial motion.

Reed, however, had done his damage with the question.

"You don't deny then, Mr. Cody, that you would kill for Courtney?" Reed asked, summing up.

"No," Blair answered point-blank.

The jury, and the gallery, was riveted.

It was impossible to tell which way they were leaning.

The jury deliberated for two days after hearing the closing arguments and the court's charge. As they filed into the courtroom, they seemed somber, and Blair sensed the bad news. It was the way they refused to look at him that gave them away. The foreman read the verdict in a deadpan voice: "Guilty."

Their verdict was another win for District Attorney-Elect William Reed.

It was another win for Michelle, and for her father.

It was a terrible loss for Blair, who whispered to Kimberly, "I know you did your best; we both know the truth."

Judge Morrisey sentenced Blair on the spot to twelve months' nonreporting probation.

One week later, in a written opinion, Judge Franklin Hester ordered that Courtney remain in the custody of her mother, with limited but specified visitation for her father.

CHAPTER FOURTEEN

INNOCENCE LOST

Courtney blamed her mother for dragging her into a chaotic world. Her only happiness was the time spent with her father, and her dreams. She would bide her time and make the best of it. That's what her father told her to do. That's what her friend Melanie told her to do.

But it was so very, very difficult.

Christmas and New Year's were an emotional roller coaster. Christmas morning was with her mom; the afternoon was with her dad. New Year's Eve was with her mom; New Year's Day was with her dad. Courtney could also tell that her dad was having a harder time with the court order than she was, which didn't help.

It hurt her to think of him in his apartment, alone. She remembered him differently, on their wide-open ranch with their horses, the two of them playing and laughing. At least he had Melanie to talk to, and be with, and she seemed awfully nice.

Her dad explained that after the holidays he had to go back to Pennsylvania for a while. He had to clear up some odds and ends at their old house and office. He was going to fly Grandma Cody back to Oklahoma. "I'll be gone for about a month," he said, "but I'll be back to spend the weekends with you, and when summer comes we'll go home together." He promised that he would call every day, and said that she should tell Melanie if she needed anything.

Courtney never told her mom about Melanie. Every time her mom and John argued, and Melanie's name came up, her mom would bristle and swear. Her mom was acting stranger and stranger lately. She was more agitated, meaner, and struck her more than once for no reason. One time it was because of the phone bill. The last time was because Courtney slammed her bedroom door too hard. The time before that, her mother pulled her hair and made her cry, then snickered.

Courtney was afraid to tell her dad about the situation at home. She didn't want him to get into trouble with the judge, which might cost him, and her, time together. Most of all, Courtney didn't want to upset him. She felt guilty enough about what her dad was going through.

Then there was John.

From the day she met him, she couldn't stand him. John never hit her or anything like that, but it was the way he would look at her, especially when her mom wasn't around. Courtney couldn't describe it, but it was a feeling of uneasiness. He was always hanging out at home, planted in a recliner, watching television in his underwear.

One morning she woke up without a blanket on and he was there looking at her. Every time she took a shower, John was in the hallway waiting for her. Once he pulled her towel off, exposing her naked body, and said that it was a joke.

Then, on a dreary Saturday afternoon in mid-February, while her mom was shopping and her dad was gone—it happened.

John had been locked in his bedroom for hours, and Courtney could hear him moving around, going to the bathroom and blowing his nose. She was in her room, alone, watching a video on horses, hanging out in her pajamas. The instructional video was boring and she fell asleep on her bed.

She was awakened when she felt a hand between her legs. She sat up, startled, and saw John standing there with nothing on. Courtney was terrified and started crying, hoping it was a nightmare, knowing it wasn't. She prayed her mother would come home; she prayed her dad would walk in and stop him.

Courtney screamed as loud as she could.

"Please don't!" she cried, but no one could hear her.

John put his hand over Courtney's mouth and pushed her back onto the bed. She bit his hand as hard as she could, but he got her pajamas off with his free hand and climbed between her legs. As he forced himself into her, a sharp pain tore through her whole body. Courtney got his hand off her mouth and screamed for help, continuing to beg him to stop.

John continued to thrust. Courtney could smell his breath and feel his sweat dripping onto her bare skin. Her head kept slamming against the headboard as her anguished cries went unheard. When she thought she could stand no more, he stopped, but continued to breathe in her face.

"Now," he said as he climbed off of her, "maybe you'll respect me a little more, you spoiled little bitch."

"Clean this mess up, too," John added, pausing at the door, still naked, "before your mommy comes home." The blood on the sheets was already staining the mattress, and her new pajamas were ruined.

Courtney could only bury her head under her pillow and cry uncontrollably.

The pain was like nothing she ever imagined. Worse than that was the feeling of shame, guilt, and helplessness. Maybe if she had locked her door or gone out to play.

She thought about taking her life. She remembered seeing a handgun in her mother's drawer by the bed. She would have done it, but John had locked his bedroom door.

Late that night, Courtney's mother finally pulled into the driveway. Courtney was sitting on the porch step, wrapped in a blanket, shivering and waiting in the darkness.

She could hear her mother yelling, "Courtney! Courtney! What happened? Talk to me!" but she could not respond.

Courtney heard the screen door open and close behind her. She turned around and saw John standing there, silhouetted by the streetlight.

Courtney closed her eyes and could feel more tears running down her cheeks. She wanted to disappear.

"John," Michelle asked, concerned, "what's wrong with Courtney? What happened?"

"I don't know, honey. I thought she was asleep," John answered innocently.

The sound of John's voice cut through Courtney like a sharp knife, but seemed so far away.

"He raped me," Courtney said, feeling detached. "He raped me in my room."

"What!" Michelle said, turning toward John and raising her voice. "You . . . you sick son-of-a-bitch!"

"She wanted it," John said.

Michelle quickly ushered the two of them into the house and threatened to call the police. For that one moment, Courtney believed in her mom, and believed her mom was on her side.

"I wouldn't do that if I were you," John said, looking straight at her mom. "There's enough cocaine in this house to put your ass in jail for years. If that isn't enough to bring you to your senses, maybe committing perjury is. Those ladies in prison would love to get their hands on your cute little white ass."

Courtney realized that she was about to lose her mom again, this time for good.

"Call Daddy. Please don't make me stay here," Courtney begged.

"No!" Michelle answered, frustrated. "You know what your father will do. You're staying here and keeping your mouth shut. If you don't, Courtney, you will never see him again. You know I mean it."

"Mom, please!"

"No! I said no!"

"This is all your fault!" Courtney shouted, enraged. "You only care about yourself. I hate you!"

Michelle slapped Courtney across the face as hard as she could, knocking her to the floor, and left the room. John immediately followed her to their bedroom, leaving Courtney alone and devastated on the kitchen floor.

Courtney rolled over on her side, and with silent tears streaming down her face and clasping her hands, prayed to God for help.

◆ ◆ ◆

Melanie was deeply troubled as she drove to Melrose Middle School.

Courtney had taken a drastic turn for the worse and she didn't know why. She sensed something was wrong when Courtney left word that she didn't want to get together with her in Mr. Johns' office. Their previous meetings together had gone so well, and Melanie felt a special attachment to this loving child who was fast becoming a young lady.

Then, Mr. Johns called and asked her to meet him at her earliest possible convenience. There was a tone of urgency in his voice.

One hour later, Melanie parked her red BMW convertible in the space reserved for visiting doctors and walked directly to the guidance counselor's office.

Outside, children were playing during their lunch hour. Melanie scanned them quickly, looking for Courtney, but she was not around.

Paul Johns had his suit jacket off and his sleeves rolled up when Melanie walked in. They had been friends for a long time. She had confided in him that she was fast becoming emotionally and romantically involved with Courtney's father.

For the past two months, Melanie and Blair had been spending their evenings together. Their involvement began shortly after Courtney's custody hearing. She really liked him, and was finding it more and more difficult to keep her distance.

"She's not doing well at all, Melanie," Mr. Johns said as the two of them sat beside each other in front of his desk.

"What happened?" Melanie asked, concerned. "Courtney seemed to be doing okay last week. I know she was having a hard time accepting the custody order. When her father left, she withdrew a little more. But . . . "

"This is different, Melanie," Mr. Johns said, interrupting. "This is worse, much worse than the regression which was to be expected. Courtney has shut down. When anybody tries to talk to her, including Mrs. Cooper, her favorite teacher, she just zones out."

"Did you try to talk to her?" Melanie asked, grasping.

"Of course," Mr. Johns answered. "I called her in this morning. I tried to find out what was going on. She just broke down and ran out. That's when I called you, Melanie, because I'm at a complete loss. I figured if anybody can get anything out of her, it would be you."

Melanie didn't know what to say. She didn't have any idea what could have happened to Courtney. It was just last Friday, only five days ago, that the two of them met over the lunch hour and took a walk to the duck pond. Courtney seemed fine then, maybe a little melancholy, but nothing like this.

Even her teacher called Mr. Johns to report that Courtney was really down and not herself.

"Something serious happened, Melanie, that we don't know about," Mr. Johns added. "When I called her home to find out what I could, her mother said that Courtney was in good spirits over the weekend, and seemed happy when she left for school."

"I want to talk to her," Melanie said, "but the time and place are going to be important. I can't go to her house, that's for sure. Maybe I should call Blair, but I hate to worry him. He's only been gone two weeks and my hope is that it's not that serious."

"What do you want me to do?" Mr. Johns asked.

"I'll write her a note that I'm here and that I want to see her. We'll send it with a messenger from your office to keep it low-key. Courtney embarrasses easily."

Moments later, Mr. Johns' young student messenger returned to the office with the sealed envelope for Courtney. The messenger told them that Courtney hadn't returned to class since she went to the guidance counselor's office earlier that morning.

◆ ◆ ◆

Pennsylvania.

Blair loaded the last of his horses onto a six-horse trailer that was destined for Rocky's farm in Lexington, Virginia. It saddened Blair to be shipping them out, with instructions to Rocky to sell them all except a young black colt and Impressive James. It's just that for the past six months they had been standing around, not getting worked, and were a lot for one ranch hand to take care of.

Loading Impressive James brought back a fond memory, one of the few for Blair in the past several months. He could still see Courtney coming into the arena in Raleigh, North Carolina, on the little gelding. She came out firing, and when the announcer said, "And your new leader, with a score of 72, riding Impressive J. James, is Courtney Louise Cody," the small crowd in the stands yelled and cheered.

Courtney's smile as she walked out of the indoor arena, with Impressive James walking behind her with his head down like a big dog on a leash, said it all.

As the horse whinnied, Blair shut the trailer door. Grandma Cody told him that it was just a matter of time before Courtney would be back where she belonged.

While home, Blair had dinner with Pat Greely to bring him up to date. He told him that he was flying back to Los Angeles in two weeks. He would not be back until the summer. Blair promised his most trusted investigator and friend that he was okay, but Pat just shook his head.

It was good to be home, in the gentle wilderness that he loved. The hustle and bustle of Los Angeles was not his element, and that would have been true under any circumstances. Yet it wasn't the same without Courtney. The void was too wide and deep.

He also missed Melanie, a lot more than he told her or admitted to himself. Melanie was so easy to talk to and never complained about anything. She loved life and laughed easily. Blair had forgotten what it was like to be with someone like that, someone he cared about deeply, someone who cared about him.

Melanie had also become an important influence in Courtney's life, at a time when Courtney was in desperate need of a mother's love. Her being in California—loving Courtney, encouraging her, giving her strength during the darkest hours of her life, doing everything she could to get her through these troubled times— helped ease his mind. Melanie would never know what that meant to him.

Blair was looking forward to seeing Melanie again, and being with her, and he wished that she could have joined him on his trip back home. He would have liked to show her the other world he lived in, where controversy, stress, courtrooms, lawyers, and judges didn't exist; maybe the next time when the circumstances would be different.

Late that night, a light snow flurried in the black sky. By early morning the fields, fence lines, and trees in central Pennsylvania would be under a thick blanket of white, powdered snow. It looked peaceful enough from the sliding glass doors of Blair's bedroom, but the fierce winds were causing major drifts and closing down the roads and highways. The school closings were already being announced on the radio.

Blair knew enough to wait it out. He had fought the winter storms before and knew that patience and timing, as in life, were everything. He was building a fire in the den, intending to spend the day at home alone, when the phone rang in his bedroom.

It was Melanie, and Blair was glad to hear from her. She said that she was doing fine, that she missed him, and that she was looking forward to his return. She said that she wished she were there with him, alone in the winter storm, where the two of them could spend precious time together.

But there was something in Melanie's tone that bothered him. He felt she was reluctant to tell him something about Courtney, and that made him uneasy. She said that Courtney was fine, but she hesitated when asked, and Blair became concerned.

He decided it was time to go back to California.

CHAPTER FIFTEEN

NEVER AGAIN

Soft shadows from the moonlit night danced spookily on the walls and ceiling in Courtney's dark bedroom. Rustling leaves outside her window made her heart race, with no one to call to for help. Her mother hadn't spoken to her since that awful night, and Courtney hid from John every time she saw him. That evening, she caught a glimpse of him in the hallway, and he winked at her mockingly.

It wasn't just her mother's threat that she would never see her dad again; Courtney was also ashamed of what had happened to her. She didn't want anybody to know—no one, not even her dad or Melanie, or her teachers or friends. She had tried going to school, but after three days found it impossible.

It wasn't that Courtney couldn't sleep—she was physically exhausted and emotionally drained. It's just that she was afraid to fall off into the darkness where her dreams spun unmercifully out of control. She would be raped by John or faceless, dark figures, over and over, and each time the dreams were in color. She would always wake up crying, calling out loud to her mother for help, but no one ever came. Courtney felt betrayed by a mother who wasn't there for her, like some terrible demon had taken her away. She had felt that way last year when her mother took off and never called, but this time was different, so different, and frightening.

Courtney promised herself that John was never going to do that again. One day, when her mom and John went shopping together, she snuck into her mother's bedroom and took the loaded gun out of the drawer. She thought about taking her life, and pointed the deadly barrel to her chest, closing her eyes. Instead, she hid the gun under her mattress, remembering how her dad taught her to shoot it. She wasn't sure if the safety was on, but thought it was because red was showing on the black handle.

◆　◆　◆

Across the hall from Courtney's bedroom, behind closed doors, John passed the hand mirror with neatly carved lines of cocaine to Michelle. She was resting comfortably in their king-size bed. The canopy had been done in smoked mirrors, and she could see herself lying there in her designer red oriental pajamas. John prepared her feast by chopping the white, powdery substance with a pinch of crack, and was serving her like a humble servant from the Queen Anne chair beside her.

Michelle had made up with John in a pact to keep things quiet. He promised her that he wouldn't touch Courtney again. He told her that he would get help in the future in one of those out-of-state clinics, where he could be anonymous. To get help immediately might cause some suspicion, and neither one of them needed that.

The two of them had been partying since Courtney went to bed. They didn't talk much, but they were feeling good and their mutual silence was emotionally safe. John may have done too much because his hand trembled slightly as he handed Michelle her next portion. He was starting to sweat profusely and was grinding his teeth. Michelle avoided those symptoms, having taken two quaaludes an hour before; one more quaalude would be enough to put her out.

The euphoria brought on by John's recipe of cocaine and crack made it easier for Michelle to deal with herself, but added fuel to her growing resentment of Courtney. Michelle was never going to forgive her daughter for busting into the courtroom weeks ago and sitting on her father's lap. That was so embarrassing to her, so humiliating in front of Judge Hester and Jim Johnson. Michelle seethed at what Courtney told everybody in chambers, knowing that her father was going to be told everything. Courtney just didn't give a fuck about her. Michelle was sure that Blair and that phony psychiatrist friend of his, Melanie, were behind Courtney's grandstand appearance.

It was still dark when Michelle finally fell into a deep, peaceful, and dreamless sleep.

◆　◆　◆

Courtney stared at the dark silhouette over her bed. It was a motionless figure that seemed to blend with the haunting shadows on the wall. Her trembling hands pulled the covers over her body. The silhouette didn't move, and Courtney prayed that this was just another terrifying dream. The shadow then disappeared. Courtney wasn't sure, but if this was a dream, it was the most realistic of them all.

The shadow reappeared and moved closer.

Courtney could feel him in the room. The familiar smell swept over her. His clammy hand, out of nowhere, pressed hard against her mouth and nose, and she turned her head to breathe.

Oh, please God, help me! Courtney prayed.

And from her inner strength, Courtney forced herself onto her side, then her stomach, reaching under the mattress with her right hand, frantically grabbing for the gun. John was all over her with his naked, sweating body, groping and feeling her, then jerked her fiercely by the hair to keep her in position.

Courtney felt the cold steel under the mattress and gripped the handle tightly. She could also feel John pulling up her nightgown, tearing at her underpants. She could hear him breathing heavily, gasping for air.

Screaming, Courtney broke loose and crashed to the floor, with the gun clutched in her hand. Scrambling, she ran out of her room toward the kitchen. She could hear John close behind her.

The quick flash of light in the kitchen startled her. Her mother was by the back door, and had flicked the light on.

Courtney stopped before running into her mother, and looked at her. Once again she felt trapped, with John behind her, still naked.

And Courtney knew that her mother was prepared to let it happen again.

"You're not going anywhere, Courtney," Michelle said, threatening, blocking the back door.

John Morgan started laughing, and approached Courtney to take the gun from her. She quickly moved out of reach and faced him. Holding the gun with both hands, she raised it and pointed it toward him.

"What are you going to do with that?" John said, still laughing at her as he took another step.

Courtney started crying again, and pleaded, "Stay away from me or I'll shoot . . . I mean it . . . I'll kill you."

John and Michelle charged Courtney at the same time. She closed her eyes, and still pointing the gun at John, pulled the trigger. The blast from the handgun sounded in the house like a bomb, and knocked Courtney up against the refrigerator.

She never saw her mother attacking from the side.

It just happened, blood was everywhere, and the rank smell of death filled the air.

Courtney, horrified, ran out the back door into the darkness.

◆ ◆ ◆

Jimmy Beyer, a top-notch homicide investigator, flicked his cigarette into the yard as he watched from the porch.

Red lights on marked police cars flashed in front of 719 Valley View Road as concerned neighbors gathered on the sidewalks to watch. Orange tape surrounded the house, and two uniformed officers were making sure nobody crossed the evidence line. Soon, a wheeled stretcher with a bloodstained sheet covering a body was loaded into the back of a white and orange ambulance. The ambulance left slowly and quietly, and headed for the morgue.

The neighbors were already whispering rumors about death and violence, and the dark, overcast sky with threatening rain added to his unsettled mood. Beyer had been through enough homicide investigations since he was a rookie cop to never jump to conclusions.

The crime scene had been secured since 6:50 a.m., and investigators from the District Attorney's Office of Los Angeles County, the California State Police Criminal Division, and the LA County Coroner's Office were already there. The man himself, District Attorney Reed, had contacted him. "This one is personal, Jim, so we'll do it together," Reed told his longtime friend.

Years of stress showed on Beyer's craggy, lined face. He worked the streets of LA where violence and senseless killings were a way of life, and now a twelve-year-old kid was out there somewhere with a gun.

A German shepherd on a leash, trained to track missing persons, was given items of Courtney's clothing to smell before being put to the task of finding her. The dog barked and yelped in the back yard, and then didn't have a clue what direction to go. It kept jumping up at Courtney's bedroom window, frustrating the handler.

Police were canvassing the entire neighborhood. They were going door to door, asking everybody if they had seen Courtney, a barefoot little girl dressed in a pink nightgown. They checked all garages and sheds. They looked into cars and truck beds. They questioned everybody in the area, stopping cars for any possible leads or sightings.

Before going inside, Detective Beyer checked his watch one more time. It was 8 a.m. The call to 911 from the occupant of the house had been made two hours ago.

Inside, the kitchen was being photographed from every angle. Blood samples were taken for analysis and photographed to preserve the splash marks. No fingerprints were lifted. A team of forensic investigators looked everywhere for the missing handgun, a search that included all shrubbery outside the house, as well as the garage, the shed, the neighbors' yards, and all trash cans for blocks.

By noon, an autopsy had been performed on the white female body at Hollywood's Community General Osteopathic Hospital by Dr. Otis Fillinger. Attached to the foot of the victim was a gray tag reading *Michelle Lynn Morgan, age thirty-seven.* In attendance were many law enforcement officials, including Detective Beyer.

Cameras were constantly flashing in the autopsy room, before, during, and after the body was cut open. Michelle Morgan was getting a photo session like she had never dreamed of. X-rays of the head and neck were taken to be kept by the pathologist.

The external examination established that there were no bruises to the face or body that required explanation. No lacerations. No defense wounds. No notable abrasions.

Blood samples were taken to be analyzed later.

Dr. Fillinger's preliminary conclusion was easy enough. The victim died when a nine-millimeter bullet lodged itself in her spinal column, but only after rupturing her lungs. The fragmented lead bullet was removed from the body and placed in an evidence bag to be turned over to the ballistics division for examination. Dr. Fillinger's estimated time of death was somewhere between 5 and 6 a.m.

"The next thing I knew, Courtney aimed the gun at her mother in the kitchen, and pulled the trigger," John said, facing Detective Beyer in the interrogation room of the LAPD.

"You witnessed Courtney intentionally kill her mother?" Detective Beyer asked. "Is that what you are saying?"

"It happened suddenly, but yes, that's what I saw, and that's what I am saying," John answered.

"Tell me again, John, one more time," Detective Beyer asked nicely, having a cup of coffee with his cooperative witness, "what was this argument between Courtney and her mother all about?"

The small room had the bare essentials: a wooden table, wooden chairs for those in attendance, adequate lighting from a ceiling fan, and a looking glass for others to observe from the outside. Cigarette smoke hung in the air and floated around John Morgan like a slow-whirling lariat.

Detective Beyer watched his eyewitness, his only witness, closely. He had questioned a lot of witnesses in the past twenty-five years, and never gave them the benefit of his thinking. He certainly wasn't ruling out the possibility that John Morgan was the killer—spouses were always his prime suspect in domestic homicides—and most of the time he was right. Detective Beyer envisioned Morgan killing Michelle in a heated argument, and the kid taking off out of fear. He also wasn't impressed with the fact that John was willing to cooperate fully, without requesting the opportunity to retain counsel, a right he was advised of earlier that morning by one of Beyer's men.

"Yes sir," John answered respectfully. "Courtney was upset with her mother and had been since she brought her out here. Courtney kept telling Michelle how she hated her, and it really got bad between them when the custody order came down. Courtney then realized that she wasn't going back to Pennsylvania with her father.

Michelle tried to be a loving mother to her, but Courtney was out of control."

Referring Beyer to the recent custody hearing, which he described as very, very bitter and ugly, John added, "Courtney's testimony on the record, in Judge Hester's courtroom, will confirm what I am telling you. After that court order, it got so bad at home between them that Courtney dropped out of school."

Detective Beyer took a final drag from his cigarette, then crushed it into the full tin ashtray on the table.

Beyer didn't like John Morgan. There was just something about him that rubbed Beyer the wrong way. Maybe it was his soft, manicured hands, or the perfume that smelled like lilacs; maybe it was his flashy gold jewelry, which John decided to wear while his wife lay dead. Yet Beyer couldn't picture him with a handgun either. He thought he was much too prissy, and doubted if Morgan had ever handled a gun of any kind.

"Have you ever owned a handgun, John?" Beyer asked.

"Never," John answered.

"Is there any possibility," Beyer asked, lighting up another cigarette, "that if we find the handgun that killed your wife, your fingerprints will be on it?"

"There is no such possibility," John answered adamantly. "In fact, I didn't even know the gun was in the house until Courtney fired it."

"Are you willing to take a polygraph?" Beyer asked.

"Right now?" John asked.

"Yes," Beyer answered.

"No problem," John said, nodding his head.

John told Beyer that after Courtney killed her mother, she ran out the back door, carrying the handgun. He said that she was dressed in her pink nightgown, and that she was barefoot. He did not know where she was, or might have gone; however, he told Beyer that "Courtney will find her father no matter where he is, or he'll find her."

CHAPTER SIXTEEN

SURRENDER

Like a scared animal, she ran in her bare feet through back yards, stopping to catch her breath, and looking around to make sure nobody was following her. Within blocks of the house, she hid the gun under a bush after covering it with tan bark. There was a pay phone by the school. Under the cover of darkness, she made it to the phone unnoticed, and frantically dialed the operator for assistance. Courtney had no money, and the operator helped her make a collect call to her father in Pennsylvania.

The phone rang and rang, and Courtney tearfully hung up. The patient operator helped Courtney make her second collect call, this time to the home of Dr. Melanie Castille.

"Hello," Melanie answered softly.

"Will you accept a collect call from Courtney Cody?" the operator asked.

"Yes, definitely," Melanie answered, her heart racing, sitting up.

"Melanie," Courtney said, crying.

"I'm here, Courtney."

"I have to find my dad right away."

"Where are you?"

"I just want to talk to my dad, please."

"Sure, honey, he's at his apartment. He's here in California. He came back yesterday when he couldn't get in touch with you. We've all been so worried. Do you have his number there?"

"Yes, thank you. Thank you very much, but I have to go now," Courtney said, still crying.

Before Melanie could say one more word, Courtney hung up.

◆ ◆ ◆

The ducks scattered on the pond when Courtney went to the rock to wait for her dad. They startled her, just as she did them, and they flapped their wings, splashing and quacking to avert danger and alert their young. The rainstorm on the horizon was threatening, and Courtney was hoping that it would hold off until her dad got there; she was already shivering, dressed in nothing but a light cotton nightgown, and her feet were bruised and sore. Courtney crouched, crossed her arms for warmth, and waited.

But not for long.

Blair pulled up by the pond, and after checking his rearview mirror, jumped out of his car and ran toward Courtney, who was running toward him. He swept her up in his arms and she buried her face on his shoulder as he carried her to the running car without saying a word. He gently put her in the back seat and told her to lie down, and that they would talk when they got back to his apartment. Courtney didn't make a sound in the back seat, having passed out from exhaustion.

Blair passed two marked police cars speeding toward 719 Valley View Road with their red dome lights flashing, but no sirens. He was going in the opposite direction, toward Melanie Castille's, and watched the tandem cruisers in his rearview mirror. After they disappeared over a hill, he could still see their red lights flashing for several seconds in the ominous sky. Blair breathed a sigh of relief, then pressed the accelerator to the floor.

It was too risky to take Courtney to his apartment. Blair knew the police would be looking for him to find her, and he wasn't taking any chances. The police were capable of busting right past him at his apartment, with guns drawn, with or without a search warrant to get her.

Based on what Courtney told Blair over the phone, which was very little, this was going to be a homicide investigation. All Courtney said when she called Blair was, "Dad, please come get me. I shot Mom by accident. I think she's dead. I'm at the pay phone near the pond."

Blair asked no questions, horrified at what she had told him.

Blair told Courtney to run to the big rock by the pond and hide until he got there. He wasted no time, putting on a pair of jeans as he ran to his car, jamming on his loafers without socks. The early morning traffic in Los Angeles was still an hour away and Interstate 5 was wide open. He drove as fast as he could, at one point over one hundred miles an hour, hoping there were no speed traps.

Blair had no idea what the details were. His immediate concern was getting Courtney away from it all until he got some answers.

To do that, he needed time.

Melanie was in a panic. First, Courtney called her at 5:30 a.m., asking for her dad, crying and hysterical. Then, Blair didn't answer when Melanie called him. Now, no calls—just silence, which left her in a lurch. She was out of her bed, pacing the floor, constantly looking at the phone as if that might help it ring.

She vacuumed mindlessly throughout the house. Melanie had a full-time maid, and the carpet did not need vacuuming, but she had to have something to do, anything to kill time, anything.

At 6:20 a.m., almost an hour after Courtney had called her, there was knocking at the door and Melanie ran to open it. Blair was carrying Courtney in his arms, and without saying a word, went straight to Melanie's bedroom to lay her down.

"What happened, Blair?" Melanie asked hysterically, following them into her bedroom.

Blair, with Courtney still in his arms, looked deep into Melanie's eyes but did not answer. Melanie could see confusion, pain, and fear.

Courtney, though still passed out, was clutching her dad as he laid her on the bed.

◆ ◆ ◆

Philadelphia, Pennsylvania.

Thomas Keating got the call from Reed. He was in his Philadelphia office alone, reading the *Wall Street Journal*, when his private line rang. He would cry later, but his immediate reaction was revenge: he told Reed he wanted the responsible party, even if it was Courtney, brought to justice.

Keating was certain that Blair was behind it, and told Reed.

"No," Reed said, "we haven't found Courtney, but we will."

"No," he added, "we haven't found Blair either. We heard that he was in Pennsylvania, and isn't scheduled to return for another week."

Keating picked up the framed picture on his desk of Michelle holding Courtney's hand. None of it made sense.

Before calling Michelle's mother, he made a quick call to his lawyers to discuss Michelle's will and the disposition of the estate. He was told that under the Wrongful Death Statute—assuming Courtney was convicted of murdering her mother—John Morgan was getting *everything*.

"Fuck!" Keating shouted, slamming the phone down.

Keating made one more phone call before calling home, and that was to his friend, Peter Hunt, the commander of the Pennsylvania State Police, requesting assistance in the search for Blair Cody. Within an hour, a white car with the Pennsylvania state emblem on the side door was coming down Blair's driveway, heading toward the house. Two uniformed officers, dressed in their traditional grays, guns holstered, checked the house and property.

Blair wasn't there.

A lone ranch hand, who was shoveling snow off the back porch, told them he didn't know where Blair was, or when he was coming back.

◆ ◆ ◆

Los Angeles, California.

Three cars from the Los Angeles Police Department were dispatched to go to Blair's apartment. The police were told that he could be there hiding Courtney, though he was supposed to be in Pennsylvania for one more week. Their instructions were to proceed with caution, to presume him armed and dangerous, and that backup was on stand-by.

One of the officers, Alex, heard that Blair was a cowboy who was deadly with a pistol and could draw from his holster at lightning speed. That same officer was told that Blair could lasso his ass from thirty yards away. He didn't know whether the boys at the station were kidding him or not, but he wasn't taking any chances.

By the time the story was fully embellished, the six officers at the scene were all wearing flak vests, and approached the apartment as if they were making a dangerous drug raid. Three crept along the building from the east, three from the west, and they met at the front door and knocked. They were relieved when no one answered.

Alex was told to stake out the place from across the street and wait, by himself. He spent the next eight hours crouched down in the driver's seat, radio on, watching Blair's front door, checking his mirrors for a rear assault.

No one showed.

◆ ◆ ◆

That evening, the local media was brought into the search for Courtney. The killing of Michelle Morgan, the only daughter of Pennsylvania's former lieutenant governor, and the manhunt for the victim's twelve-year-old daughter, was a sensational story. It was the lead story on the six o'clock news, WHYM, with background footage of the house at 719 Valley View Road secured with orange tape. The attractive, petite reporter with a bobbed hairdo stood in front of the evidence line with her mike in hand, reporting live.

A picture of Courtney was then flashed on the screen with a typed-in description of her weight, ninety pounds, and height, four feet ten. That recent photo of Courtney—toothy smile, teased curly hair, with her flowered western blouse—was aired in the greater Los Angeles metropolitan area. The next morning Courtney's picture would appear on the front page of the *Los Angeles Times,* captioned "Missing Child."

◆ ◆ ◆

Blair sat in Melanie's living room and watched the eleven o'clock news. For the past two hours, since Courtney fell asleep on the couch, Blair hadn't said a word. Her school picture on the television screen set off another explosion in his heart, and Melanie, who was sitting near him, held his hand tightly.

Courtney told him about the rape. The thought of John laying a hand on Courtney, let alone raping her, was more than he could take.

Blair was going to find John Morgan.

Courtney also told him how John tried a second time, and how she fought him off, and ran. She almost made it out of the house—she was going to call her dad, or Melanie, or the police, anybody—but her mother blocked the door.

"Mom said that I wasn't leaving," Courtney recalled, as she relived the horrible night.

"John came running toward me," Courtney added, crying, "and he was still naked, and I was scared, and Mom wasn't doing anything to help me. So I . . . I pointed the gun at him and pulled the trigger with my eyes shut."

Blair held his arm around Courtney and could feel her body trembling.

"I don't know what happened after that, Dad," Courtney continued, "except when I opened my eyes, Mom was on the floor bleeding, and I ran. I didn't mean to shoot Mom."

Blair's only regret was that she hadn't fired a second shot into the balls of Morgan.

Blair had already called Kimberly, and that evening the three of them—Blair, Melanie, and Kimberly—had a conference call over what to do. It was agreed that Kimberly would meet with District Attorney Reed first thing in the morning, alone. She would offer to surrender Courtney to the authorities, accompanied by her father. Blair would put up his ranch, which had an appraised value of $1.8 million.

"If Reed says no," Blair added, "there will be no surrender."

◆ ◆ ◆

The next morning, Reed agreed to the terms of surrender. He told Kimberly that he wanted a fax of the deed to Blair's ranch. Blair simply nodded when Kimberly got back to him.

With Melanie's help, Blair explained to Courtney what they had to do, which was to report to the police station where she would be fingerprinted and photographed. Courtney understood that she was to do exactly as she was told by her father, which was to make no statement regarding what happened to anybody. Blair guaranteed Courtney that they would be leaving the police station together, and the three of them would be flying home to Pennsylvania that night.

"Melanie, too?" Courtney asked, wiping the tears from her eyes.

"Yes, Melanie, too."

"Good," Courtney said as she reached for Melanie's hand.

By noon, Blair drove Courtney to the LA police headquarters, where Detective Beyer was waiting with the paperwork.

"Mr. Cody," Beyer said, getting right down to business when the two of them walked in, "my name is Detective Beyer and I am the arresting officer in this case."

"I'm her father," Blair said.

"I have the unpleasant responsibility of serving these arrest papers on your daughter, Mr. Cody, charging her with murder in the first degree for the intentional and premeditated killing of Michelle Lynn Morgan on or about February 25, 1996, at approximately 5:30 a.m."

"Just give me the paperwork," Blair said, holding out his hand, "and let's get the booking over with so we can go on our way."

"Is she willing to make any statements?" Beyer asked.

"No."

"I'm interested in the gun," Beyer said.

"I'll see what I can do," Blair told him.

"Fair enough," Beyer remarked, knowing that wasn't part of the deal for her release.

It tore Blair's heart out watching Courtney get fingerprinted in the room set up for booking criminals. Beyer was gentle enough rolling Courtney's fingers, one at a time, over the ink card ... and the picture-taking with flashing bulbs was painless enough ... but the whole thing seemed surreal to Blair, so far removed from the world he and Courtney lived in not that long ago.

CHAPTER SEVENTEEN

FUNERAL

The slow procession to Michelle's gravesite consisted of four cars with funeral flags flapping in the wind: a black, polished Cadillac hearse carrying the body of Michelle Lynn Morgan; a black, polished Cadillac limousine, driven by a uniformed chauffeur, which carried Mr. and Mrs. Thomas Keating and their minister; a black Lexus driven by John Morgan; and an unmarked police car carrying two plainclothes detectives, which John requested to assure his safety.

The funeral for the daughter of Pennsylvania's prominent politico was private. The Keatings did not want the media circus, and planned accordingly.

The burial was on a pleasant hill at the Rolling Green Cemetery. Michelle's wooden casket, laced with creamy white silk, was carried by representatives from the Hoffman Funeral Home as the family followed it to the canopied opening in the ground. Fresh red roses, which were Michelle's favorite, draped the casket and wreaths adorned her headstone. The granite headstone had a carving of an angel playing a harp.

Mr. Keating watched as the casket was gently placed above the deep, dark opening in the ground. Mrs. Keating wept openly. Mr. Keating, consumed by his anger, did not. The sight of Morgan made him sick in the stomach.

Keating and Morgan weren't talking to each other. They had already argued about burying Michelle under her married name, in California no less, with the sparsest of arrangements. John's lawyers explained that under California law a surviving spouse determines the name on the headstone, the appropriateness of the arrangements, and the burial place.

The Keatings had no say in these final matters.

The Keatings were also reminded by John's lawyers that John was in line to inherit Michelle's entire estate if Courtney was convicted of her death. John had his lawyers give it to them in writing, so there would be no misunderstanding at the time of distribution.

The prayer and vigil for Michelle were kept short. The minister likened Michelle to the angel on the headstone playing a harp—a gentle soul, sweet, kind, always thinking of others, never herself. "She will fly among the clouds above us in heaven," the minister said.

John had his head bowed with his eyes closed in prayer. The detectives, assigned to protect Mr. Morgan, stood on either side of him at his request.

Within the next hour, John was going back to New York on the next plane, leaving Michelle alone on the hill.

◆ ◆ ◆

Every week, first thing Friday morning, Reed would meet in the library of his office with a well-trained team of prosecutors. Most of his soldiers were young men and women in their late twenties and early thirties, recent graduates of the top law schools in the

West. His legal staff consisted of eleven hundred lawyers, but only the top echelon had the privilege of meeting with the boss.

They all dressed professionally, in conservative business suits with silk ties or scarves. Many of the men wore suspenders and vests, while the women favored two-piece matching outfits, never slacks. The more experienced and more talented prosecutors got the better cases, which were the higher-profile cases, the more challenging ones. Very often, a particular case became desirable because of the defense attorney on the other side; beating a good defense attorney was a rush to these feisty litigators, and added a notch on their belts.

Reed's staff called him "the General," and he liked that. The more senior members of the office were called "captains" and "lieutenants." Everybody else was a soldier, and certain staff members got nicknames; there was "the Sniper," "the Bomber," and "Bayonet." Reed's favorite prosecutor in the office was Larry Coleman, who had been prosecuting cases in Los Angeles for twenty-five years. Larry was a career man and made no bones about it. He looked like a career prosecutor, too—clean-shaven, short cropped hair, medium build—and resembled game-show host Bob Barker.

Larry always said that running the DA's office of Los Angeles County was like a game show. "Sometimes you win, sometimes you lose" was his favorite saying. But game or no game, every prosecutor in his office dreamed of becoming a crack-shot trial lawyer; some of them already were, others thought they were but weren't, and some never would be.

"Okay, everybody," Reed said, beginning the staff meeting, surrounded by his top ten litigators. "Any scheduling conflicts should be taken up with Larry after this meeting.

"Jane, congratulations on your verdict this week. I heard you had a hell of a closing argument," Reed added, looking at Jane.

"Thank you, General," Jane beamed. She had just convicted a major heroin dealer.

"Where are we on the case involving the murder of the baker . . . what's his name?" Reed asked.

"Mr. Giovanni," said Nick Lighter, a senior prosecutor who was assigned to the case.

"Right," Reed continued. "Where are we on that one, Nick?"

"They're all pleading guilty. The two older boys folded first, and the youngest one just last week. They all agreed to forty years' imprisonment. We should have asked for the death penalty, but we wouldn't have gotten it, not in this fucking city anyhow."

Everybody in the room laughed at Nick's comment. Los Angeles was a wild card in certain kinds of cases. The riots that occurred after some verdicts were well known to all of them.

For the next half hour, everybody discussed the heavy case load, who was trying what, which cases were pleading out, which judges were available, and problems with witnesses, victims, and certain police officers.

The staff agreed that the secretaries, though generally over-worked, were handling it well. But the receptionists, especially one named Karla, were screwing up too many messages.

"Anything else?" Reed asked before adjourning the conference.

"Just one thing, General," Nick piped up. "I thought I saw on television that you personally are going to try the Courtney Cody case."

"That's right, Nick," the General confirmed with a smile. "Do you want that case or what?"

"I was just wondering if you still remember how to try a big case," Nick said, joking.

Due to the election, Reed hadn't tried a significant case for almost a year. Plus, the elected district attorney rarely stepped onto the battlefield where cases are won and lost, and reputations are made and destroyed instantly.

"I remember how to try a case," Reed said with a lot of confidence, accepting the joke.

"Good luck," Nick said, winking, proud of his general.

To Reed, getting back into the courtroom felt good. He loved trying cases, kicking ass, putting juries in the palm of his hand.

Reed considered himself a fearless trial lawyer. He could win a case—and hadn't lost a case in ten years—with or without evidence, whether the defendant was guilty or not.

Juries loved him. Reed knew how to play to their fears and sympathies. He spoke their language, and impressed upon them that a verdict for the District Attorney's Office of Los Angeles was a verdict for themselves; a guilty verdict meant one more criminal off the streets, and a safer community for their children. Reed's stock phrases were always timely, and delivered with emotion and passion.

"Is it true, General," Jane asked, "that Blair Cody is going to defend his daughter? That's this morning's headline."

"You got it," Reed answered, watching his staff closely for their reaction.

Reed could feel the wave of silence sweeping over his office. A father representing his daughter for the murder of her mother eclipsed everything in that room. In a way, Reed resented his staff's fascination with Blair's announcement. He also resented the media's hype.

Blair Cody was going to try a case against *him*? Who in the hell did he think he was?

Maybe Blair thought he was going up against a country prosecutor in Oklahoma, or some farm boy in Pennsylvania. Reed doubted that Blair was ready for Los Angeles, California.

Reed had heard all about Blair's reputation in the East, how he could try a case. Reed was told that five years ago, Blair had acquitted Mark Steadman, the multi-millionaire corporate executive who was charged with killing the governor of New Jersey. Reed heard about Cody's defense of three American soldiers accused of unauthorized killings in Vietnam; the indictments were dismissed. He also heard how Blair represented a six-year-old child who lost his eyesight when playing with a "child-proof" disposable lighter that ignited in the boy's face; the jury's verdict was $12 million.

One of Reed's prosecutor friends from Pennsylvania, an old law school buddy, called him. "Don't underestimate Blair Cody in the courtroom," Reed's friend warned. "He's capable of anything, especially when defending his daughter." A judge called Reed into chambers to tout Cody's reputation.

Reed was sick of hearing how Blair was some kind of legal guru or tough cowboy. Even Detective Beyer was buying into that shit. He told Reed that his investigation of Cody was confirming a lot of rumors.

Reed wasn't impressed.

As he told Kimberly and Beyer, Reed was looking forward to their showdown on the courtroom floor. He promised Beyer that Blair's daughter was going to jail for the rest of her life.

◆ ◆ ◆

Courtney would wake up in the middle of the night, drenched in sweat from fear. She hated falling off to sleep and facing her demons. Melanie, who insisted on sleeping with her for a while, would read to Courtney at all hours to get her through the night. Often, Blair would sit by their bed protectively.

It was difficult for all of them.

The best tutors for Courtney were brought to the house. Blair wanted her home, away from all the gossip. He wanted it that way until the trial was over, and prayed for the day when Courtney could get on the bus with her bookbag and go to school.

Courtney's friends came over whenever they could to play, and she would go to their homes on the weekends. But the kids had already heard about the shooting from their parents, and sometimes were cruel. Blair could see it.

Blair had Rocky bring Impressive James, plus a quiet, aged mare for Melanie, and his own horse back to the ranch. He enjoyed watching Melanie learn to ride, with Courtney teaching her. The three of them would go for hours at a time up a timber road that disappeared into the wilderness. The trails were a calm respite, and once a light snow fell when they were high on the ridge, erasing the way back home.

Blair was also falling in love with Melanie, and sometimes that worried him. He didn't know, no one knew, what the future held for any of them. Courtney had a trial coming up on a charge of murder. If convicted, she would go to jail. There was no way Blair could live with that, and he fought to put it out of his mind.

The damage Morgan had done to his daughter was forever, and all of Melanie's psychiatric schooling and training wasn't going to change that. Blair only hoped that in time his child would get better. The whole thing with her mother was an accident. That bullet was meant for John Morgan.

Blair never talked about how he felt; he never talked about what he was going to do; he never even talked about his defense of Courtney. Late at night, he would read the file, over and over, getting ready for a trial that he could not afford to lose.

He was doing what he had to do.

He had already waived Courtney's preliminary hearing, which meant that none of them had to fly back to Los Angeles to hear John's fucking lies. Reed had already turned over Morgan's written statement to Kimberly.

Blair had also notified the court that he wanted a jury trial for Courtney, and was not making an issue of her adult status under California's new law. He was not going to petition to have her transferred before a juvenile judge. He could not leave her fate in the hands of a judge like Hester. Though it was extremely risky, he was going to take his chances with a jury.

The jury selection was scheduled to begin on April 29, but Blair wasn't waiting that long to confront John Morgan, his daughter's accuser and rapist. He had Pat Greely looking for John, full time, and Pat had spent the previous week in New York trying to find him.

Reed knew Blair had the right to question John about the case—though he warned Blair that if anything happened to his eyewitness, he would be their first suspect—so Reed told John to disappear until the trial. "You have the right to be unavailable" was how Reed put it.

And John made himself unavailable. He disappeared into the vast jungle of New York. He left no forwarding address, and changed his name and credentials. He even changed his looks by growing a beard and cutting his hair. That's what Greely learned after two weeks in SoHo.

John made one little mistake, however, that was going to cost him.

He had listed 719 Valley View Road for sale with a reputable real estate agency, LoeMax Realty. Kimberly saw it advertised in the paper and called Blair immediately.

Suddenly, Blair became interested in buying a house in the Hollywood Hills, and this one sounded perfect. It was in the Melrose School District, on a quiet street, and had a swimming pool. He called LoeMax immediately, offered the full purchase price under the name of Rocky B. Jones, and wired $50,000 down. An immediate settlement date was the buyer's only condition, having offered the asking price of $300,000 as is.

The agent got back to "Rocky" within hours. "The seller," the nice agent said, "has agreed to your settlement date. He will be flying in from New York next week to close the deal at our office."

CHAPTER EIGHTEEN

SETTLEMENT

The real estate agent, Patty Newman, was excited. She had been with LoeMax Realty for one month when the call came in, and this was her first big sale on commission. The neatly typed settlement sheet on the conference room table showed the agency getting seven percent of $300,000, or $21,000. Patty's cut was $10,500—not bad for a twenty-seven-year-old housewife who just passed the California real estate exam.

Waiting in the settlement room, alone, was the buyer. He told Patty that he was acting on behalf of Rocky Jones. He said that he was a lawyer, had the closing papers with him, and a certified check for the balance in full, plus the closing costs. There was no need for a representative from a bank to approve any mortgage because he had the cash.

"Terrific," Patty said.

"Mr. Morgan is on his way," she added reassuringly. "The poor man's wife was recently killed by their daughter, who must have been on drugs," she said in a hushed tone, leaning toward him.

She had no clue who Blair was, nor did she ask him his name. All she cared about was the check, and told him the deed was on the table for his review. She also said, twirling her natural curls, that she had never dealt with a lawyer wearing jeans and cowboy boots.

Blair sat calmly reviewing the documents, not reading a word on the printed pages. He thought Patty was a friendly little thing, and occasionally looked out the window for John's arrival. He had waited one week for this settlement, which seemed like an eternity, and was looking forward to meeting "the poor man."

Soon, a white convertible Porsche Boxster sped into the parking lot. Blair quickly moved away from the window, and peering through the sheers, watched John emerge from the car. He was dressed in black alligator shoes and carrying an alligator briefcase, sporting a white silk shirt open at the collar, with a sparkling diamond "J" hanging from his thick gold chain.

Several moments passed, and Blair could hear them talking in the outer room. Patty was her friendly self and said that all the details were taken care of "pursuant to my commitment to excellence." Morgan told her that he didn't need a lawyer, didn't like them, and could do this on his own. Finally, Blair heard Patty say, "Let's go in and we'll get this started, Mr. Morgan. The buyer is ready to settle."

I'm ready to settle all right, Blair thought.

Blair didn't get up from his chair at the far end of the table, but watched them enter. The venom in Blair's heart surged at the sight of Courtney's rapist, as John followed Patty into the room through the only door.

When they locked eyes, Morgan knew. Fear swept over his face as he pushed Patty toward Blair and ran out the open door as fast as he could.

Blair went after him.

Morgan made it to his car, and with his tires squealing and smoking, got out of the parking lot. Shifting the five-speed frantically, grinding the gears, he accelerated from 0 to 60 in nine seconds.

Blair wasted no time getting into his BMW Roadster, jamming it into gear, and jumping a low concrete curb to give chase. Melanie's red performance car with flared fenders and wide tires had its own acceleration package and a top speed electronically limited to 155 mph.

Patty watched her settlement leave the parking lot faster than it came in, with stones, gravel, and dust flying all over the place.

Blair, losing ground at 120 mph, followed John onto Route 11, a winding road that went up the majestic Pacific coastline, with turns and hills that wove in and out of cliffs for miles. Blair knew this treacherous coastline, for Melanie had taken him there to show him the view of the ocean and the jagged cliffs. There were scenic overlooks where powerful waves slammed into cliffs, displaying nature's awesome might. The road snaked around for miles, and the high point of this raceway was known as "God's View."

As Blair took a hairpin curve wide open, he caught a glimpse of Morgan's white Porsche disappearing over a hill.

Blair's heart was racing faster than the 6,000 rpm's under the hood of his roaring machine. The car's compression ratio didn't hold a candle to the compression in his chest as he caught another glimpse of the white Porsche cresting another hill. It didn't matter that he was a mile away, maybe more; Blair put the accelerator to the floor.

Suddenly, after the next hairpin curve that tied into a straight-away, Blair saw a police car bolt out of nowhere. With the loud siren activated and the red domelight swirling, the Chevrolet Caprice Classic pursued the Porsche Boxster.

From a distance, Blair saw the cop, and shaking his head in frustration, slowed down.

But Morgan wasn't slowing down.

Wide open, Morgan approached the cattle chute—a horseshoe curve that went around God's View with a posted twenty-mile-per-hour speed limit, featuring a 1,500-foot jagged ravine to oblivion. The speeding Porsche never had a chance as it crashed through the wooden guard rail, leaving no skid marks as it literally took flight, at first skyward before plunging downward. The crash and explosion of metal against rock created a ball of fire that careened and tumbled to its final resting place in the belly of the ravine.

Officer Alex Haines stood outside his car, looking downward from the top of God's View in utter disbelief. He had never witnessed anything like this in his career. He actually saw the car flying in the air, at first soaring upward before it began its long, breathtaking descent. The explosion was the loudest he had ever heard, and Alex could feel the crashing of the car all the way down as he watched it.

Blair could see black smoke billowing from the ravine before he reached the top. He pulled into the tourist parking lot within seconds, and unnoticed, walked over to the edge where Alex was standing. Below, the fire was still raging and the thick smell of gas and death filled the air.

"What happened, officer?" Blair asked after several moments of silence.

"I'm not sure," Alex answered. "All I know is the guy flew by me at 155 miles an hour and never slowed down."

"Were you pursuing him?" Blair asked innocently.

"Yeah," Alex said, "but I didn't make him go faster. I wasn't closing in on him either with my Caprice. He did this to himself."

"I know you had nothing to do with this," Blair agreed. "The crazy son-of-a-bitch was flying."

"He literally flew when he went through the guard rail," Alex recounted. "He actually went upward before he plunged to the earth. It was unbelievable."

"I bet."

"I'm glad you witnessed this thing, buddy. You know how crazy litigation is these days. I don't want to be accused of a reckless pursuit that caused his death when I had nothing to do with it," Alex said defensively.

"You had nothing to do with this accident, officer," Blair assured him. "It was his own doing."

"Thanks, mister," Alex responded, feeling better. "I'm going to have to prepare a written report on this one, but first I think I should check on the wreckage to make sure the guy's dead."

"I'll go with you," Blair volunteered.

Alex and Blair, together, hiked down the 1,500-foot ravine. It was a steep drop, and both of them had to grab onto bushes and branches all the way down to keep from falling. They created minor rock slides as they went, and their journey to the bottom took half an hour. Alex was sweating profusely and breathing heavily, dreading the thought of climbing back up.

Blair was the first to arrive at the scene. He could see the charred remains of John Morgan's body strapped into the front seat, which came to rest a hundred yards from what was left of the car. The corpse, with eyes wide open, was blackened with ash and smelled like burnt skin. The nearby car was still smoldering and no longer looked like a white Porsche; it too looked dead.

"He's dead all right," Alex said when he finally arrived.

"Yep," Blair agreed.

"How are we going to get back up there?" Alex asked, looking up the steep ravine he had just trekked down.

"Very slowly," Blair answered as he too looked up, charting the easiest route to the top.

Alex and Blair took their time ascending the monstrous cliff, resting frequently, occasionally sitting on rocks to catch their breath and wipe the sweat from their brows. Alex, though twenty years younger than Blair, was soaked with perspiration and was having a much harder time than his new partner. Alex's new police shoes were killing his feet, and his holstered handgun felt like twenty pounds and getting heavier; he carried his police hat in his left hand.

This hike was not easy for Blair either. He willingly waited for Alex at several points, and neither one of them talked on the way up to save energy. Blair was glad when they finally scrambled up the last leg to the top of God's View and were resting comfortably in Alex's cruiser with the air conditioner on. Their exhausting hike had taken over an hour, but for Blair, who witnessed John Morgan's demise, it was worth it.

Blair listened as Alex, who was still breathing heavily, radioed for assistance. He called in for an ambulance but said the driver was dead. He requested an accident reconstruction expert due to the circumstances. No, he didn't know who the victim was. No, he couldn't get a license plate number from the wreckage. Yes, they'd better bring a helicopter or they would be walking their asses off.

Soon, a helicopter hovered overhead and located the wreckage without difficulty. Blair watched as John Morgan was lifted out of the ravine, still strapped to the driver's seat. Other assistance — a fire truck with siren blaring, an ambulance that would go back empty, and an LAPD marked cruiser — arrived at different intervals.

Alex sat in his cruiser, writing his police report. He carefully noted the date, time, and place. A sketched diagram illustrated the vehicle in question going airborne "at a speed of 158 mph, according to calibrated radar." The box for the entry of witnesses was at the bottom of the page, and Alex quickly jumped out of his car before his only witness left the scene.

"Sir!" Alex yelled as Blair was getting into his car. "I need your name."

Blair turned around and waited for the officer. "Certainly," he said as Alex prepared to write it down. "My name is Blair Lee Cody."

Alex looked up, startled by his partner's name. "You're Blair Cody? Are you the lawyer from Pennsylvania that we were just looking for? The lawyer with the kid? The cowboy?"

"Yes," Blair answered.

Alex smiled and shook his head. "I can't wait to tell the boys back at the station," he said as he wrote down Blair's name. "You know, I was on one of your stakeouts. I just can't believe you're my witness."

"I'm on your side all the way, officer," Blair replied, giving Alex a friendly pat on the back with his left hand.

Blair liked Alex, and was willing to come forward for him if needed. He was willing to testify that Alex had nothing to do with this accidental death, or suicide. The victim was traveling at 155 mph and killed himself when he lost control of his fancy Porsche at the top of God's View. Other Mario Andretti wanna-bes had fallen victim to this tricky course—twelve to be exact, over the past ten years—that's what Melanie had told him.

"Will you do me a favor?" Blair asked after giving Alex his Pennsylvania address and telephone number, and promising his availability on a phone call.

"Sure," Alex said.

"I have something in my glove box that I promised Detective Beyer. Would you give it to him for me?" Blair asked.

"You know Detective Beyer?" Alex asked.

"Yeah."

"Sure, what is it?" Alex inquired.

Blair told Alex not to get excited as he removed a nine-millimeter handgun from the glove box of the BMW. He emptied all the rounds, including the one that was chambered.

"Give this gun and these rounds to Detective Beyer."

"Sure," Alex responded, putting the rounds in his pocket and the gun in his belt. "Will he know what this is for?"

"He'll know," Blair answered.

◆ ◆ ◆

It was almost midnight when the last commuter flight touched down on the wet Harrisburg runway. Blair's flight from LA was delayed in Pittsburgh because of rain and dense fog, but he was finally home.

Melanie watched for Blair from his Chevy Suburban, the motor softly running, as a few weary-looking passengers crossed in front of her, lugging their suitcases. Courtney was sound asleep in the back seat with her head resting comfortably on a soft pillow, covered with a goosedown comforter. Melanie was glad that Blair was back safely from his "business trip."

She didn't quite know, however, what the trip's purpose was. Blair had told her that he was returning to California to wrap up some loose ends, and to prepare for Courtney's upcoming trial. He didn't tell her what that entailed, and Melanie was afraid to ask.

He had been gone two days, and hadn't called. That wasn't like Blair.

Melanie called Kimberly to find out if she had heard from him, but Kimberly had not; in fact, she didn't even know that Blair was on the West Coast. That took Melanie by complete surprise since Kimberly was his best friend and local counsel.

Blair was so secretive. Melanie had accepted that and trusted him, but his mysterious ways often confused her. She didn't understand why he never opened up, especially to her, the woman he loved. This latest disappearing act was the ultimate intrigue.

"We're going home," Blair said to Melanie as they hugged outside the truck. He then glanced into the back seat and saw Courtney sleeping peacefully.

"Fine with me," Melanie said, comforted.

"I'll drive," Blair offered.

Melanie stared ahead as he drove toward the ranch, with the windshield wipers rhythmically clicking back and forth. The light drizzle and drifting fog impaired her visibility. Blair said that he would explain everything once they got home, and nodded toward the back of the truck where Courtney was still sleeping.

It was after 1 a.m. Courtney did not wake up, but clung to Blair as he carried her to her bedroom.

That night, before Blair and Melanie fell asleep in each other's arms, they talked in bed.

Blair told her that he went to California for one reason, and one reason only.

"I went out there to find John Morgan," Blair said, as if Melanie should have known that.

He told her how Kimberly called to let him know that 719 Valley View Road was for sale, and about the prearranged settlement at the offices of LoeMax.

He described how John unwittingly showed up for his money, and how he was there waiting for him.

He told Melanie about the high-speed chase up the cliffs to God's View.

And all about Alex.

And how John Morgan lost control of his Porsche on that hairpin curve which Melanie knew about. He described how John crashed through the wooden guard rail on the left and plunged 1,500 feet to his death.

"John Morgan is dead?" Melanie asked, incredulous. The whole story seemed so unreal to her, so frightening.

"Yes," Blair answered, "he burned to death."

"Jesus!" Melanie gasped.

"He deserved it," Blair said unsympathetically.

"How can you be positive that he's dead?" Melanie asked.

"Because I walked down the ravine with Alex to make sure," Blair answered. "He was still strapped in the driver's seat, which was thrown from the car, and was burnt to the size of a monkey. The gold 'J' was still dangling on his neck."

Melanie almost laughed at Blair's imagery, but she knew that he was serious. Melanie didn't know what to say, or how she felt. She was glad that John Morgan was dead, but Blair's presence at the scene of his death worried her.

She desperately wanted to believe the details of Blair's version, that Morgan plunged to his own death, that Blair didn't run him off the road and kill him.

But there was a haunting uncertainty in her heart.

"What were you going to do to him, Blair?" Melanie asked.

At first, Blair just lay there looking at the ceiling. The silence in the room was deafening as Melanie imagined what he had intended. "Melanie," Blair answered quietly, looking at her, "I honestly don't know. I just had to confront him."

Blair told her that when he left California, nobody knew the identity of the charred body. He explained that an autopsy, through dental records, would confirm that it was John Morgan. The Porsche looked like burnt black scrap metal, and the license plate was destroyed, but the engraved serial numbers on the frame would trace the car to the airport car rental agency, and then to John Morgan.

"Kimberly doesn't know either?" Melanie asked.

"No, not yet. I'll explain everything to her when the time comes," Blair answered.

"Reed's going to go crazy," Melanie added.

"I know."

"What about Alex?" Melanie wondered.

"He was just doing his job."

"What about you?" Melanie asked, worried.

"I'm fine," Blair said, and sounded like he meant it.

Blair and Melanie agreed to tell Courtney in the morning that John Morgan was never going to hurt her again.

That night, Blair slept soundly.

Melanie didn't sleep a wink.

When Courtney was told—especially about how her dad was there and saw Morgan's dead body—her only response was "Good!"

CHAPTER NINETEEN

BONKERS

Detective Beyer, who attended the autopsy, cut the melted, corroded chain with the diamond "J" from the cadaver, and placed it carefully in an evidence bag. He left immediately for District Attorney Reed's office, where Reed was waiting.

The engraved serial numbers on the frame confirmed that the car was once a white Porsche Boxster rented to John Morgan at the LA Airport.

The forensic pathologist, with the dental records flown in from New York, confirmed that the charred human remains on the steel examination table were those of John Morgan.

"I intend to get to the bottom of this monstrous fuck-up, no matter what it takes," Reed told Beyer once Morgan's identity was confirmed. Beyer knew that Reed was frantic over the recent events, and that he would blame Officer Haines for everything. Alex Haines had already typed up his accident report identifying his witness, and had completed the favor asked of him by handing Detective Beyer the gun and ammunition. Beyer was convinced that Alex was at the wrong place, at the wrong time, doing his job. He was also convinced that Cody was nobody to fool with.

Beyer lit up another cigarette as he watched Alex settle into a comfortable leather chair across from Reed. From the tapping of his pencil on the desk, it was obvious that Reed was enraged.

"John Morgan," Reed screamed, without wasting any time, pointing his pencil at Alex, "was the husband of the woman murdered by her daughter! Blair, your new friend, is Courtney's father and the defense lawyer in this case!"

Alex just sat there.

The look on Alex's face told Beyer he was clueless. He didn't know the identity of the victim, and once told, didn't make the connection. He's still excited about the fact that he met "the cowboy," Beyer thought.

"John Morgan, you asshole," Reed continued, still screaming, "was the eyewitness to that murder, our only fucking eyewitness! My lead witness is dead!"

"Well, Mr. Reed," Alex said apologetically, "I didn't kill him. I had nothing to do with it. He just went over the cliff by himself. I didn't make him do it. Ask Mr. Cody if you don't believe me."

Reed slammed his fist down on his desk so hard that Alex jumped out of his seat. Detective Beyer just stood off to the side with his hands folded across his chest, watching. He thought Reed was being a little hard on the guy.

Beyer didn't believe for one second that this hapless son-of-a-bitch was recruited by Blair Cody into some kind of grand conspiracy. Alex was just watching for speeders on canyon run, and found one.

And Blair Cody lucked out, big time.

"Was Blair Cody chasing him?" Reed asked Alex, gritting his teeth.

"No," Alex answered innocently, "he was behind me."

"I know he was behind you, Alex, but was he chasing Morgan before you got in the fucking middle?" Reed asked, seething.

"How would I know that?" Alex said defensively, shaking his head in bewilderment. "I was in front of him."

Beyer almost laughed out loud. Alex was like an innocent child getting scolded for something he didn't do.

"Well," Reed asked, trying a kinder approach, "isn't it a fact that you saw Cody chasing Morgan, trying to run him off the road, forcing Morgan to go faster. Isn't that what you saw, Alex?"

"I think you're trying to put words in my mouth," Alex said, getting angry. "I didn't see any such thing. I saw this guy fly by me at 155 miles per hour, according to my radar gun, and the asshole didn't make the hairpin turn at God's View. He thought he was at the Indy 500. He went over the cliff on his own. That's what I saw."

"That's what I saw," Reed repeated, mocking Alex.

"And Blair didn't pull up until after the idiot crashed in the ravine," Alex added, digging it in.

Reed stood up and let out a long sigh.

"All right, Alex," he said, "you've made your point. You can go now."

"Thank you, sir," Alex said, standing up.

"One final question," Reed said.

"What's that?" Alex asked, still standing.

"Cody just handed you a loaded nine-millimeter handgun and told you to give it to Detective Beyer, just like that?"

"He unloaded it first, after he took it out of his glove box. He then told me that Detective Beyer would know what it was for. The chain of custody has been documented, if that's what you are worried about," Alex answered.

"Good-bye, Alex," Reed said, frustrated.

"Good-bye, sir," Alex returned, leaving the room.

There was an awkward silence in Reed's office after Alex left. Detective Beyer, with his arms still folded across his chest, didn't say a word. Reed sat still, thinking everything through.

Beyer knew the dilemma they were both in.

The trial of Courtney Cody was six weeks away. She was a juvenile who was charged as an adult under a California state law that provided for tougher prosecutions of violent young offenders. The law permitted the District Attorney's Office of Los Angeles County to automatically try her as an adult for certain crimes involving deadly weapons.

Like murder.

How were they going to convict Courtney Cody of murder in the first degree, which carried a mandatory life sentence, without John Morgan?

Reed cleared his throat, then he told Detective Beyer, "If Cody thinks for one second that the state of California is going to throw in the towel because of Morgan's death—a death he orchestrated— he's out of his fucking mind."

Detective Beyer didn't say a word. John Morgan was an important witness. Maybe they should offer Cody a deal.

"We have enough without him," Reed added. "Did you check the ballistics out on that handgun?"

"Yes," Beyer answered, without a whole lot of enthusiasm.

"Well?" Reed asked.

"It checks out."

"That was the gun used to kill Michelle Morgan?"

"Yes," Beyer answered. "The groove marks on the bullet removed from the body match the groove marks in the barrel. In addition, the bullets removed from the gun by Mr. Cody and given to Alex match the one taken from the body."

"Perfect," Reed said.

"You think?" Beyer asked.

"Yes, I think," Reed snapped, annoyed at Beyer's pessimism. "It's the gun, for Christ's sake."

Beyer knew Reed well enough to let him vent, but Beyer was convinced that Reed wasn't thinking clearly on this one—or more importantly, taking Cody seriously enough. It didn't make any sense to Beyer that Cody would voluntarily surrender the smoking gun to the authorities just because he said he would.

Especially since the defendant was his daughter.

It just didn't add up, and Detective Beyer had investigated hundreds of homicide cases, and dealt with a lot of criminal defense lawyers. Twenty-five years in the business and he had never dealt with anybody quite like Blair. He considered the recent events—though he would never tell Reed—a masterful piece of work on Blair's part, and everything was falling into place for him.

Cody fascinated Detective Beyer. When he waived Courtney's preliminary hearing, an unheard-of move in murder cases, Beyer was suspicious. Reed said that Cody simply didn't want to bring Courtney back from Pennsylvania and put her through a hearing that would generate anxiety and adverse front-page publicity.

Beyer wasn't convinced. He thought that Cody didn't want John Morgan's transcribed testimony.

To Beyer, there was a method to Cody's madness. A witness' transcribed testimony may be read to the jury if the witness is unavailable at the time of trial. Now, there was no transcribed testimony to be read to the jury, and no witness.

Beyer did not have to remind Reed that their case now rested on circumstantial evidence. Dr. Fillinger, who did the autopsy, would confirm the manner of death. They had their lab technicians, the best around, to prove the gun was the murder weapon. The transcripts of the custody hearing, and the stenographer who saw Courtney storm into the courtroom, would lay out the motive. Courtney's school records would also confirm her absence the week before her mother died.

"No one else was in the household on the night in question, right?" Reed asked.

"Except John Morgan," Beyer reminded him.

"You said yourself," Reed reminded Beyer, "that Morgan didn't kill Michelle."

"That's what I said, General," Beyer responded. "I don't believe Morgan did it, but Blair Cody is capable of putting it on him, and you know it."

"Then how in the fuck did Courtney end up with the gun?" Reed fired back, obviously having considered Cody's possible defense.

"I don't know the answer to that, Bill," Beyer replied, "but I don't know how we ended up with it either, or why."

"Maybe your boy Blair Cody isn't as smart as you think he is," Reed remarked sarcastically.

Detective Beyer didn't believe that for one second. This most recent development with John Morgan flying over a cliff and killing himself, and Blair Cody showing up within seconds, was not a coincidence.

Beyer didn't know what more Reed needed to wake up to the seriousness of his adversary.

◆ ◆ ◆

Thomas Keating crushed his cigar into the ashtray on David Wallace's desk. Despite the "Please No Smoking" sign on the wall, and the ungodly early hour to be smoking cigars, both Keating and Doc Bunt were huffing and puffing away on large Havanas. Wallace cleared his throat and could feel the burning in his eyes as he listened patiently.

It was 8 a.m. Courtney was going to trial in two weeks. The vast halls of McNett, Wallace & Johnson were empty, but would soon be crawling with lawyers and staff.

Keating had flown in from Philadelphia to make sure that everybody understood what was at stake, and who the players were. Pennsylvania's former lieutenant governor was getting his own dose of publicity in the East, especially from the *Philadelphia Inquirer*, which had a distribution of over four million copies daily. The publicity regarding the death of his daughter, at the hand of his granddaughter, was terrible.

And now, the prosecution's only eyewitness flies off a cliff.

The most recent story in the *Philadelphia Inquirer*, complete with Blair Cody's picture on the front page, was that Blair was going to be representing his daughter. The undisputed facts were sensationalized and tied into the Keating name: Keating's daughter was murdered; Keating's granddaughter, now twelve, was the accused; and she was being represented by his former son-in-law.

That last article in the *Inquirer* sent Keating scurrying to the West Coast. He wasn't convinced that they understood what Blair Cody was capable of, especially in the courtroom, or outside of the courtroom, for that matter.

"Blair Cody killed John Morgan," Keating stated flatly.

"I can understand why you feel that way, Tom," Wallace began, "but there's no evidence of that."

"Of course there's no evidence of that," Keating snapped angrily. "That's my fucking point. What you don't understand is who you're dealing with."

Wallace glanced at Bunt for some help.

Doc Bunt, picking up the cue, gently interjected. He told Keating that he personally talked to District Attorney Reed, who was very upset about this development. Reed wanted Keating to know that now he was more determined than ever. "He also told me to inform you that he's trying this one personally and that you have nothing to worry about," Bunt added.

"Nothing to worry about, my ass," Keating fired back. "Reed doesn't know. He doesn't have a fucking clue what he's up against. I read that Blair, because he wants a jury to hear this case, isn't even fighting the certification process."

"That's true," Wallace confirmed.

Keating made it emphatically clear that he didn't care that Courtney was his granddaughter. If Courtney killed her mother, then she was to be prosecuted to the hilt. If that meant that she was to spend the rest of her life in prison, then so be it. That's what Keating told the *Philadelphia Inquirer*, and all the local television stations, at a recent press conference in the City of Brotherly Love.

That's what he was telling Wallace and Bunt.

The final business matter was the distribution of Michelle's estate. Wallace explained that since Morgan was dead, Mr. and Mrs. Keating were in line to get everything.

"But only if Courtney is convicted," Wallace pointed out reluctantly.

◆ ◆ ◆

Courtney liked the retired high school English teacher with the funny-looking glasses that were too big for her face—she looked like Sally Jessy Raphael, sort of—but home tutoring wasn't the same as going to school. There were no friends to talk to or play with, no one to pass notes to, and instead of going to the cafeteria for lunch, Courtney would eat with Mrs. Bogadello in the kitchen. She also missed riding to school on the bus.

"Make sure, honey," Mrs. Bogadello cautioned as she wrote down Courtney's homework for the weekend, "that you read chapter six in your history book and do the review questions."

"I will," said Courtney.

Courtney knew why she was not going to school. She knew that she had to go back to California to stand trial, in front of a jury, just like on television. Her dad and Melanie explained everything to her, over and over, but they never talked about what would happen if the jury found her guilty.

But Courtney knew.

Courtney knew that if the jury found her guilty, she would go to jail, maybe forever. She read that in one of the newspapers.

The only jail cells Courtney had ever seen were on television. She had talked with friends about it once, a long time ago, and they told her there were rats and spiders in them. She also heard that they didn't have lights, and if you were bad, the guard would slide moldy bread and warm water to you under the door.

She asked her dad about going to prison if she was found guilty, and he just looked at her. She had never seen her father look so sad. He finally said, "Don't worry about that, Courtney. Your dad's never going to let that happen."

Her dad got so upset that day, he had to leave for a while. Courtney didn't know where he went, and she didn't know what she had done to upset him so much.

Melanie—thank God for Melanie—was a big help that day. She put her arms around Courtney and said that her dad was under a lot of pressure. Melanie then made lunch for the three of them and that night took her to the movies to see *The Lion King*.

"Your dad and Melanie will be home in about an hour. Are you sure you'll be all right here by yourself?" Mrs. Bogadello asked as she packed her books and things into her canvas bag, preparing to leave.

"I'll be fine," Courtney answered, wanting her to go.

As soon as Mrs. Bogadello's Volvo station wagon went down the driveway, disappearing around the first curve, Courtney ran to her bedroom to change. She wanted to ride Impressive James before it got dark.

Putting the saddle on was the hard part, even harder than sticking the bridle in his mouth, because of its weight and her having to pull so hard to tighten the cinch. Her gelding kept moving in the cross-ties, making things more difficult. But finally, after a struggle, she strapped on her spurs and mounted.

Courtney loped circles in the groomed riding pen on the hill. A cool spring breeze kept the horse fresh, and Courtney zipped up her coat to keep warm. She could see from the hill that her dad wasn't home, and decided to go on a trail ride to the north side of the property. Even though it was almost dark, and her dad told her never to trail ride alone, Courtney thought she had time before nightfall. The north side was a bluff that overlooked the valley, and fun to get to because of the stream that had to be crossed. The thick pines were plentiful with white-tailed deer, and Courtney was sure that she knew the trail, having traveled it many times with her dad. Like she had done so many times before, Courtney pressed her spur gently into the side of her horse and coaxed him forward. Impressive James responded to Courtney's command.

Courtney felt safer out here, away from it all.

She was glad John Morgan was dead. He would never hurt her again. She knew her dad killed him, no matter what he said.

This trial in California just didn't make sense. She hadn't meant to kill her mother. She had thought John Morgan was going to get her again, and she could still see his naked body coming after her. She could still hear the shot ring out that was intended for him, and she always would.

As Courtney climbed the steep on Impressive James, several rocks beneath them rolled down the hill, and her young horse scrambled for his footing. Courtney grabbed the horn of her saddle until they made it to the crest.

The other night, she dreamt about her mother. It was a dream filled with fond memories, when her mother lived with her dad. The dream went back a long time ago, to when Courtney was four years old and her mother took her to the circus. In the dream, the two of them were laughing at the clowns, eating cotton candy, and holding hands in the crowd.

Everything was different now. There was no more laughing or holding hands. That had changed some time ago, long before the move to California. Her mother had betrayed her, lied to her, physically abused her, and sided with John Morgan in a conspiracy of silence. Her mother's not doing anything after John raped her was so very painful. Courtney's fond memories of her mother were fading.

Why hadn't the judge listened to her? She had told the truth about everything, but he would not let her go home with her dad. If only he had, none of this would have happened. It was all his fault.

The sun on the horizon was setting quickly, and darkness was falling.

Courtney turned around to head home and noticed that the stretch of pines was no longer familiar without light. The trail disappeared, the known landmarks weren't there. A cold wind softly whispered, and Courtney pulled up her collar to keep warm. She wanted to run her horse but didn't know which way to go. She kept going, not looking back, praying that her path was the right one and she would be home soon.

Courtney pressed forward, the low-hanging pines brushing against her. Then restless Impressive James lowered his head and pulled to the right. Courtney thought she could hear the stream and hastened her pace to a clearing, but it was only the wind.

She suddenly knew, without a shadow of a doubt, that she was lost.

◆ ◆ ◆

When Blair walked into the house from the garage with Melanie, he sensed that something was wrong. There were no lights on, no television, no radio, no voices. Mrs. Bogadello's car was gone, and the house was unlocked.

Melanie immediately called Mrs. Bogadello while Blair checked the house looking for Courtney, but no, Mrs. Bogadello said, Courtney did not go with her. She also explained that she had left an hour before and Courtney had been there.

Blair told Melanie to wait by the phone while he checked the barns. He took his cell phone with him, and she was to call if Courtney showed up. Panic was fast setting in. His heart was pounding, and the knot in his stomach was tightening, as he ran across the yard. Had Courtney been kidnapped again? By whom? Michelle was dead; Morgan was dead. Thomas Keating? Then he thought: Could she have run away?

The first stall he checked was Impressive James'. The horse was gone, as was Courtney's tack, and a fleeting moment of relief washed through him. She was riding, and though it was dark, all he had to do was find her.

Immediately, Blair tacked up his best trail horse and headed for the north fork in the direction of the cliffs. He would have to cross a stream, which had its own element of danger, but it was the fastest way to get there. Because night had set in, Blair moved quickly across the terrain that he knew so well.

The top of the distant hill was a silhouette, and Blair strained to see movement. As much as he didn't want to think about Courtney going down the jagged side of the north fork, he had to consider the possibility, and fear once again swept over him.

Blair circled a thicket on his way to the top of the hill, which flushed several deer, spooking his horse.

Courtney was not on the bluff, and Blair rolled back and headed for the pines. Once he got into the center of the pine grove, he stopped and listened. He thought he could hear movement on the soft floor, and yelled for Courtney. Blair heard Courtney yell back, and following the sound of her voice, soon found her. She was on foot, walking her horse, with tears streaming down her face. Blair dismounted and, hugging her, told her that he was going to take her home, that everything was okay.

He realized that he wasn't angry, only scared, and that his life was never going to be the same. When it came to Courtney, he would do whatever had to be done.

TWENTY

HEAT

Reed was excited, but feeling the pressure.

He was pacing back and forth in his library, alone, like a caged lion about to be released into an arena. He envisioned that arena filled with people, cheering him on to do justice, to draw blood, to win.

The media were clamoring about the upcoming case, which had a different spin every time Reed picked up a newspaper. Last week, the sensationalism focused on the fact that the victim was the daughter of the wealthy and powerful Thomas Keating, Pennsylvania's former lieutenant governor and chairman of the state Republican Committee.

The murder's having taken place in the prestigious Hollywood Hills was also a fact that got the media's attention. Domestic killings in downtown LA may have been routine news—almost always between warring spouses, or between estranged spouses and paramours—but a twelve-year-old daughter killing her mother in the upscale suburbs of Los Angeles made terrific headlines.

"I am personally going to prosecute this horrendous crime committed with an adult level of sophistication," Reed added for the media in dramatic fashion.

The most recent release from his office was that Courtney's father—Blair Cody—was going to represent her. That story drove the media wild!

FATHER TO DEFEND DAUGHTER was the headline in *USA Today*.

MURDER VICTIM'S EX-HUSBAND TO DEFEND DAUGHTER was LA's front-page angle, complete with pictures of Courtney and Blair.

CODY TO DEFEND DAUGHTER FOR MURDER was Philadelphia's lead story.

Added to that explosive mixture was Blair's reputation in the East as a top-notch courtroom performer, who was going up against LA's biggest gun, District Attorney William Reed.

At a recent staff meeting, a young assistant innocently remarked that Blair Cody's reputation was awesome, and Reed went into a tirade. After that, things got quiet throughout the office. No one dared mention that their "General" was feeling the heat.

Reed checked his watch and glanced at the clock above the main library door.

In ten minutes, he was going to have a private staff meeting, which included his two most trusted courtroom advisors: Larry Coleman, his first assistant and office administrator, whose friendship and loyalty had withstood the test of time; and Jane Baskin, his top homicide prosecutor and an accomplished trial strategist.

Reed also asked Detective Beyer to be there for his input.

In addition, Reed had personally invited Dr. Francine Patterson, a forensic jury consultant, to join them. He had already made up his mind that Dr. Patterson was going to help him pick this jury. She had a nationwide reputation for picking cooperative juries, and that's exactly what he wanted.

Reed had seen enough runaway juries in Los Angeles, and he

wasn't taking any chances with their integrity. He wasn't interested in a jury that was impartial. He wanted a jury that would run with him all the way to the gallows. And Dr. Patterson, a forensic psychologist who specialized in human behavior, was to lead the way. She was a long-haired redhead—thirty-two, single, opinionated, and vain; she always credited herself anytime her side won a case, regardless of the facts.

It was 7:30 p.m., and everybody was on time.

Reed sat at the head of the table, with Larry Coleman to his left and Jane Baskin to his right. Jimmy Beyer sat across from Francine Patterson at the oversized table.

Reed had asked Beyer to devote full time to the Cody case, though LA had a ton of unsolved cases. Some were more serious to the law enforcement community than a domestic killing in the Hollywood Hills. In fact, one of Beyer's men, Officer Donivon— married, with four small children at home—was killed in a shoot-out during a drug raid some weeks earlier. Officer Donivon had been with the LAPD for seven years before he took the surprise bullet in the neck, well above his flak vest. Donivon's killer was still at large, and Reed knew that.

"The trial is less than two weeks away," Reed began, feigning calm, his hands folded neatly on the table, "and I have assembled the four of you because I trust your collective judgment."

Coleman and Baskin nodded their heads appreciatively.

Beyer said nothing.

Patterson smiled. More than once she crossed her legs provocatively, but Reed was preoccupied and missed the subtle hint.

"I think our case is open and shut," Reed continued. "I can prove that Courtney had the sole motive and opportunity to kill her mother, did kill her mother, and thereafter fled with the gun in hand. What I want to talk about is what the defense is going to do, how we can counter it, and what kind of jury we want in anticipation of the defense."

Reed then stood up and unveiled a color-coded chart, outlining his case. Emblazoned in red were the words:

MOTIVE

OPPORTUNITY

DATE

TIME

PLACE

POSSESSION OF GUN

FLIGHT

Coleman, as he examined the exhibit, rocked back in his leather chair. With his hands folded behind his head, he opined that because the defendant was a cute little girl, the defense had a weighty sympathy factor. He said that Blair could concede the shooting by Courtney, present evidence that she was being abused by her mother, and argue self-defense. Or, he added, Courtney killed her mother in an emotional rage, which would reduce the verdict to manslaughter.

"You're probably right," Baskin agreed, "and he'll follow up with expert testimony about how abused children react, and how Courtney was just a child, with a child's mentality, on the night in question."

Reed walked around the table, putting two and two together. Earlier that day, he got a frantic call from Dr. Goldstein, who had just been subpoenaed by the defense. Some asshole P.I. from Pennsylvania served his office, but never said a word to him about his appearance.

"Real cute," Reed said out loud. "Blair's calling Michelle's expert, Dr. Goldstein, to prove his case."

"That's consistent with my theory of the defense," Coleman interjected, "because on page 101 of the custody hearing transcript, Dr. Goldstein testified that Courtney's wishes weren't relevant because she was just a child."

"I'll take care of Dr. Goldstein," Reed said knowingly.

Detective Beyer watched the lawyers brainstorming, arguing over what Blair Cody was going to do in court. He wasn't convinced that Blair was going to concede that Courtney fired the killing shot. That concession would expose Courtney to a compromised verdict, possibly voluntary manslaughter, which carried ten years in the state of California. Blair Cody wasn't going to do that!

Beyer also wasn't convinced that anybody in that room was capable of figuring out what Blair Cody was going to do. Cody came from a world that they didn't understand. Their law books didn't mean shit when it came to dealing with a guy like that. Cody had instincts, especially when he was fighting for his daughter's life. Beyer wasn't even convinced that Cody was going to show up.

"What do you think, Detective Beyer?" Reed asked, looking over at him.

"What do I think?" Beyer asked back.

Reed nodded his head.

"Well, I don't think you people can figure out a guy like Blair Cody."

"Don't start that shit," Reed snapped.

"I don't believe for one second that Cody's going to concede that Courtney killed her mother!" Beyer shot back, looking hard at Reed, one on one. "Now that Morgan is dead and can't testify, we can't even use his written statement since Cody waived the preliminary hearing. He could put it all on Morgan, assuming Blair shows up," Beyer added.

"You . . . " Reed tried to interject.

"Let me finish," Beyer said, interrupting Reed.

Dr. Patterson sat up during this heated exchange between two warriors. Coleman and Baskin stayed out of it; their "General" and LA's top homicide cop were having it out.

Beyer insisted that Blair would never concede Courtney fired the gun. He painted a convincing scenario for his attentive audience. Morgan killed Michelle, and in the scuffle dropped the gun. Courtney picked up the gun off the floor and ran.

"You said yourself, Jim," Reed reminded him, "that Morgan didn't do it."

"I did say that, but Cody didn't," Beyer answered, defending his theory.

Reed, as if he were addressing the jury, stressed that Courtney fled the scene; she never called the police, or the ambulance, or the neighbors to report that her mother had been shot. Even her flight to avoid prosecution was planned.

"The reason she didn't call," Reed said passionately, "is because she didn't care that her mother was dead, and because she was hiding from the law."

"I like it," Coleman said, praising his boss.

"I do, too," Baskin concurred. "Flight is classic evidence of guilt."

Beyer had to admit that Reed's closing argument had a lot of merit; at least it sounded good.

Dr. Patterson, when asked, said that she had reviewed the psychological profile of Courtney and everything else in Reed's file. She believed that Cody's defense would be one of justification. She pointed out that though Courtney wanted to live with her father, she never alleged abuse by her mother or John. And Blair Cody could call all the child psychiatrists he wanted, including Dr. Melanie Castille, to testify that Courtney was a mere child incapable of forming the specific intent to kill.

Before leaving, Dr. Patterson stood up and shook everybody's hand—holding onto Reed's hand tenderly—promising them a winning jury. She said that the jury would have no sympathy for a kid who killed her mother under any circumstances.

"Good," Reed said with satisfaction.

◆ ◆ ◆

A lone vulture circled the ravine below God's View, where the Porsche once rested, floating in mid-air, scanning for morsels. The condor of death had been having a feast in the area for weeks, but the search for food was now taking longer with each passing day.

With the warm sun in her face, and the ocean breeze blowing

her auburn hair away from her eyes, Kimberly Wells watched from the top of the mountain where Blair once stood.

Pat Greely had asked her to take him there. He had been in Los Angeles for the past week at Blair's request, with very specific instructions: to serve subpoenas on Dr. Goldstein and others; to review the physical evidence at the crime lab; and to spend time with Kimberly since they were going to be working together.

Kimberly was casually dressed in blue jeans and a long-sleeved denim blouse.

Pat Greely was dressed in a pin-striped business suit, with a solid blue tie, looking like the federal agent he once was.

Kimberly's forest-green Jeep Cherokee was the only vehicle parked in the tourist parking lot, and an occasional car would pass by at the posted speed limit of twenty miles per hour on the peak.

"Unbelievable," Greely said.

"Yeah, 155 on this curve," Kimberly answered, still looking down over the cliff in amazement.

"He was running scared from something," Greely added.

"You got that right, Pat," Kimberly responded, looking right at her new partner, shaking her head without having to say any more.

Kimberly hadn't heard from Blair, who was acting stranger than ever. She heard from Melanie all the time; that's how she found out the eerie details about Morgan's death. The newspaper account, a headline story, had never mentioned that Blair was at the scene.

As local counsel, she had filed the necessary paperwork, but knew nothing about Blair's defense.

"He's a funny guy," Greely said, breaking the silence. "If it makes you feel any better, Kimberly, I don't know any more than you do."

"Well, it doesn't," she answered with a slight laugh.

"You know," Greely added, "we finally found Hector."

"Really?" Kimberly said with surprise. "How'd you find him?"

"Once Courtney was charged with murdering her mother, Hector found us. He called Blair two days ago. He said his conscience had gotten the better of him, particularly since he read in the newspapers that Courtney was facing a life sentence. He offered to help and he's on board."

"I needed him at Blair's PFA hearing. I needed him at the criminal trial. How can he help us now?" Kimberly asked.

Greely just shook his head. "I don't know."

He then showed Kimberly the crumpled piece of paper that he took out of his pocket. Blair had asked them to photograph the outside of 719 Valley View Road, and then measure the distance on foot to the Melrose Middle School; specifically, to the pay phone and then to the pond. They were also to time their walk.

Kimberly was to check with Reed for any last-minute discovery, or for any new evidence that may have arisen in the case. Kimberly, who knew everything about the case, couldn't imagine there being any new evidence.

But she had just received several pages of questions from District Attorney Reed for the prospective jurors to answer in writing. They were clearly designed to eliminate any juror who might be sympathetic to a child-abuse defense.

Melanie told Kimberly that Blair would deal with those questions personally, and not to worry about them.

"We'd better get going," Pat finally said as the condor made a low-flying sweep in the valley.

"I agree," Kimberly responded. "The trial is in three days."

◆　◆　◆

Courtney's suitcases were neatly packed and sitting by the front door.

Their flight—Courtney, Blair, and Melanie's—would depart from the Harrisburg International Airport for Los Angeles at 7 a.m. the next morning.

The trial, starting with jury selection, was two days away.

The three of them would stay at Melanie's condominium.

Melanie had never experienced such fear and anxiety in her life. The thought of Courtney going to trial in front of a jury, and the possibility of that child being taken right from the courtroom to prison for the rest of her life, was terrifying. There was nothing in the world that could help ease Melanie's pain, or prepare Courtney for the upcoming event.

Courtney was a child, too young to fully appreciate what was at stake. Melanie took comfort in the fact that her dad, and Kimberly, would be with her.

Blair, who knew the stakes, was going to up the ante. Every card he had had been dealt to him by Reed and the system. Now it was time to put all the chips on the table, and play those cards.

CHAPTER TWENTY-ONE

PUZZLES

April 29, 1996.

9:30 a.m.

Los Angeles County Courthouse.

Blair, holding Courtney's hand, walked through the throng of cameras and reporters without saying a word. The media kept their cameras trained on them, capturing footage that would grip the West Coast. Philadelphia's Channel 6 zoomed in on Courtney walking up the courthouse steps, while an Action News team reported live at the scene.

"Is Courtney going to take the witness stand?" one reporter asked, thrusting a microphone in Blair's face.

"Mr. Cody," another reporter yelled as he walked backwards, "will you allow Courtney to make a statement?"

Reporters, clamoring for the best position and sound bite, fired questions from every direction:

"Have any plea negotiations been entered into?"

"How long is this trial going to take?"

"What is your defense going to be?"

"Do you anticipate a favorable verdict?"

Blair didn't slow down as he walked through the excited crowd with Courtney. He looked straight ahead, and Courtney did the same, as they fought their way to the elevators. Inside, uniformed sheriffs helped clear the way, hustling people around in the hallways, trying to maintain some semblance of order and dignity. Blair understood legal theater, and at one time enjoyed it. But that was years ago.

This time he wasn't going to play to the crowd, or the media, or the packed gallery in the back of the courtroom. This time the only audience that mattered to Blair would be Courtney's jury. He hoped to pick twelve people who would render a verdict based on the evidence, uninfluenced by anything they may have seen, read, or heard.

◆   ◆   ◆

For four days, working late into the evenings, the lawyers grilled 142 prospective jurors. Reed asked all of the questions for the prosecution, seeking to establish a personal rapport, and Dr. Patterson took notes. Kimberly did the questioning for Courtney, introducing her to each of the prospective jurors as the defendant, and introducing Blair as "Courtney's father, who will be trying the case on her behalf."

Blair intentionally avoided eye contact with his prospective jury. He paid no attention to Reed, or his personnel, or the cardboard boxes in neat stacks by the prosecution table. He sat beside Courtney, in deep thought, while Kimberly studied the thick volume listing jurors' names, addresses, marital status, and occupations. Kimberly's questioning of the prospective jurors was a textbook example of efficiency.

Finally, the selected jury—consisting of eight women and four men, with two male alternates—would be sequestered. The science teacher, who sat in the back row, kept staring at Blair. The engineer, who Blair predicted would be the foreman, kept glancing at Courtney.

◆ ◆ ◆

The back of the small courtroom was packed. The opening arguments would set the stage, and the gallery would take sides from that moment on. They would cheer to themselves whenever evidence would be presented that scored points for their team. Many onlookers knew enough to get there early for a good seat, and the faces in the audience would change from day to day.

District Attorney Reed, with Dr. Francine Patterson by his side, was waiting at the prosecution table for the trial to begin. Reed was dressed in a blue suit and conservative tie for the occasion. Dr. Patterson was also dressed in a blue business suit, with solid-blue, high-heeled shoes. Assistant District Attorney Coleman was wheeling in a dolly loaded with cardboard file boxes, all neatly labeled and tabbed.

"Ladies and gentlemen of the jury," Judge Clarence Morrisey said, looking at them and addressing them informally, "the case of California versus Courtney Louise Cody is about to begin. At this point, you have heard no evidence. If you remember the film that you saw several days ago, you will remember that the defendant in a criminal case is presumed innocent. You will remember that the prosecution has the burden of proving its charges beyond a reasonable doubt. In this case, the defendant, Courtney Cody, has been charged with murder in the first degree, meaning the malicious and premeditated killing of Michelle Morgan, her mother. This alleged murder took place on or about February 25, 1996, at 719 Valley View Road."

Blair listened without expression as Judge Morrisey's voice echoed in the courtroom. Having been tried and sentenced by Morrisey months ago, Blair had a feel for this judge, his legal philosophy and eccentricities. He had a tendency to be consistent with his rulings, right or wrong, and even-handed. Blair did not get that feeling in Judge Hester's courtroom.

"Mr. Reed," Judge Morrisey said, shifting his gaze to the prosecution's table, "are you prepared to open to the jury?"

"Yes, Your Honor," Reed said, standing and nodding his head.

After adjusting his tie and carefully placing his hands on the podium in front of the jury, he began, at first slowly, but in a resonant voice. Blair watched as Reed dealt the cards, flashing them to the jury.

Reed used all the stock phrases, but delivered them well. He told the attentive jury that an opening argument is not evidence, but is like the picture on the box of a puzzle. His picture would be supported by the pieces in his box, which consisted of testimony, physical evidence, and pre-existing courtroom documents. "Once you assemble these pieces," Reed said, raising his voice, "you will see Courtney Cody is the killer."

Blair knew that Reed was on a roll. The jury was hanging on his every word. Several jurors shook their heads in disgust as the grisly details were laid out. Reed's description of Michelle bleeding on the kitchen floor, left to die, was riveting.

Several jurors were upset by Courtney's flight and her failure to call the police. Reed called such evidence the corner pieces to their puzzle, and snaking his fingers together to show the fit, ended a dramatic opening.

After picking up his papers from the podium, Reed returned to the prosecution's table, but not before pausing and giving Courtney a cold look.

Courtney didn't know what to do.

The jury saw it.

Blair saw it.

And an artist, who was doing sketches for the TV networks, caught it.

◆ ◆ ◆

After Reed's opening, Judge Morrisey took a fifteen-minute recess for the jurors to collect themselves.

The once-silent gallery broke into private conversations that continued into the hallways. Blair could hear the reviews, and Reed had done well; even the news reporters, who were generally critical, agreed that he had presented, and promised, a very good case.

Blair watched as Reed took the opportunity to shake the hands of his supporters and well-wishers. Dr. Patterson stayed by his side, with Coleman, but Detective Beyer kept out of the limelight.

Keeping to himself in the well of the courtroom, with Courtney, Blair would soon make his own first impression. Courtney had on a blue and white striped dress, like something a kid would wear to school. Her feet barely touched the floor in the oversized chair at the defense table. It was so difficult for Blair as Courtney looked all around the courtroom, overwhelmed by the marble walls and high ceilings.

Nobody—not Kimberly, or even Melanie, who was sitting in the front row with the general public—had any idea what Blair was going to do. Reed and Coleman, with their pens ready to write down Blair's promised defense, certainly didn't.

Finally, the moment had arrived. Blair could have delayed his opening until the prosecution rested, but didn't. It was time to fight back.

Dressed in a conservative, dark gray suit, Blair walked to the podium. Several of the jurors looked down; the old engineer did not. The rest seemed willing to hear him out.

"Ladies and gentlemen of the jury," Blair began, without any introduction or polite amenities, but with a magnetism that captured the jury, "when this case is over, the picture on the box of Mr. Reed's puzzle isn't going to have Courtney anywhere on it."

Without wasting any time, Blair told the jury that Courtney did not kill her mother.

And quickly added, he would prove who did.

"You see, ladies and gentlemen," Blair continued, knowing he had their undivided attention, "I know who the killer is. I know who had the motive. I know who threatened her, and who had the opportunity."

Blair turned around and faced Reed, and still addressing the jury, pointed out that their district attorney never mentioned to them that John Morgan—Michelle's husband and Courtney's step-father—was the only other person in the house on that fateful night.

Nobody on the jury was looking down now. Two divorced women in the back row, with children of their own, were glaring at Reed, who had never said a word about *that*.

Before Blair sat down, he walked straight over to Reed's table and looked hard at him. He then moved closer and whispered, "Don't you ever, ever look at my daughter like that again."

Reed didn't know what to do, but was obviously ruffled.

Blair didn't give a fuck.

He was ready to try this case, and fully intended to play by the rules—Reed's rules, Reed's deck.

CHAPTER TWENTY-TWO

REED'S HAND

A blown-up photograph, in black and white, depicted Michelle lying on the kitchen floor, with blood oozing from her mouth and neck. Michelle's eyes were wide open, staring at the jury in horror. They seemed unsettled with death in their faces, but Blair was unmoved.

He told Courtney not to look, and she didn't.

The medical examiner, who performed the autopsy, said the bullet entered the jaw bone, went through the trachea, and lodged itself in the spinal column. The bullet was removed from the body and given to Detective Beyer.

Prosecution Exhibit 2 was a picture of the blood on the refrigerator; 3 was the outlined body on the floor, done in black chalk; 4 was Courtney's bedroom, which depicted her unmade bed and personal belongings; and 5 was the open back door that led out of the kitchen. Reed uncovered the blow-ups, one at a time, and walked them in front of the jury as a uniformed officer explained the obvious.

Officer Weaver, young and enthusiastic, said that upon his arrival he could hear John Morgan crying softly in the bedroom. He added, without prompting from Reed, that Morgan appeared distraught and sad, and was clutching a framed photo of Michelle.

The photo of Michelle, dressed in her wedding gown, was given to the jury to pass around.

Weaver waited, sitting erect, for Blair's cross-examination. He was a credible witness with a Boy Scout appearance, which included freckles and short red hair parted neatly at the side, showing his receding hairline. The large photograph of the open back door remained on the easel facing the jury.

"Officer Weaver," Blair asked as he approached the easel, pointing to the back door that led into the darkness, "did you dust the outside door knob for fingerprints?"

Weaver hesitated and then simply answered, "No, sir."

◆   ◆   ◆

One by one, the high-profile anchor reporters from LA's networks took the witness stand. They, too, had participated in the search for Courtney and the gun.

Reed dimmed the lights in the courtroom and played, on closed-circuit TV, their news broadcasts asking "for any information that may lead to the whereabouts of Courtney Cody, who is being sought in connection with her mother's death at 719 Valley View Road, in upscale Hollywood Hills."

Whenever Courtney's picture would flash on the television screen, or when Reed showed the jury Courtney's picture on the front page of their newspaper, the jurors would compare the image with the girl who was sitting in the defendant's chair.

A uniformed officer, who ended the parade of witnesses, testified that he was in charge of the search. He kept putting the two together—"the search for Courtney and the gun"—as he described how the dogs were brought out to help, but to no avail.

Reed had presented enough evidence of flight that he was sure to get a jury instruction from Judge Morrisey at the conclusion of the trial. The judge would instruct the jury that "if you find that the defendant was a fugitive, you may consider that flight as evidence of guilt."

◆ ◆ ◆

In his opening, Reed had told the jury about the incident in Judge Hester's courtroom, and the opinionated stenographer who had transcribed the proceedings filled in the details. "She practically busted the door down," the stenographer recalled, "and disrupted the proceedings."

Courtney had caused a big commotion, according to the stenographer, and told Judge Hester in chambers that she wanted to live with her father and did not want to live with her mother and John Morgan.

Contrary to Courtney's wishes, the stenographer added, custody was awarded to her mother.

Reed's motive card was laid on the table, and the jury got the picture.

Reed was feeling good. The signals he was getting from the jury, especially the engineer and the divorced housewives with children, suggested a guilty verdict.

He believed that if Blair presented no defense other than the insinuation that Morgan may have done it, he was finished. And just in case Blair had more than insinuation and innuendo to implicate Morgan, six reputable witnesses were flying in from New York to portray him as an altar boy.

In addition, Reed was going to prove to this jury why John—his only eyewitness to the murder, and Blair's scapegoat—was rendered unavailable. He had plenty of proof that Blair was responsible for

Morgan's death, which conveniently eliminated Courtney's accuser. That insolent Blair Cody, Reed thought, was out of his league.

◆ ◆ ◆

Patty Newman, the real estate agent from LoeMax, walked into the courtroom with her file. She was poised when she came in, with her name card on her lapel, but did a double take when she saw Blair.

She kept glancing at Blair during her testimony, and when asked by Reed if he was the one who showed up at her offices to buy 719 Valley View Road, she answered, "Definitely."

Blair nodded when she pointed her finger accusingly, acknowledging her identification. He could feel all eyes in the courtroom— the jury's, the judge's, and the gallery's—focus on him.

Patty Newman talked fast, but her detailed recollection was accurate and her file complete. She thought she was selling the house to Rocky Jones. Her seller was Mr. John Morgan, and the minute he saw Blair Cody, alias Rocky Jones, in the conference room, all hell broke loose. Morgan pushed her out of the way and ran, with Blair in hot pursuit. From the conference room window, she witnessed their sudden exodus. Her seller peeled out of the parking lot in a white Porsche, her buyer gave chase in a red BMW, and her settlement went *poof.* Their departure time, she said, was exactly 11 a.m.

Blair almost smiled as the agent told her story, and he remembered it well. There was going to be a time for cross-examination, but not with this witness, and he thanked her as she was excused. The jury didn't need a calculator, Blair thought, to figure out that Morgan was going airborne at God's View within minutes.

"That's right," Alex testified as he faced the jury, "John Morgan was traveling too fast for conditions when he went over the cliff at 11:15 a.m. The speed limit was twenty miles per hour."

Officer Haines was coming off as a truthful law enforcement officer who witnessed an accident.

"Officer Haines," Reed said from the prosecution's table, "tell this jury how fast Morgan was going when he passed your radar trap."

Alex, without looking at his typed report, answered, "155 miles per hour."

"And when he went over the cliff?" Reed asked, standing up.

"154 miles per hour, sir," Alex answered respectfully.

Blair was sure from the jury's reaction that they had all traveled the scenic route, and couldn't imagine that speed.

"Officer Haines," Reed asked with a pause, alerting Alex to the importance of his next question, "was there a vehicle traveling in the same direction that would have been directly behind Morgan's Porsche if it were not for your intervention?"

Alex didn't respond at first.

Judge Morrisey leaned forward to hear.

"Yes, sir," Alex answered, "driven by Mr. Blair Cody."

Blair had everybody's attention now, including Kimberly's and Melanie's. With Reed doing the questioning, Alex told the jury how Blair pulled up in a BMW within seconds after the crash. "According to my notes, we both went down to check on the driver, just in case he was still alive," Alex added.

Confirming for the jury that the driver was dead, burnt beyond recognition, Alex stated that he later learned the victim's identity.

"Yes," Alex testified, "Mr. Cody handed me a nine-millimeter handgun and eight rounds, and asked that I give them to Detective Beyer."

Before Alex stepped down, Blair approached the witness and whispered, "You did fine, Alex, and I'm not going to ask you any questions. I hope this whole thing didn't cause you any problems."

Reed didn't know what the fuck was happening, and objected.

Judge Morrisey didn't know what Reed was objecting to, but sustained it because Blair hadn't asked permission to approach the witness.

Alex just sat there and waited to be excused.

The media, however, didn't wait as they ran to their phones with the story.

◆ ◆ ◆

Exhibit 12, Reed's final exhibit, was the gun. The fragment removed from Michelle's body was of the same caliber, and the groove on the fragment matched the barrel groove.

"Perfectly," the expert said, pointing to a large drawing on the easel showing the exact match-up.

"No doubt," he said, "the bullet removed from her body came from this handgun."

Reed took the gun from the agent and placed it on the jury's rail for them to observe. The ominous black handgun was now theirs, and Reed had proven a chain of custody that went back to Courtney. He had proven motive, opportunity, date, time, and place. In the process, he proved why Morgan wasn't there, and the district attorney of Los Angeles, on behalf of the state of California, had met his burden.

Reed's presentation was over. He had proven his case beyond a reasonable doubt. He imagined the sound of silent applause in the courtroom as he scanned the gallery for their approval and appreciation.

"I rest my case," Reed said, looking at Judge Morrisey.

His hand was now on the table, and though not a royal flush, certainly four of a kind would be hard to beat.

CHAPTER TWENTY-THREE

THE SHUFFLE

"Mr. Cody," Judge Morrisey said, "are you ready to proceed?"

"Yes, Your Honor," Blair said.

"Call your first witness."

"I call Hector Marquez."

Not having access to Blair's witness list, Reed wasn't sure what the point was. Maybe Blair was calling Hector to prove that Courtney was kidnapped from her home, to lay the groundwork for Courtney's justification defense. Reed's confidence wasn't shaken in the slightest.

He was intrigued, however, by the fact that Blair had found this witness.

Hector, with his short-sleeved shirt exposing his massive arms, told the jury in his broken English how he—with his brother, Sylvio, and four other workers—entered the home of Blair Cody and took everything. He testified that he was hired by Michelle Cody to move out the furnishings. He did not know where he was going to take them after that. He did not know, he said, that a child was going to be kidnapped.

For the rest of the morning, Hector described the grueling trip west, how Courtney rode with him, and how Michelle smashed Courtney in the mouth with the telephone. He did not tell the jury that he went to Courtney's aid. He did not tell the jury how he grabbed Michelle's arm and pulled her off Courtney. Blair had told him not to volunteer *that* information, but to tell the truth if asked by Reed.

"Mr. Marquez," Blair asked, wrapping up his direct examination, "did Michelle tell you why she was taking Courtney in the middle of the night?"

"Yes," Hector answered, "she said that she was afraid of you. She said we had to hurry, because if you caught us, you would kill her. And maybe even me."

Once again, Blair took the hit, and ended his direct on that suspended note.

Reed asked no questions on cross-examination, and Blair knew why. Reed knew enough to let sleeping dogs lie.

Courtney smiled when Hector, her trucking buddy, winked at her as he left the courtroom.

◆ ◆ ◆

Over the lunch hour, Pat Greely supervised the technicians who were setting up the headsets for the jury, the court, the prosecution, and the defense. A speaker was also put into place for the gallery, and the media, to hear.

When Reed walked into the courtroom and saw the setup, he asked Blair what was going on. Blair said he was going to play a tape for the jury.

"What tape?" Reed asked, curious.

"Your tape," Blair answered.

"What in the hell is going on?" Reed demanded.

Rather than deal with him, Blair sent word to Judge Morrisey that he wanted a "brief meeting in chambers to discuss an offer of proof." Blair's offer would answer Reed's question, and then some.

All the attorneys, and Beyer, attended the conference in Morrisey's chambers. For the first time in a long time, Blair felt in control. Nobody knew it, but everything was falling into place for him, just as he had planned. He was looking forward to exposing his defense, and the reaction that was sure to follow.

"Mr. Cody," Judge Morrisey began in a friendly tone, "Mr. Reed wants to know what's on the tape and how it's relevant to this proceeding."

"Mr. Reed wants an offer?" Blair asked.

"Exactly," Judge Morrisey said.

"The tape, Your Honor," Blair responded, "is the 911 tape which was previously authenticated in this courtroom by Mr. Reed. This tape is of Michelle's call to the police, reporting an assault on her person and a threat on her life. This call was placed by Michelle within twenty-four hours after Hector Marquez told me where Courtney was."

"Objection, Your Honor," Reed interjected angrily. "This tape is not relevant to this proceeding. It has nothing to do with John Morgan . . . "

But Judge Morrisey signaled to Reed by waving his hand to let Blair finish.

"This tape, Your Honor," Blair continued, ignoring Reed, "supports my contention. My defense in this case—which I told the jury in my opening—is that Courtney did not kill her mother. This tape is a piece in my own puzzle box for the jury to consider."

"Your Honor," Reed railed, "that tape has nothing to do with John Morgan!"

"Let him finish, Mr. Reed," Judge Morrisey said. "Go on, Mr. Cody," he added, looking at Blair.

"My defense, Your Honor," Blair continued in a cold, matter-of-fact tone, "will prove who killed Michelle Morgan in the early morning hours of February 25, 1996. I have the evidence to prove it, and this tape is the first step in that direction."

Judge Morrisey shook his head in amazement.

Kimberly held her breath.

"Hector Marquez was also a step, if I'm hearing you right, counselor," Judge Morrisey said.

"That's correct, Your Honor," Blair assured him. "You're hearing me right."

Reed looked nauseous, and Blair loved it.

"The 911 tape can be played for the jury," Judge Morrisey ruled without hesitation. "It is clearly relevant," he added as he stood up, signaling to everybody this conference was over. He then started to zip up his robe to return to the courtroom where the jury was waiting.

Reed was stunned. This case had just made a U-turn and was heading for his table.

Coleman and Baskin looked pale.

Detective Beyer had an I-told-you-assholes look on his face.

◆ ◆ ◆

Only the principals knew.

The jury didn't have a clue.

When Blair explained to Courtney what he was doing, she looked at him with fright in her eyes. She was a mere child, thrust into a world she did not understand. He told her to trust him, that nobody was going to separate them again.

Blair then called the 911 operator who had been on duty on August 7, 1995. She testified that pursuant to the subpoena, she had brought the call tape that was received by her from Michelle Cody on August 7, 1995, at 2100 hours. She said that she had reviewed it, and that it accurately reflected what she personally heard.

"May I now play this tape for the jury?" Blair asked.

"You may," Judge Morrisey ruled, and looked to Pat Greely, who immediately instructed the jury on how to work the headsets. He then started the tape for everyone to hear.

The large speaker, in the well of the courtroom, immediately came to life.

"This is 911, may I help you?"

"This is an emergency." The voice that careened off the walls of the courtroom, and reverberated in the jurors' ears, was that of a terrified woman.

"Go on."

"My name is Michelle Cody and I have been assaulted. My life has been threatened and I don't know what to do." Blair watched the jury's interest rise as the tearful Michelle stated her location, that she was calling from a pay phone, and that her daughter was waiting in a hotel room.

"Do you know who did this to you?" the operator asked.

Before Michelle could answer, Blair saw several jurors quickly turn the volume up on their headsets.

"Yes, my ex-husband, Blair Cody," Michelle replied with desperation in her voice. "He came out here unexpectedly from Pennsylvania, and he's trying to take my daughter. He threatened to kill me, and I am terribly frightened because I believe that he's going to do it. Please, please help me," she sobbed.

The operator, who was listening from the witness stand, had immediately determined Michelle's location and instructed her to go to the nearest police station, where officers would be waiting to assist her.

Everybody in the courtroom heard Michelle hang up, and the audible dial tone disconnected them from her desperate plight. Blair let the dial tone play for a few seconds, and then there was dead silence in the courtroom.

Blair had the jury's attention. They were staring at him with confusion and contempt. The gallery was also stung by the realization that the killer was standing in front of them, mingling with them.

Even dead, Michelle was a convincing witness.

◆ ◆ ◆

Blair got his next witnesses from Reed's own deck.

He called the police officers who had arrested him outside Michelle's home following her call to 911. Blair confronted them with their previous testimony, and they testified, agreeing with each other, that "Mr. Cody was lying in wait outside the home of Michelle Cody, at 719 Valley View Road in Hollywood Hills. It was August 8, 1995. It was after midnight."

The officers had previously portrayed Blair as a stalking killer waiting in his car for his ex-wife to return. Their perceptions and opinions remained unchanged.

Blair then pulled Michelle Morgan out of her grave for the jury to hear her previous testimony under oath. Blair called the Clerk of Courts of Los Angeles County to read Michelle's testimony from the custody hearing.

Reed screamed, "Objection! Hearsay!"

But Judge Morrisey overruled Reed's objection.

Michelle Morgan's testimony continued to mesmerize everyone.

"'Yes,'" the clerk read, "'Blair Cody is dangerous. Though he has never exhibited any violence toward Courtney that I know of, he is capable of anything. Five years ago, he killed a man in the state of Oklahoma by putting a handgun in his mouth and pulling the trigger. I know the killing was ruled justifiable by the coroner's jury and the district attorney, but that doesn't change the fact that Blair is unpredictable. I know that I'm afraid of him, and believe that if given the opportunity, he would kill me.'"

Blair smiled to himself. How was Reed going to challenge that sworn testimony? Michelle Morgan was his victim. Michelle Morgan was his witness.

Blair's proof was coming from the jury's own police department, their elected district attorney who swore to uphold the law, and from Reed's own witnesses, including Michelle Morgan.

Blair was proving that *he* killed Michelle—that he had the background, propensity, motive, and opportunity—and would prove it beyond a reasonable doubt.

CHAPTER TWENTY-FOUR

FINAL PIECES

Blair had a few more pieces for Reed's puzzle.

Before he could get them to the jury, however, he had to get himself and Courtney through the swelling media throng on the courthouse steps. They were getting more aggressive for a comment from Blair, who was now being headlined as "KILLER ATTORNEY."

That morning, Blair stopped at the top of the steps and faced them all. Courtney clutched her father's arm as he spun around. The cameras were rolling and flashing, and all the reporters were waiting for a comment, though some stepped back. He was, after all, a possible killer.

"Any comment, Mr. Cody?" the NBC affiliate's reporter asked, nervous to be closest to him with his camera crew.

"My only comment, ladies and gentlemen," Blair replied, "is that my daughter did not kill her mother."

"Who did?" several reporters asked simultaneously.

"On that question," Blair responded, "you'll have to wait and see, but in the meantime, I'm pleading the Fifth."

◆   ◆   ◆

When District Attorney Reed objected to the relevance and impropriety of such opinion testimony, Blair confronted Judge Morrisey with the court's previous ruling during his trial. He read Reed's argument and authority directly from the transcript as to why Dr. Goldstein's opinion was admissible. Judge Morrisey shook his head in bewilderment, and agreed with Blair's position.

Dr. Goldstein, who had been kept waiting in the crowded hallway, took the witness stand with an attitude. He didn't have any idea what Blair wanted, and didn't appreciate the short notice.

He had made up his mind that he was going to zing Blair at every opportunity.

Though surprised by Blair's questions, Dr. Goldstein had his memory refreshed when Blair showed him his testimony from the previous trial. The doctor looked over to Reed for some guidance, but Blair caught him, and brought it to the attention of the judge and jury, which embarrassed the expert.

Angrily, and with emphasis, Dr. Goldstein testified that "certain people are dangerous." He said that "it is genetic, and cultivated by their life's experiences." It was his expert opinion that "Blair Lee Cody falls into that homicidal category, and I believe Blair Cody would have been capable of killing Michelle Cody Morgan if adequately provoked."

Blair flipped several pages in the transcript and put it in front of him.

"Read this," Blair demanded, pointing his finger at the relevant passage.

"Certainly," Dr. Goldstein said sarcastically. He shifted in his chair and faced the jury, as he had done many times before to drive a point home.

"'Ladies and gentlemen,'" Dr. Goldstein began, "'Mr. Cody's history is most revealing, and supports my expert opinion. Five years ago, he killed a man in a fit of rage in Lawton, Oklahoma. The report indicates that the assailant was interested in his father's money, and during that incident, which resulted in his father's unfortunate death, Blair Cody took a handgun and placed it in the mouth of the man, and pulled the trigger.

"'I have the picture in my file,'" Dr. Goldstein continued, giving Blair a smug look, "'taken from the *Oklahoma Times,* which shows the body of the victim with his head partially attached.'"

"Objection!" Reed shouted, startling and confusing Dr. Goldstein.

"On what grounds?" Judge Morrisey asked.

"The picture, Your Honor," Reed answered, collecting himself, "is inflammatory."

"Your objection is sustained," Judge Morrisey ruled, and instructed the jury that the picture was too inflammatory for their view.

Blair then asked Dr. Goldstein to describe for the jury the picture that he relied on, in part, to form his expert opinions about Blair.

Dr. Goldstein's description made the jury sick, but not as sick as Reed.

◆ ◆ ◆

Courtney was looking more innocent with each passing moment. She sat between her dad and Kimberly, and unlike her dad, was not a hard read. Her confusion, fear, and occasional boredom were apparent. She shifted in her chair, wanting to go home, and several times cried.

Blair, with the pain surging in his heart, stayed focused and determined.

Defendant's Exhibit 1 was the temporary custody order awarding Courtney to her mother; 2 was a protection from abuse order stating that Blair was a threat to Michelle's life; 3 was Blair's conviction, on December 12, 1995, of assault and battery, and threatening to take the life of Michelle Cody; 4 was the final custody order, dated December 19, 1995.

And Blair Cody, the monster they created—the civil lawyers, District Attorney Reed, and the system—was not done with them. They had branded him a killer. They took Courtney from him. They were responsible for the rape of his daughter. They intended to send Courtney to prison for the rest of her life.

No, Blair wasn't done with them yet.

His case was winding down, but not before the addition of the final pieces. Like so much of Blair's case of self-incrimination, his evidence came from Reed, who had created it all.

Detective Beyer, when called by the defense, acknowledged that the gun was registered to Blair. The prosecution had no evidence that it had ever left Blair's possession; in fact, Beyer admitted, the gun was given to them by Blair on the day Morgan died.

Blair now had the gun where it belonged—on him, where it arguably had never left.

Defendant's Exhibit 5 was handed to Detective Beyer before he was excused from the witness stand. Beyer identified the piece of paper as part of an airline ticket.

"Tell the jury, Detective, the specifics of the ticket you are holding in your hand," Blair prodded.

"It indicates that you, Blair Cody, departed Harrisburg, Pennsylvania, on February 24, 1996, and arrived in Los Angeles at 9 p.m., that date. You flew on USAir, flight number 716," Beyer answered, shaking his head.

The jury, in their deliberations, would figure out that Blair landed in LA eight hours before the murder.

With that conclusion, and gun in hand, Blair rested.

The silence in the courtroom hung in the air.

◆   ◆   ◆

The jury retired to deliberate at 2 p.m.

Nobody, except the judge and the jury, left the courtroom.

Everybody started talking about who was going to win, how long the jury would be out, and several reporters bet among themselves on the deliberation time.

At 2:30 p.m., the jury had a question. They submitted their question to Judge Morrisey on a handwritten note through the tipstaff.

District Attorney Reed and Coleman, and Blair and Kimberly, waited nervously for Judge Morrisey to unfold the note and read it into the record. Judge Morrisey read it to himself first, without expression.

"Let the record reflect," Judge Morrisey said, looking to the stenographer, "that the jury has submitted a question. All counsels are present in chambers, and this is the question that will be made part of the record in this case.

"'Why,'" Judge Morrisey began, reading from the note, "'based on the evidence presented, doesn't the District Attorney's Office charge Blair Cody with the killing of Michelle Cody?'"

Everybody knew.

The case was over.

Kimberly didn't know what to think. She was ecstatic for Courtney, but afraid for Blair.

Blair kept his composure.

"I'm going to tell this jury," Judge Morrisey said without any input from counsel, "that this question cannot be answered by the court, and that they should render a verdict as to Courtney's innocence or guilt, not Blair Cody's, which is a separate matter."

The jury's question, and Judge Morrisey's answer, was read in open court. All bets in the courtroom were paid on the spot.

Blair whispered to Courtney, and then to Melanie, that the case was over, and they were going home.

At 2:45 p.m. the jury filed into the jury box, one by one, smiling at Courtney, who smiled back.

The engineer was the foreman, just as Blair had predicted. He announced the jury's verdict loud and clear: "We the jury, in the case of the State of California versus Courtney Louise Cody, find the defendant NOT GUILTY."

CHAPTER TWENTY-FIVE

GOING HOME

The jury listened appreciatively as Judge Morrisey thanked them for their time and service. He told them that they did not have to talk to the media, or anyone, about their verdict. He spoke with sincerity, and then asked the lawyers whether there was anything else before they were excused.

Reed, looking defeated, shook his head.

Courtney, with her dad's permission, walked over to the jury foreman to thank him. It was a touching farewell. The other jurors moved closer to shake her hand before they filed out of the courtroom, but would not look at Blair.

The jurors were going home. They had done their civic duty with honor.

Thomas Keating was also going home. His lawyers, in flowing legalese, gave Keating the news: now that Courtney had been acquitted of killing her mother, she would inherit the "Morgan estate," which included the house and the remaining $350,000 in her mother's accounts.

District Attorney Reed had no comment. He instructed Coleman and his staff to take the same position. To prosecute Blair Cody for the murder of Michelle Morgan would be a public acknowledgment that he had prosecuted an innocent child; Reed was not going to end his career on that note, or because of Blair Cody.

On the other hand, Reed knew that the media were going to be on his ass if he did nothing about Blair. The son-of-a-bitch proved to the world, on the front page of every newspaper in the fucking country, that he murdered his ex-wife. The jury's question was read in open court, for God's sake. How could Reed walk away from that?

"You have no choice," Beyer told Reed. "You see, you can't touch Blair. After the verdict, he and Courtney came to see me. He had Courtney give me a taped confession. Bill, she told me what we already knew. *She* killed her mother.

"She said it was an accident, because the bullet was intended for John Morgan, who was trying to rape her. She said Morgan had already done it once before. I believe the kid, Bill."

"And if we charge Blair with the murder of Michelle," Reed said, "we're fucked. Courtney takes the witness stand and clears her father."

"You've got it, my friend," Beyer replied. "This case is over."

"What do I tell the media?"

"You tell them this case is over," Beyer answered. "You tell them you stand by your initial charge."

Detective Beyer lost no sleep over the acquittal of Courtney Cody. He had seen it coming, and had tried to warn Reed about Blair. Beyer's instincts told him that the jury's verdict was right, even if Courtney did it.

Judge Clarence Morrisey would forever be intrigued by what happened in his courtroom. He thought Blair Cody was everything they said he was, and regretted that he would never see him in his courtroom again. He hoped, but kept it to himself, that Blair would not be charged with the murder of Michelle.

Kimberly Wells was sent the deed to 719 Valley View Road, with a note from Blair that the house was hers "for your love, loyalty, and unfailing representation." Before he left California, Blair embraced Kimberly to let her know how much she meant to him.

Pat Greely was paid a hefty sum, and he would always be there for his buddy, Blair.

◆ ◆ ◆

Blair was finally home.

The evening sun was setting on the distant horizon, and Courtney was playing with two friends from school in the driveway. The three children were on roller blades, jamming a puck with their field hockey sticks. That fall, Courtney would be boarding her school bus once again, with her baseball cap and backpack.

Blair watched Courtney from the porch. She was already calling Melanie "Mom."

Melanie had sold her condominium and offices in California for a handsome profit, and was looking forward to counseling children in the East. She had converted Blair's law offices into a modern counseling center, and was backed up with appointments.

Impressive James and two young colts ran the fence line, bucking out.

Blair loved Melanie, and their new life. They would soon be married on the ranch, up on the hill overlooking the valley. The invitation list was short, but Rocky and Kimberly were coming.

There were young horses to be broken, a lengthy softball schedule with Courtney back on the mound, and Blair was looking forward to a little boredom.

Blair Cody wasn't trying any more cases.

He put to rest the killer in Oklahoma, who took his father's life.

He put to rest John Morgan, who raped his daughter.

He put to rest the system that had failed him, and violated Courtney. She was guilty of innocence, and nothing more.

He had done it. By their rules. Playing their game. Using their cards. It was over.

almost American Girl

AN ILLUSTRATED MEMOIR
ROBIN HA

almost American Girl

BALZER + BRAY

IMPRINTS OF HARPERCOLLINS*PUBLISHERS*

All the art featured in the background of the chapter
openers comes from comics I created as a teen.

Disclaimer

This book is a memoir and a work of creative nonfiction. Some names
and identifying details have been changed to protect the privacy of
the individuals involved. I have compressed some events and made
two or more people into one. I did my best to re-create the events
depicted in this book as faithfully as I could, by digging deep into
my memories, diaries, letters, photos, and various artifacts I've saved
from the past. The events that I didn't personally witness have been
fictionalized based on what I've been told by the people involved in
them. *Queen's Quest* (depicted in this memoir as my favorite Korean
comic book) is a made-up series, combining existing Korean comics
that I used to love as a kid.

Balzer + Bray is an imprint of HarperCollins Publishers.
HarperAlley is an imprint of HarperCollins Publishers.

Almost American Girl: An Illustrated Memoir
Copyright © 2020 by Robin Ha
www.epicreads.com
ISBN 978-0-06-268510-0 — ISBN 978-0-06-268509-4 (paperback)
Typography by Robin Ha and Dana Fritts
Hand lettering by Alison Carmichael
19 20 21 22 23 SCP   10 9 8 7 6 5 4 3 2 1
❖
First Edition

TO MY MOTHER,
WHOSE TENACITY HAS TAUGHT ME
NEVER TO GIVE UP

Chapter 1

The End of the World
as I Know It

I grew to five feet six inches by eighth grade, yet remained flat-chested. I felt like a giant next to the tiny girls in my class. Even though I was obsessed with Korean girls' comics, which were mostly about romance, I had no interest in real boys.

NO, THANK YOU.

Unlike the dashing heroes in comics, real boys were weird and covered in zits.

I DON'T KNOW WHICH ONE TO TAKE! THEY'RE ALL GOOD.

WHAT ARE YOU DOING? COME EAT NOW!

JUST A MINUTE!

HURRY UP! WE'RE GONNA BE LATE.

COMING!

I SHOULD JUST LEAVE THE MATH WORKBOOK.

MOM, THIS SONG IS FROM BEAUTY AND THE BEAST!

IT MEANS "WHERE ARE YOU GOING?" REPEAT AFTER ME. WHERE . . .

WEAH . . .

ARE . . .

AH . . .

YOU . . .

YU . . .

OFF TO?

OHFU TO.

Mom listened to Good Morning English on the radio every morning, which taught English through popular American films.

*Speaking in KOREAN.   *Speaking in ENGLISH.

3

HA HA!

♪ (gibberish musical notes) ♪

LUK DARE SHI GOZ DAT GURL IZU STRANGEEEE....

YOU SOUND SO FUNNY!

I had learned English for a year and a half in middle school, but it still sounded like gibberish to me.

WHY DO YOU BOTHER LEARNING ENGLISH?

Trickle

Coffee

BECAUSE EVERYONE SPEAKS ENGLISH AROUND THE WORLD.

♪ (gibberish musical notes) ♪

BUT NOBODY SPEAKS ENGLISH IN KOREA. IT'S USELESS.

IT'S GOOD TO KNOW ENGLISH FOR TRAVELING. REMEMBER LAST YEAR? WE FOUND OUR WAY BACK TO THE HOTEL IN GUAM 'CAUSE I KNEW A BIT OF ENGLISH.

Mom and I had gone on a vacation outside Korea every year since I was nine. So far, we had traveled to Guam, Saipan, Hawaii, Thailand, Malaysia, and Singapore.

DID YOU EMPTY THE TRASH CAN IN YOUR ROOM?

I THINK SO.

And this summer, we were going to Alabama, in America. Why Mom picked this destination was a mystery to me. But I trusted her.

My mom always made all the decisions regarding our lives by herself, and so far it had worked out for both of us.

TO THE AIRPORT.

DID YOU PACK YOUR MATH WORK-BOOK?

I... DON'T KNOW.

America seemed as unreal to me as a fairyland.

Other than the Hawaiian beaches full of tourists . . .

. . . all I knew about America was from the movies and TV shows like *90210*.

MOM, WHAT'S IN ALABAMA?

WE'RE VISITING MY FRIEND WHO LIVES THERE.

WHO'S YOUR FRIEND?

HIS NAME IS KIM MINSIK*. IF WE GET ALONG WITH HIM WE MIGHT STAY A LITTLE LONGER IN AMERICA.

WE'RE GOING TO AMERICA! AREN'T YOU EXCITED?

YEAH. WHAT'S ALABAMA LIKE? I'VE NEVER HEARD OF IT.

* Korean names are in reverse order of American names. The family name (last name in English) comes before the given name (first name in English). So instead of Minsik (given name) Kim (family name), Kim Minsik is the correct order for a Korean name.

After the longest flight of my life, we landed in Huntsville International Airport.

WELCOME TO ALABAMA! HOW WAS YOUR FLIGHT?

IT WAS FINE, MR. KIM! THIS IS MY DAUGHTER, CHUNA.

He was an ordinary middle-aged Korean man with a kind smile.

HI, CHUNA. I'VE HEARD A LOT ABOUT YOU FROM YOUR MOM.

HI.

I wondered what kind of friend he was to my mom. How did they meet and how long had they known each other?

I'LL CARRY YOUR LUGGAGE. FOLLOW ME.

THANKS.

I had so many questions but felt too weird to ask Mom about it.

MY BROTHER IS WAITING TO PICK US UP. MY ENTIRE FAMILY IS EAGER TO MEET YOU.

WE'RE MEETING HIS ENTIRE FAMILY?

HELLO, MS. SHIN. IT'S SO NICE TO FINALLY MEET YOU! I'M MR. KIM'S SISTER-IN-LAW.

HI, MRS. KIM! NICE TO MEET YOU TOO. THIS IS MY DAUGHTER, CHUNA.

YIKES! I DON'T LIKE TALKING TO ADULTS.

HONEY, SAY HELLO TO HER.

HELLO, NICE TO MEET YOU.

Mr. Kim, his brother, and his sister-in-law were not that different from any other adults that I had met in Korea. They always asked the same questions.

MY KIDS ARE SO EXCITED TO ASK YOU ABOUT KOREA. THEY WERE ALL BORN HERE. HOW OLD ARE YOU?

I'M FOURTEEN.

MY OLDEST DAUGHTER IS ALSO FOURTEEN.

DO YOU GO TO CHURCH?

NO.

I'LL TAKE YOU GUYS TO MY CHURCH. YOU WILL LOVE IT!

UH . . . OKAY.

HOW ARE YOUR GRADES?

SHE'S AT THE TOP OF HER CLASS!

WOW, THAT'S IMPRESSIVE!

MOM, STOP.

WHAT'S YOUR FAVORITE SUBJECT?

I LIKE ART. . . .

SHE'S WON EVERY ART COMPETITION AT SCHOOL!

HER TEACHERS THINK SHE HAS REAL TALENT.

I'D LOVE TO SEE HER ARTWORK.

MOM, PLEASE STOP!

Modesty was not one of my mom's virtues.

SHE'S BEEN DRAWING EVER SINCE SHE WAS BORN....

MOM!!!

BLAH BLAH BLAH.

FORGET IT.

I had never seen such endless flat land before. Everything seemed to bear the immense weight of the sky.

WHAT A PRETTY SONG!

I'VE NEVER SEEN SUCH A HUGE HOUSE BEFORE!

WELCOME TO OUR HOME.

HA HA. THIS ISN'T BIG AT ALL BY AMERICAN STANDARDS.

The entire house was covered in carpet, unlike the linoleum floors in Korea. How did they keep it clean?

COME IN AND MAKE YOURSELVES COMFORTABLE.

LET ME INTRODUCE MY CHILDREN.

THIS IS GRACE, MY OLDEST.

HI, NICE TO MEET YOU.

AND MY SECOND, ASHLEY. SHE'S TWELVE YEARS OLD.

HI.

AND MY YOUNGEST, DANIEL. HE'S EIGHT.

HI.

WELCOME!

HELLO.

AND MY MOTHER AND MY DAUGHTER LENA. SHE'S FIFTEEN. SHE MOVED TO AMERICA WITH ME LAST YEAR.

I wondered what all these Korean people were doing here in the middle of nowhere in America.

Meet the KIM FAMILY

Name: Yunsik Kim
Younger brother of Minsik Kim. Married to Sujin Kim. Father of Grace, Ashley, and Daniel. A college professor.

Name: Grace Kim
Age: 14
The oldest sister. Straight-A student. Plays several sports.

Name: Minsik Kim
Older brother of Yunsik Kim. Divorced, with two daughters. Moved from Korea a year ago. Temporarily lives with Yunsik's family. Owns a fish market.

Name: Ashley Kim
Age: 12
The middle child. Straight-A student. Running for class secretary this year.

Name: Sujin Kim
Married to Yunsik Kim. Mother of Grace, Ashley, and Daniel. Owns a deli.

Name: Kyungja Kim
Mother of Yunsik Kim and Minsik Kim. Lives with Yunsik's family. Worries about her family a lot.

Name: Daniel Kim
Age: 8
The youngest son. Straight-A student.

Name: Lena Kim
Age: 15
Moved to Alabama with her father. Misses her mother and younger sister, who live in Los Angeles.

I sat with the kids in the TV room while the adults were in the living room.

12

HYA!

YOU GUYS HAVE IT HERE TOO? THAT'S SO COOL!

WE WEAR GYM PANTS UNDER OUR SKIRTS SO WE CAN DO THE HIGH JUMPS.

IT GETS SUPER HARD. ONE OF MY FRIENDS BROKE HER ANKLE DOING IT.

AFTER SCHOOL WE GET SOME TREATS FROM THE FOOD STANDS AROUND BACK.

호떡 500원

MY FAVORITES ARE *TTEOKBOKKI** AND *BUNGEOPPANG**.

AND ALSO *TWIGIM** AND *TTEOKKOCHI**.

AND *HOTTEOK**. I LOVE THEM ALL!

THERE ARE SO MANY LITTLE CAFES WITH DELICIOUS SNACKS IN MY NEIGHBORHOOD.

팥빙수

I LOVE EATING *PATBINGSU** WITH FRIENDS ON HOT DAYS LIKE THIS.

13

Hagwon friends: Sunhee, Jeongwon, and Minkyung

Hagwon teacher

I HAVE TO GO TO *HAGWON** TO STUDY AFTER SCHOOL. BUT IT'S OKAY BECAUSE MOST OF MY BEST FRIENDS ARE IN *HAGWON*.

AFTER *HAGWON*, WE CHECK OUT STATIONERY STORES . . .

. . . AND SNACK PLACES. WE OFTEN RUN INTO OTHER FRIENDS FROM SCHOOL THERE.

THEN WE GO TO THE COMICS STORE.

My best friend, Jaehyun

14

WHAT ABOUT YOU, *EONNI**? DO YOU READ COMICS TOO?

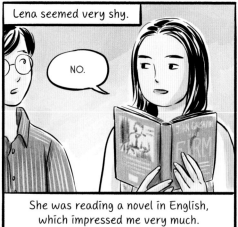

Lena seemed very shy.

NO.

She was reading a novel in English, which impressed me very much.

The music I heard earlier in the van was playing on TV.

WHAT SONG IS THIS? I LIKE IT!

IT'S THE THEME SONG FROM THE NEW *BATMAN* MOVIE.

OH, I KNOW *BATMAN*! DO YOU WATCH THE CARTOON?

NO WAY! CARTOONS ARE FOR KIDS.

Soon, Grace and I ran out of things to talk about.

16

 Mr. Kim's sister-in-law told me that I'd be sharing a room with Grace.

 I went to the bathroom to take a shower and noticed...

NOT 100% waterproof?

...it was covered in carpet, which was so weird to me because Korean bathrooms were covered in tile.

 AT LEAST THE INSIDE OF THE SHOWER IS TILED.

 I JUST HAVE TO BE CAREFUL NOT TO SPLASH . . .

Ack!

It was hopeless.

eek!

HOW DID I MANAGE TO GET EVERYTHING WET?

I GOTTA GET OUT OF HERE BEFORE ANYONE FINDS OUT I MADE THIS MESS.

Yaawn

WHAT TIME IS IT?

I had the worst jet lag.

WHAT DAY IS IT TODAY? IT'S BEEN A WEEK SINCE I GOT HERE.
IT FELT LIKE A LOT LONGER THAN THAT.

MONDAY	TUESDAY	WEDNESDAY	THURSDAY	FRIDAY	SATURDAY	YESTERDAY
I ARRIVED.	NASA Space Center	NOTHING.	NOTHING.	...WENT SHOPPING. Bruno's	NOTHING.	WE WENT TO CHURCH.

IT'S SO QUIET.

MOM?

HELLO, ANYONE HOME?

Grace was always busy going to practice.

SEE YOU TONIGHT.

Ashley and Daniel were a lot younger than me.

MOM!

Lena kept to herself.

SHE THINKS SHE'S TOO COOL TO HANG OUT WITH ME.

I GUESS I'M LEFT ALONE AGAIN.

Gurgle

Mr. Kim's sister-in-law always left something for me to eat.

For Chuna

STALE MAYO, KETCHUP, AND CHEESE. THREE OF THE MOST VILE FOODS!

YUCK!

MORE CHEESE, HAM, BREAD, YOGURT . . .

IS THERE ANYTHING SPICY OR EVEN JUST PLAIN RICE AND *KIMCHI**?

EVERY CORNER IN SEOUL IS FULL OF STORES AND PEOPLE. WHAT DO KIDS DO FOR FUN IN THIS TOWN?

HEY, BARRY!

Bow

WoW

BARK!

BARK!

Huff

Barry was the family dog. No one paid much attention to him, so whenever I went outside to play with him, he got so excited.

BARK!

YOU MUST BE THIRSTY.

Pff!

YOU AND I ARE LIKE KINDRED SPIRITS, LONELY AND BORED OUT OF OUR MINDS.

LET'S GET YOU SOME FRESH WATER.

I WISH I COULD TAKE HIM INSIDE TO COOL OFF.

STOP, BARRY!

BUT MR. KIM'S BROTHER SAID, "DON'T LET BARRY INSIDE! HE'LL GET THE CARPETS DIRTY."

BARRY!

Half an hour later...

BARK!

OKAY, THAT'S ENOUGH!

BARK BARK

WHEW, I GOTTA TAKE A SHOWER. BYE, BARRY.

CLICK

CLICK

CLICK

I could read and write simple sentences in English, but listening was a totally different story.

CLICK

I CAN'T UNDERSTAND A SINGLE WORD.

Even so, I watched TV for hours because there was nothing else to do.

THE NEW ISSUE OF THE COMIC MAGAZINE *WINK* COMES OUT TODAY. I HOPE SIR BJORN IN *QUEEN'S QUEST* HAS SURVIVED THE LATEST ISSUE.

I COULD BE EXPLORING JAEHYUN'S NEW NEIGHBORHOOD WITH HER.

WE COULD ALSO GO FOR *TTEOKBOKKI* IN MY HOOD.

MRS. KANG'S CART IS THE BEST.

GAHH

GrrR

THIS IS THE WORST VACATION EVER!

THANK GOD SCHOOL STARTS NEXT WEEK. I DON'T THINK I CAN TAKE ONE MORE WEEK OF THIS.

GRRR

Later that evening...

HAVE YOU BEEN SLEEPING ALL DAY?

NO.... WHERE WERE YOU? I AM SO HUNGRY, MOM.

WHY DIDN'T YOU EAT SOMETHING?

I HATE ALL THE FOOD HERE. WHAT DID YOU DO ALL DAY?

I WAS LOOKING FOR AN APARTMENT.

AN APARTMENT? WHY?

I HAVE SOMETHING VERY IMPORTANT TO TELL YOU. COME UPSTAIRS WITH ME.

WHAT ABOUT MY FRIENDS? MY THINGS AND MY COMICS?

I'LL DO MY BEST TO HAVE YOUR THINGS SENT HERE.

BUT WHAT ABOUT MY FRIENDS? THEY DON'T EVEN KNOW THAT I'M HERE!

Sigh~

BWAA

Just like that, everything I loved was suddenly snatched away from me.

Chapter 2

My Only Sunshine

MOM!

CHUNA!

STOP

SCRAM!

ARE YOU OKAY?

Uh huh

WOW, MOM! YOU SCARED HIM AWAY WITH JUST ONE LOOK!

NEVER APPROACH A STRAY DOG!

BUT THAT DOG DIDN'T LOOK LIKE A STRAY. HE WAS CLEAN!

IT DOESN'T MATTER. A DOG IS A DOG. HE CAN STILL BITE.

I WISH I HAD MY OWN DOG. THEN I WOULDN'T HAVE TO PLAY WITH ANY OTHER DOGS. CAN I PLEASE HAVE ONE?

WE'VE TALKED ABOUT THIS ALREADY. DO YOU KNOW HOW MUCH WORK IT IS TO TAKE CARE OF A DOG?

I WILL DO ALL THE WORK! YOU WON'T HAVE TO DO ANYTHING. PLEASE!

I SAID NO.

WILL I EVER GET TO HAVE A PET OF ANY KIND? ALL MY FRIENDS HAVE PETS.

I BET THEIR MOMS DON'T HAVE TO WORK TWELVE HOURS A DAY LIKE YOUR MOM DOES.

I was born in Seoul, Korea, in 1981. It was always just me and Mom. My parents separated when I was a baby.

DO YOU NEED ANY ART SUPPLIES?

OH, YEAH. I RAN OUT OF GLUE STICKS.

Mom had been a hairdresser. I spent all of my childhood at her salon.

I had my own corner where I drew and made toys out of empty boxes of perm solution.

33

Panel 1: I was in my own world.

Panel 2: I was an only child, but I didn't want any siblings.

COME ON— IT'S TIME TO GO HOME.

Panel 3: But I always dreamed of having a pet.

Woof Woof

LOOK WHAT I MADE. IT ACTUALLY MOVES!

Panel 4: Then one day, my dream came true.

I'M HOME....

Panel 5:

Wee.

WHAT ARE THESE BIRDS DOING HERE?

ONE OF MY CLIENTS GAVE THEM TO US. DO YOU LIKE THEM?

Panel 6:

YES!

PRRR

I instantly fell in love.

I couldn't wait to get home from school to play with the birds.

BYE!

BYE!

SOMEBODY'S IN A HURRY.

HEY, SKY AND CLOVER, DID YOU GUYS MISS ME?

When the salon wasn't busy, I took the birds out and let them fly around.

OH NO!

SPLAT

ARE YOU OKAY?

35

I vowed to never speak to my mom again.

WILL YOU STOP CRYING ALREADY?

'NIGHT.

I PACKED YOUR FAVORITE SPICY SQUID FOR LUNCH TODAY.

HOW WAS SCHOOL TODAY?

THESE BELT FISH ARE GOING TO BE SO YUMMY, I CAN'T WAIT TO FRY 'EM UP!

RISE AND SHINE! BREAKFAST IS READY.

After a few days, I gave in. I couldn't not talk to my mom forever. She was my only family. She was my everything.

IT'S GOING TO BE A BEAUTIFUL SUNDAY TOMORROW. WANT TO GO TO THE CHILDREN'S GRAND PARK?

...OKAY.

I remember missing those parakeets so badly, but I can't recall missing my father at all.

Mom told me that he had visited me at least once a month when I was young. There are photos of us together to prove it.

But I can't remember my father's voice, how he laughed or smelled, or how he made me feel.

The only "real" memory I have of my dad is a nightmare I had when I was five or six.

He was kidnapping me and taking me away.

Even in this nightmare,

I could only see the back of his head.

39

Mom didn't spoil me by buying me things, but she spoiled me in other ways.

TWO TICKETS, PLEASE.

She worked long hours, six days a week. Yet she took me wherever I wanted to go on Sundays. I remember one gloomy autumn Sunday, I begged my mom to take me to my favorite place in Seoul, Children's Grand Park.

The entire park was almost deserted except for us.

YAY! THERE'S NO LINE ANYWHERE!

Soon it started sleeting, but I didn't want to go home.

BRRR! WE SHOULD GO HOME, HONEY.

BUT MOM! WE CAN FINALLY SIT IN THE LAST ROW!

Viking was the most popular ride, and the best seat was in the last row, which everyone fought over on busy days.

ARE YOU READY?

YES!

WOOHOO

The ride seemed extra fast and high that day.

Soon the ride became too scary for us to handle.

KYAAAA~!

The sleet made the railing slippery. Mom and I held on to the railing for our dear lives.

STOP

THE VIKING

PLEASE STOP!!

The operator stopped the ride because we were the only passengers.

OH, THANK GOD!

No ride intimidated me after that.

41

A few days later...

POOR THING. THE FLU THIS YEAR IS REALLY NASTY.

YES, I TOOK HER TO THE DOCTOR AND GOT HER SOME MEDICINE. I HOPED HER FEVER WOULD GO DOWN.

COUGH

When I got sick, I had to stay at the salon because there was no one at home to look after me and Mom had to work.

NO!

COME ON! IT'S JUST A SPOONFUL.

It must not have been easy for her to take care of me all by herself.

I was a sickly child and she often had to stay up all night to nurse me.

BLEGH

But she never complained and always got up on time to open her salon.

Z z z

THANK GOD, HER FEVER FINALLY BROKE.

She gave me such a complete sense of protection. She was my rock.

SHE REALLY IS THE APPLE OF YOUR EYE, MS. SHIN.

I thought nothing bad could ever happen to me as long as my mom was with me.

Boy, was I wrong about that....

HOW COULD YOU DO THIS TO ME? YOU SHOULD HAVE TOLD ME BEFORE WE LEFT!

Back in Huntsville, Alabama, August 1995

I DIDN'T KNOW HOW THINGS WOULD WORK OUT BEFORE WE GOT HERE AND I DIDN'T WANT YOU TO FEEL STRESSED.

YOU DIDN'T EVEN GIVE ME A CHANCE TO SAY GOODBYE TO MY FRIENDS!

SOON YOU'LL MAKE NEW FRIENDS....

YOU'RE THE WORST!

I had no way to contact my friends in Korea.

EVERYTHING I DO IS FOR YOUR OWN GOOD.

HOW DO YOU KNOW WHAT'S GOOD FOR ME WHEN YOU JUST TOOK AWAY EVERYONE AND EVERYTHING I LOVE?

HEY, IT'S GRACE. YOU OKAY?

KNOCK! KNOCK!

WHERE AM I?!

IT WAS JUST A DREAM. I'M STILL IN ALABAMA.

Sigh

In the sea of Korean people in my dream, I realized I didn't belong to any of them. Without my mom, I was lost.

KNOCK
KNOCK

DINNER IS READY. COME DOWN.

I didn't have a choice but to stay with my mom.

YOU MUST BE HUNGRY!

YOUR NEW AUNT MADE MISO SOUP FOR YOU.

And I had to at least try to make the most of it.

Chapter 3

My Name Is Robin

51

No one knows her past.
No one knows her name.
She is a mystery.

WHO ARE YOU? PLEASE, I MUST KNOW YOUR NAME!

MY NAME IS...

...

I had never thought about what American name I would like to have.

UMM...

This time, I could pick the coolest name ever, but I had no idea what names were trendy.

My stepcousins, stepsister, and I looked through their yearbooks for inspiration.

HOW ABOUT SARAH OR JENNY?

TOO GIRLY.

COURTNEY?

THEY ALL SOUND TOO GIRLY FOR ME.

HMM... THERE ARE SOME BOYS' NAMES THAT GIRLS CAN HAVE.

We picked a handful of gender-neutral names from the yearbook.

I LIKE THEM ALL.

WELL, YOU HAVE TO CHOOSE ONE.

I was always drawn to androgynous female characters in Korean and Japanese comics because I was a tomboy too.

My stepcousins taught me this American thing....

EENY, MEENY, MINY, MO, CATCH A TIGER BY THE TOE....

ROBIN! THAT'S A PRETTY NAME. YOU'LL FIT IN RIGHT AWAY AT SCHOOL.

REALLY? YOU THINK SO?

The R sound doesn't exist in Korean, so I spent all night practicing my new name.

LOBIN LOOOBIN RRRR... ROBIN RRRRRRRROBIN ROBIN.

But no matter how many times I said it out loud, I just couldn't picture myself with this new name.

The dreaded first day of school came.

It was surreal to be surrounded by so many non-Korean kids.

COME ON. LET'S GO. WE'RE GONNA BE LATE!

OH, OKAY, ASHLEY.

THAT'S YOUR 교실·옆문 OKAY?

HUH? COULD YOU REPEAT THAT?

UGH, 알겠어요.

Ashley spoke Korean with an American accent and often used English instead of Korean words, which made it hard for me to understand her.

I felt terrible being a burden and making her late to class.

THANKS....

GULP

SQUEAK

MUST LOOK NORMAL.
LOOK NORMAL. LOOK NORMAL.
LOOK NORMAL. LOOK NORMAL.
LOOK NORMAL. LOOK NORMAL.
LOOK NORMAL. LOOK NORMAL.
LOOK NORMAL. LOOK NORMAL.
LOOK NORMAL. LOOK NORMAL.
LOOK NORMAL. LOOK NORMAL.
LOOK NORMAL. LOOK NORMAL.
LOOK NORMAL. LOOK NORMAL.
LOOK NORMAL. LOOK NORMAL.
LOOK NORMAL. LOOK NORMAL.
LOOK NORMAL. LOOK NORMAL.
LOOK NORMAL. LOOK NORMAL.
LOOK NORMAL.

BUT . . . WHAT IS NORMAL HERE?

Chapter 4
How To Deal With Turds

OH. OKAY.

I felt like an animal in the zoo.

I was finally able to relax once class began.

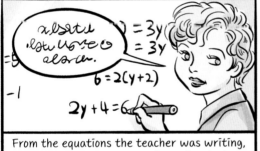

From the equations the teacher was writing, I understood she was teaching the algebra that I'd already learned last year in Korea.

I CAN'T UNDERSTAND ANYTHING SHE'S SAYING, EVEN THOUGH I KNOW THE ANSWERS TO THE EQUATIONS.

Soon I found myself struggling to keep my eyes open.

I resorted to doodling to fight the boredom.

MULTIPLYING FRACTIO

When I was around five years old, Mom introduced me to her favorite comics.

READ FROM THE LEFT TO THE RIGHT PANEL.

IT'S SO COOL!

It was her way of getting me into reading.

Since then, I have never stopped reading comics of all genres.

My favorite was a girls' fantasy series called *Queen's Quest*.

The heroine, Princess Eshika, was cursed and cast out of her kingdom by an evil witch.

She had to find a way to break the curse and return to her homeland.

THE NEXT VOLUME OF *QUEEN'S QUEST* MUST BE OUT ALREADY....

THE CLASS IS ALREADY OVER?! I HOPE THE TEACHER DIDN'T SEE THAT I WAS DOODLING THE WHOLE TIME.

I almost got lost trying to find the next classroom

HOW WEIRD IS IT THAT THE STUDENTS HERE HAVE TO RACE TO THEIR NEXT CLASS? IN KOREA, TEACHERS ROTATE AND THE STUDENTS STAY IN THE SAME ROOM.

CHEN...NA HEI?

YU CAN KOHL ME LO...ROBIN.

2nd period: Social Studies

I SHOULD AT LEAST TRY TO PAY ATTENTION.

3rd period: French

THIS IS TORTURE, I'VE NEVER FELT SO BORED IN MY LIFE.

4th period: Science

RRING

HOW EMBARRASSING! I CAN BARELY KEEP MY EYES OPEN.

20

I WANT TO MAKE FRIENDS, BUT I'M SCARED THEY WILL LAUGH AT MY TERRIBLE ENGLISH.

AT THIS RATE I AM DEFINITELY SITTING ALONE DURING LUNCH.

ACK!

CHING CHANG CHONG!

WHY DID HE BUMP INTO ME? AND WHY IS HE DOING THAT TO HIS EYES?

This was my first encounter with racism. In a way my lack of English was a blessing because these racist taunts had no meaning for me yet.

OH, IT'S ASHLEY! MAYBE I CAN SIT WITH HER DURING LUNCH!

HEY, ASH...

...LEY.

Cafeteria

CHITTER CHATTER

CHATTER
CHATTER
HA HA!
CHAT
HA HA
WOW

OH NO, IT'S AUNT'S SANDWICH AGAIN.

Lunchtime in Korea used to be my favorite.

I never knew being in a crowd of people could make me feel so alone.

I USED TO BE JUST LIKE THOSE GIRLS. NOW I AM A LOSER WITHOUT ANY FRIENDS.

WHAT IN THE WORLD ARE THEY EATING?

WHY IS ALL THE FOOD HERE SO GREASY?

WHAT I WOULDN'T GIVE TO BE EATING RICE AND KIMCHI WITH MY FRIENDS RIGHT NOW.

HEY!

ᴏ‑ᴛ ᴛᴠ ᴏ‑‑‑ᴠ … CHINA?

HE'S THE BOY WHO BUMPED INTO ME IN THE HALLWAY. WHAT DOES HE WANT?

SORI... WAT?

HI, I. AM. BRYAN. WHAT. IS. YOUR. NAME?

OH, I ACTUALLY UNDERSTAND WHAT HE IS SAYING!

I AM HAVING A CONVERSATION WITH AN AMERICAN BOY!

HI. MY NAME IZU ROBIN. NISU TO MEET YU.

68

WHAT'S GOING ON?

EAT YOUR SHIT SANDWICH, CHING CHANG CHONG!

IS SHIT A BAD WORD? HE WAS MAKING FUN OF ME THE WHOLE TIME!

After that day, these boys taunted me whenever they saw me.

I WILL NOT CRY. I MUST NOT GIVE THEM THE SATISFACTION!

BUT DAMN IT! I CAN'T STOP MY TEARS FROM COMING.

I CAN'T HELP BUT FEEL ASHAMED...BUT FOR WHAT?

69

HA HA HA HA HA HA HA

I've always known that people pick on others just for being different.

Back in Korea, when I was little . . .

. . . I didn't notice anything wrong with my family.

Mom gave me everything I needed.

I thought my life was great. I was completely unaware of the outside world.

Soon, it was time for me to leave my mom's sheltered nest.

LISTEN TO YOUR TEACHER AND BE A GOOD GIRL!

I WILL, MOM!

TODAY, YOU'RE GOING TO DRAW YOUR HOUSE AND YOUR FAMILY.

YOU DRAW VERY WELL, CHUNA! BUT YOU HAVEN'T FINISHED YET.

NO, I'M DONE, MISS KIM.

BUT YOU FORGOT TO DRAW YOUR DAD! AND DON'T YOU HAVE ANY SIBLINGS?

NO, I ONLY LIVE WITH MOM.

IS YOUR DAD DEAD?

NO, WE JUST DON'T LIVE TOGETHER.

IF YOUR DAD IS ALIVE, WHY DON'T YOU LIVE TOGETHER?

I DON'T KNOW.

THEN WHO MAKES THE MONEY?

MY MOM DOES.

I realized what I thought was perfectly normal wasn't normal at all.

And not being normal meant bad.

I was too young to understand just how rigid Korean society could be.

I told my mom what happened at school.

Being discreet about my family life became second nature to me.

HA HA HA
WAA

I made friends and we loved to...

...wreak havoc.

OUCH!

YOU'RE NEXT, CHUNA!

HA HA, NO WAY!

My mom's salon was at a mall that was full of family-owned businesses.

Beh~

HEY!

All of the store owners' children played together without any adult supervision.

Whoa!

Gotcha!

WHAM

CRASH

I wanted to protect her
as much as she had protected me.

I tried to be extra good.

HOW WELL-
BEHAVED YOUR
DAUGHTER IS!

THAT'S
MY GIRL.

Mom was a master at diverting gossip by working extra hard to be successful.
When I was a toddler we lived in a dingy room in the back of a tiny hair salon.
By the time I was in middle school, Mom became the owner of the biggest
hair salon in the neighborhood and bought us a large three-bedroom apartment.

Hair salon

Our apartment

1984 1994

Our home

She also became the head of a group of
local beauticians who gave free haircuts
to seniors and children with special needs.

And I was her warrior apprentice.

DON'T FIGHT
WITH TURDS HEAD ON.
IN THE END YOU'LL BE
COVERED IN THEM AND IT
WON'T MATTER WHO
STARTED IT.

And cast out in a strange and hostile land.

Chapter 5

Family Cuts Deeper Than Strangers

The first month of school went by, and things had not changed much.

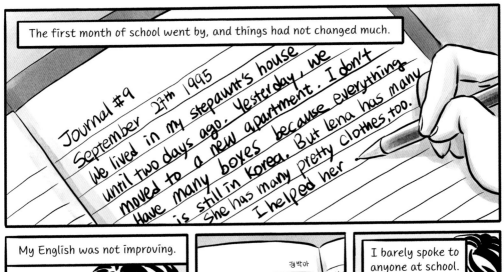

Journal #9
September 27th 1995
We lived in my stepaunt's house until two days ago. Yesterday, we moved to a new apartment. I don't have many boxes because everything is still in Korea. But Lena has many. She has many pretty clothes, too. I helped her —

My English was not improving.

HMM...HOW DO AMERICANS SAY 정리하다?

Prr...

정박아

portional taxation.
정리(廷吏) a court clerk.
정리(定理) a theorem.
정리(整理) (정돈) arrangement; (re.) adjustment; (해제·해소) liquida-tion; settlement(청산); (감원) cur-tailment. ∼하다 put (the room) in order; arrange; readjust; dis-pose ((of one's ...)) (처분); (배 체·청산) liq... ...ttle (clear off) ((one's a... ...uce (the staff)) (감원). ‖ ∼와(교통의)

SO MANY DIFFERENT WAYS TO SAY THE SAME THING.... WHICH ONE OF THESE IS RIGHT?

I barely spoke to anyone at school.

I GUESS I'LL GO WITH THE FIRST ONE.

The only person I connected with at school was Mrs. Halls, my English teacher.

She knew that eighth-grade English would be too hard for me. So she told me that we could write to each other in a journal instead.

She also brought me children's books to read.

AR

It took me an hour to read one children's book because I had to look up every other word in the dictionary.

ARGH, A FIVE-YEAR-OLD AMERICAN KID COULD READ THIS FASTER THAN ME.

GOOD JOB, ROBIN.

Getting Mrs. Hall's response back in my journal was the highlight of my day...

...even though it was hard for me to decipher what she wrote.

Robin I am so proud of you. I am very glad that you write a lot in class. Q: How was your day so far?

P...R...O...U...D... PROUD...THERE IT IS!

HOW... WAS...YOUR...DAY... SO...FAR? SO FAR? LIKE IN DISTANCE? OR LIKE SOFA, THE COUCH?

I KNOW WHAT ALL THESE WORDS MEAN, BUT I CAN'T FIGURE OUT WHAT THEY MEAN TOGETHER!

...so pl... m very glad... u write a lot in class. Q: How was your day so far? I will answer tomorrow

I'LL HAVE TO ASK LENA WHAT "SO FAR" MEANS WHEN I GET HOME.

My relationship with Lena was challenging.

IT MEANS "UNTIL NOW."

OH... I SEE.

I had no idea how to act like a sister. And Lena was secretive about her personal life. I assumed she missed her real sister in LA.

I wanted to at least become her friend.

LENA, IT'S YOUR FRIEND MIKE AGAIN.

OKAY, I'LL TAKE IT IN MY ROOM.

DON'T HOG THE PHONE LIKE LAST TIME.

But she turned out to be very different from my friends back home.

I was used to hanging out with goofy tomboys like me. Lena was demure and feminine: the kind of girl that my friends and I would mockingly refer to as a princess.

Shiny, straight hair

Clear skin

Skinny arms

Petite figure

Trendy clothes

Frizzy hair

Dorky glasses

Pimples

Big shoulders

Chubby arms

Baggy, unfashionable clothes

I felt like an ogre next to her.

She had a closet full of cute clothes that she had brought from Korea and that her mother in LA sent her as gifts.

YOU CAN BORROW THEM IF YOU LIKE.

THANKS, BUT THEY ARE TOO SMALL FOR ME.

I never cared about clothes or making myself prettier until I met Lena.

MOM, PLEASE CAN YOU BUY ME THIS JACKET?

NO. WHAT'S WRONG WITH THE JACKET I BOUGHT YOU LAST TIME?

Lena's grandmother pitied Lena because her parents were getting divorced.

GRANDMA, CAN I HAVE THIS?

OF COURSE, MY DEAR.

Lena's room was next to mine and our walls were thin. I could hear her talking to her American friends on the phone.

BLAH BLAH

I'LL NEVER BE AS SMALL OR PRETTY AS LENA AND I'LL NEVER BE ABLE TO SPEAK ENGLISH LIKE HER.

Whenever I heard her girlish giggle, I wanted to punch her through the wall.

POP!

HA HA HA HA

CAN SHE BE ANY LOUDER?

BLAH BLAH HAHA

I HATE IT HERE!

This was the first time I felt truly jealous of someone.

85

Apart from English, the only class I liked was band.

My stepcousins and Lena were also in band and played flute.

THANK GOD NO ONE CAN REALLY HEAR HOW BADLY I AM PLAYING.

Even though I was terrible at flute, I loved the harmony we created together. Band was the only class where I felt like I could truly blend in.

It was the only class in which I didn't need to speak to participate.

ATTENTION! ⟨⟩ NEXT TUESDAY WEAR YOUR BAND UNIFORM. OKAY?

HMM... IT SOUNDS LIKE SOMETHING IMPORTANT. I NEED TO ASK SOMEONE WHAT HE SAID.

But I couldn't get over my fear of sounding like a bumbling idiot when I spoke English.

I GUESS I HAVE TO ASK ASHLEY ABOUT THIS EVEN THOUGH I REALLY DON'T WANT TO.

In Korea I walked to school and wasn't used to riding the bus anywhere. I always felt anxious about getting on the wrong bus or getting off at the wrong stop.

I DON'T KNOW WHICH BUS I'M SUPPOSED TO TAKE.

OH NO, THEY ARE ABOUT TO LEAVE! WHAT SHOULD I DO?

HEY, WHAT ARE YOU DOING? COME WITH ME.

DIDN'T YOU HEAR MY MOM TELLING US TO WAIT AFTER SCHOOL FOR HER TO ꧁ꩍ?

SORRY. I MISSED THAT.

Since the beginning of school, Ashley had avoided me.

ꩍꩍꩍ!

The stepfamily didn't know how Ashley treated me behind their backs.

HOW WAS YOUR DAY?

IT WAS OKAY.

MOM...?

SPEAK KOREAN, ASHLEY.

UMM, THE BAND TEACHER SAID SOMETHING TODAY ABOUT WEARING OUR UNIFORM NEXT TUESDAY. WHAT'S HAPPENING ON TUESDAY?

I HAVE NO IDEA.

She always answered my questions with a smirk, which made me wonder if she was telling me the truth.

My mom was busy helping out at my stepfather's fish market, so I was left at my stepaunt's house after school a lot.

The stepchildren were much more comfortable with English. So when there were no adults around, they all spoke in English...

...which made it impossible for me to join their conversations.

THEY DON'T EVEN TRY TO INCLUDE ME.

I turned to drawing to make myself feel better. But...

Drawing used to bring me joy, but now it was just making me sad.

WHAT'S THE POINT OF DRAWING ESHIKA OVER AND OVER? I'LL NEVER FIND OUT WHAT HAPPENS TO HER.

Next Tuesday, first period.

ATTENTION *(unintelligible)*

I CAN'T UNDERSTAND A THING THIS ANNOUNCEMENT IS SAYING. I HOPE IT'S NOT SOMETHING IMPORTANT.

I spotted my band teacher, Mr. Johnson, in the hall on the way to class.

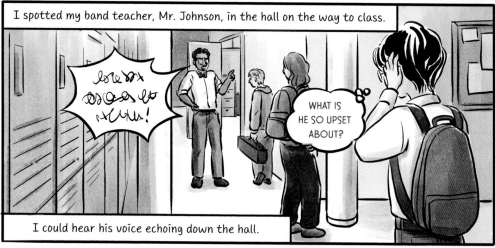

(unintelligible)!

WHAT IS HE SO UPSET ABOUT?

I could hear his voice echoing down the hall.

HEY! WHY DIDN'T YOU COME TO THE CLASS PICTURE THIS MORNING?

CLASS...PICTURE?

DIDN'T YOU HEAR THE *(unintelligible)*?

I AM SORRY. I DIDN'T KNOW!

I wasn't the only one who missed the photo. More than half of my class had missed it, and that's why Mr. Johnson was so upset.

I DON'T KNOW WHY THE OTHER KIDS MISSED IT. IT'S UNFAIR FOR HIM TO BE MAD AT ME. I EVEN WORE MY UNIFORM.

I WISH I COULD EXPLAIN MYSELF, BUT I CAN'T FIND THE RIGHT WORDS IN ENGLISH!

When I saw Ashley in the hallway with her band uniform on, my heart filled with rage.

I BET SHE DIDN'T TELL ME ON PURPOSE!

CHITTER CHATTER

I had no friends to vent my frustration to.

So I wrote about it to Mrs. Halls.

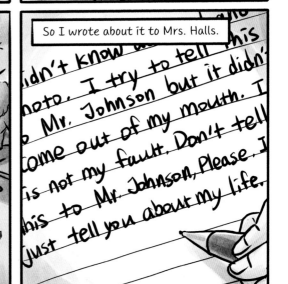

didn't know ... his
...oto. I try to tell this
.. Mr. Johnson but it didn'
...come out of my mouth. I
...is not my fault. Don't tell
...his to Mr. Johnson, Please. I
...just tell you about my life.

Mrs. Halls wrote me back.

Robin,

I am so sorry that you missed when yearbook photos are to be taken. I should have made sure you understood that.

Mr. Johnson is really a kind person at heart. He doesn't mean to scare you, but he has so many band students every day and he sometimes forgets things. He also forgot that English isn't your first language. I won't tell Mr. Johnson. I know it's really hard for you, but you **MUST** stand up for yourself.

You have learned a lot this year. Now you understand so much in English! I'll write more later.

Yours,
Mrs. Halls

SHE'S RIGHT. I MUST BE ABLE TO ASK FOR HELP AT SCHOOL.

AND I CAN'T LET ASHLEY TREAT ME LIKE THIS ANY LONGER.

I had wanted to see if I could handle Ashley by myself. But it was time for Mom to know.

WHAT A LITTLE BITCH!

HER PARENTS SHOULD KNOW ABOUT THIS!

All the adults confronted her that evening.

HAVEN'T YOU LEARNED ANYTHING ABOUT HELPING OTHERS IN THE BIBLE?

WE ARE SO DISAPPOINTED. I THOUGHT YOU WERE BETTER THAN THIS.

HOW COULD YOU BE SO HEARTLESS? ROBIN IS YOUR COUSIN. YOU HAVE TO HELP HER!

I DON'T HAVE TO HELP HER IF I DON'T WANT TO! IF YOU YELL AT ME AGAIN, I WILL LIE TO HER ABOUT **EVERYTHING**!

COME BACK HERE! *YOU'RE GROUNDED!*

FINE — I DON'T CARE!

I'd never seen a Korean kid disrespect an adult like that.

She was my new family and she hated me.
The anger and helplessness that I felt toward
Ashley brought back a bad memory from my childhood.

1990, Seoul, Korea

YAY, RECESS!

RINGG

Third grade had begun.

HUH, THAT'S WEIRD. MY DRAWING ISN'T THERE.

As days went by, I had a growing suspicion that my new teacher didn't like me.

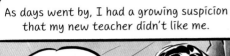

FOR THE LAST TWO YEARS MY ART HAS BEEN UP THERE. WHY DOESN'T MY NEW TEACHER LIKE IT?

When students scored 100 on a test, they got a gold star. One day I scored 100.

YAY, I GOT A GOLD STAR!

HUH? MAYBE THE TEACHER FORGOT MINE?

It was a small reward, but I worked hard for it.

PARDON ME, MS. LEE. YOU FORGOT TO GIVE ME A GOLD STAR....

HOW DARE YOU? AN INSOLENT LITTLE BRAT LIKE YOU DOESN'T DESERVE A GOLD STAR!

NOW SCRAM AND LEARN YOUR PLACE!

I...I'M SORRY.

During classroom cleanup time, my teacher would scold me....

YOUR AREA IS ALWAYS THE MESSIEST!

NOT ALL THIS TRASH IS MINE!

I thought maybe my teacher was being hard on me because she knew I was fatherless.

I AM GOING TO MAKE MY AREA SPOTLESS!

I was determined to prove to her that I was good.

But no matter how hard I tried, Ms. Lee ignored my efforts.

WHO KNOWS THE ANSWER TO THE QUESTION?

...ANYONE?

She always picked me for the worst possible tasks.

EEK!

CHUNA, SOMEONE VOMITED IN THE HALLWAY, GO CLEAN IT UP.

I never complained and always obeyed her.

NOW, GO EMPTY THE TRASH CAN.

YES, MA'AM.

But her behavior toward me only got worse.

Whenever I made a mistake,

YOU TWO, I TOLD YOU TO BE QUIET! CHUNA, COME UP HERE AND HOLD OUT YOUR HANDS.

Ms. Lee punished me more harshly than the others...

THIS IS FOR YOUR DISOBEDIENCE!

WHIP

... and humiliated me in front of the whole class.

SOB

GO STAND OVER THERE WITH YOUR HANDS UP SO EVERYONE CAN SEE WHAT A DISGRACE YOU ARE.

I thought that maybe I really was bad and just needed to work harder.

KEEP YOUR ARMS STRAIGHT AND QUIT CRYING!

Hick

Hick

I kept my ordeals at school a secret from my mom because I was ashamed.

SOMETHING'S WRONG. I'M TAKING YOU TO THE DOCTOR!

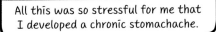

All this was so stressful for me that I developed a chronic stomachache.

The doctor couldn't find the cause of my illness.

MAYBE THE CAUSE IS PSYCHOLOGICAL. IS SHE MAYBE HAVING TROUBLE AT SCHOOL?

Mom took me aside and demanded that I tell her everything.

NOTHING'S GOING ON AT SCHOOL!

WHATEVER IT IS, DON'T BE SCARED. I'LL ALWAYS PROTECT YOU.

YOU WON'T GET MAD AT ME?

NO, OF COURSE NOT.

MOM, MY TEACHER HATES ME AND I DON'T KNOW WHY!

Once the dam was broken, I couldn't hold it in. I told Mom everything.

I expected my mom to scold me for not being a better student.

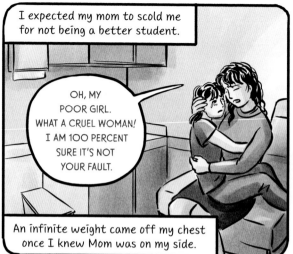

OH, MY POOR GIRL. WHAT A CRUEL WOMAN! I AM 100 PERCENT SURE IT'S NOT YOUR FAULT.

NO MATTER HOW BADLY SHE TREATS YOU, BE STRONG AND STUDY HARD.

An infinite weight came off my chest once I knew Mom was on my side.

Knowing that third grade would end in a few months helped me to get through it.

THIS YEAR WILL FLY BY AND YOU WILL GET A MUCH BETTER TEACHER NEXT YEAR.

I HOPE SO.

And my fourth-grade teacher turned out to be one of the best teachers I'd ever had.

Ashley's spitefulness seemed far more upsetting than that of my third-grade teacher, because she was my new family. This problem wasn't going to go away in a few months.

The only way to be free of her tyranny was to learn English.

Chapter 6
A Ghost of Me

Two months had gone by and I was still friendless at school.

I could barely remember how to start a conversation.

The last time I had talked to someone at school was with Bryan.

HEY, CHING...

NO!

This time, I was ready.

BRYAN, YU AH MEAN. YU BATHEH ME AGAIN, I TELL THE TEACHEH ABOUT YU. OKAY?

I had practiced these sentences at home so I could tell him off without stuttering.

And it worked. He didn't bother me again.

Eventually, the novelty of being the foreigner wore off.

There were several kids at school that I wanted to be friends with.

One of them was Sarah.
She was in my algebra class.

A couple of weeks ago...

HEY, [unintelligible]!

I AM SORRY. WHAT?

WAS THAT [unintelligible]?

AH... I DON'T UNDERSTAND.

ARE YOU DEAF OR SOMETHING?

I couldn't think of a comeback quickly enough.

NO....

SHE'S NOT DEAF.

SHE JUST DOESN'T UNDERSTAND ENGLISH WELL.

WELL, SHE MUST BE STUPID THEN.

SHE JUST MOVED FROM KOREA, YOU IDIOT!

Since then I looked for Sarah and sat near her at lunch.

With each passing day, I hated myself more than the day before.

And there was nothing to comfort me at home. All my cherished things were back in Korea.

I couldn't even cry freely in my room because Mom never knocked before coming in.

CHUNA, IT'S DINNERTIME.

ARE YOU CRYING AGAIN?

NO....

DON'T LIE. YOUR FACE IS ALL RED.

MOM, I CAN'T DO THIS ANYMORE. I WILL NEVER LEARN ENGLISH. I'D RATHER DIE THAN GO BACK TO SCHOOL.

STOP SAYING SUCH FOOLISH THINGS. YOU WILL LEARN ENGLISH SOON.

HOW DO YOU KNOW THAT?

QUIT MOPING AROUND. GO WASH YOUR FACE AND EAT DINNER.

I AM NOT HUNGRY.

FINE THEN. DON'T YOU HAVE HOMEWORK TO DO?

WHAT'S THE POINT OF DOING HOMEWORK?

But I always did my homework anyway.

The old habit of being an overachiever just wouldn't go away.

I stayed up past midnight to finish my homework every night.

I fell asleep exhausted, dreading the morning.

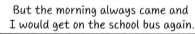

But the morning always came and I would get on the school bus again.

FLOP

NTY PUBLIC SCHOOLS

But once morning came...

...I realized nothing had really changed.

...Or had it?

HEY, IS THAT *SAILOR MOON*?

NO, THIS IS KOREAN. *SAILOR MOON* IS JAPANESE.

COOL! I DRAW CARTOONS TOO.

DO YOU KNOW *PYROCAT*?

I DON'T KNOW THAT ONE. HOW DO YOU KNOW *SAILOR MOON*?

eme ev voor eeon uine eve xem?

AH, SORRY, CAN YOU PLEASE SPEAK MORE SLOWLY?

OH, OKAY. COMIC BOOK STORE. ezuox JAPANESE ee on THERE?

When I couldn't quite figure out what people were saying...

...I often faked it by just nodding to avoid awkwardness.

UM...

emer READ OTHER evere

UH-HUH.

BYE.

BYE.

But I knew I couldn't fool anyone for long.

I saw her a few times again in the hallway.

SHE MUST THINK I AM A WEIRDO AFTER OUR AWKWARD CONVERSATION.

I drew in my notebooks more often at school, hoping that she or someone else would notice me.

But nobody did.

Jaehyun and I were best friends in fourth grade.

We didn't have the same classes again after fourth grade, but we were inseparable all the way into middle school.

Sometime in fifth grade, I noticed Jaehyun looking a bit distant.

HEY!

OH, HEY.

ARE YOU OKAY? YOU SEEM SAD LATELY.

OH...CHUNA. YOU COULD TELL?

I HAVEN'T TOLD ANYONE. BUT... MY PARENTS AREN'T LIVING TOGETHER ANYMORE.

DO YOU THINK IT'S PERMANENT?

I THINK SO.

I'M SO SORRY.

This was the first time I realized that the other kids' families weren't perfect either.

I CAN'T BELIEVE YOU COULD TELL THAT I WAS DEPRESSED.

OF COURSE I CAN TELL. I'M YOUR BEST FRIEND!

YOU'LL BE OKAY.

We didn't discuss our family problems again after that.

At the beginning of summer in eighth grade, Jaehyun moved to a different neighborhood.

I'LL CALL YOU AS SOON AS I GET BACK FROM MY TRIP TO AMERICA!

YOU BETTER!

We were sad that we wouldn't be going to the same school anymore, but we promised to hang out with each other as often as we could.

Jaehyun called me several times during that summer.

WHY ISN'T SHE PICKING UP? DID SOMETHING HAPPEN TO HER?

Finally, she went to my mom's salon and found out that I had moved to Alabama.

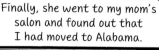
Miss Jung

DO YOU WANT HER ADDRESS IN AMERICA?

It turned out that Jaehyun wasn't the only one to ask about me. When I didn't show up to school, a bunch of my other friends also went to the salon and got my address.

While I was wallowing in my sorrow, my friends in Korea were actually trying to get in touch with me.

One by one, more letters from my friends in Korea started to arrive.

"...That's so cool that you are living in America now! Eat lots of butter so you can roll your Rs..."
— Sunhee

"...The new stationery store opened at the mall. They have a sticker photo booth. Wish you were here..."
— Minkyung

"...I made you a mix tape of my favorite songs. Did you know Taiji Boys came out with a new album?..."
— Jeongwon

"This postcard came with Wink magazine this month. You love Queen's Quest, so I'm sending it to you..."
— Hyunjin

Stay strong and stand tall. I'll do the same in my new school. Miss you! —Jaehyun

Even though my friends weren't with me, knowing that they cared gave me strength.

I got through the school day, dreaming about the letters that would be waiting for me at home.

Reading about my friends' lives in Korea made me miss Korea even more.

페시지엉

노래방

THEIR LIVES SEEM SO FUN. WOULD THEY EVEN BE ABLE TO UNDERSTAND HOW BORING MY LIFE IS NOW?

Making international phone calls was outrageously expensive back then.

I missed talking to my friends, but I just couldn't afford it, so letters would have to do.

Once I mailed out my letters...

... the waiting game began.

First week.

IF MY FRIENDS WRITE BACK RIGHT AWAY, THEIR LETTERS SHOULD ARRIVE HERE BY THE END OF NEXT WEEK.

Second week.

DID THEY GET MY LETTERS? MAYBE THEY GOT LOST IN THE MAIL....

Third week.

MAYBE MY FRIENDS DON'T CARE ABOUT ME ANYMORE.

Fourth week.

MY FRIENDS HAVE FORGOTTEN ABOUT ME. I HAVE NO FRIENDS ANYWHERE!

CHUNA, CALM DOWN. I'M SURE THE LETTERS WILL ARRIVE SOON.

YOU DON'T KNOW WHAT MY FRIENDS ARE THINKING!

YOU'RE TOTALLY OVER-REACTING!

Then the letters started arriving again.

SEE!

Sorry for taking so long....

One day my stepaunt came over to our apartment.

SISTER-IN-LAW, CHUNA HASN'T MADE ANY FRIENDS AT SCHOOL. SHE IS VERY LONELY.

POOR THING! COME TO CHURCH WITH ME. I'LL INTRODUCE YOU TO THE GIRLS THERE.

EEK!

I had stopped going to stepaunt's church after the first week in Alabama because I found it too boring. But saying no now would be rude.

HELLO, ROBIN! MY NAME IS DIANE. YOUR AUNT TOLD ME YOU ARE FROM KOREA? I *enmem* LEARN ABOUT YOUR COUNTRY.

HI. NISU TO MEET YU.

Diane had never met any foreigners before. She was very excited.

WHAT ARE YOU DOING FOR *eeswww*? IT'S TOMORROW! DO YOU WANT TO GO *afzweu* WITH ME?

SORRY ... WHAT?

YOU KNOW, TRICK OR TREAT. ON HALLOWEEN.

OH. HALOWIN! IN KOREA, WE DON'T HAVE IT.

YOU SHOULD COME OVER TO MY HOUSE FOR HALLOWEEN!

October 31, 1995

HOW COOL! I FEEL LIKE I AM IN A FAIRY TALE.

HI, ROBIN!

WELCOME! I'M DIANE'S MOM.

WHERE'S YOUR COSTUME?

HI. WHAT IS ... COSTUME?

WOW, I CAN SEE THE TOP OF HER BOOBS!

I had never seen a girl my age dress so revealing before.

YOU KNOW, LIKE, I'M A DEVIL GIRL! YOU NEED A COSTUME FOR TRICK-OR-TREATING.

OH NO, I DON'T HAVE ANYTHING.

OKAY. I HAVE ~~some~~ COSTUMES. ~~Jesus~~ YOU CAN ~~use~~ ONE.

THANK YOU.

I HOPE IT'S NOT AS REVEALING AS WHAT SHE'S WEARING.

119

YOUR HOUSE IS BEAUTIFUL.

THANKS, SWEETIE. WOULD YOU LIKE SOME *(signs)*?

EEK, I DON'T LIKE AMERICAN SWEETS, BUT IT WOULD BE RUDE TO REFUSE.

AH... THANK YOU.

OH, I LIKE GRAPES!

POP!

YUCK! IS THIS GRAPE ROTTEN? I WANT TO SPIT IT OUT BUT I DON'T WANT TO LOOK RUDE!

GAG

YOU OKAY?

This was my first encounter with olives.

WHAT IS THIS?

THEY ARE OLIVES.

OLIVES?

YEAH. I HATE THEM BUT MOM ALWAYS *(signs)*.

COME! I'LL SHOW YOU THE COSTUMES.

THIS IS MY COSTUME FROM LAST YEAR. YOU LIKE IT?

AHH... WHAT IS IT?

IT'S A PIRATE! YOU KNOW, LIKE *해적이야*.

OH, I KNOW PIRATE!

OH NO, IT'S SHOWING SO MUCH SKIN!

YOU LOOK SO CUTE!

BOTH YOU GIRLS LOOK GREAT!

HAVE FUN!

OKAY, SO WE ARE GOING TO KNOCK ON THE DOOR AND SAY "TRICK OR TREAT."

TREAT OA TREAT.

NO, TRICK OR TREAT.

TRICK OA TRICK

TRICK OR TREAT

TRICK OA TREAT.

OKAY, THAT'S GOOD ENOUGH.

ARE YOU READY?

UH, YES!

WHAT DOES THIS "TRICK OR TREAT" MEAN ANYWAY?

OKAY, HERE WE GO!

TREAT OR TREAT... NO— TRICK OR TREAT. I BETTER NOT MESS THIS UP!

TRICK OR TREAT!

TRICK OA TRICK!

OH, HELLO!

WHAT ARE YOU GUYS?

UM...

I AM A DEVIL GIRL, SHE'S A PIRATE.

HERE YA GO, DEVIL GIRL!

YOU TOO, KONNICHIWA!

I AM NOT JAPANESE, WITCH LADY.

BYE, GIRLS!

THIS IS SO COOL!

YAY — LOOK AT ALL THIS CANDY!

Our first trick-or-treat was a success.

HOW ABOUT THIS HOUSE?

NO, LET'S GO OVER THERE!

NOW TO THAT HOUSE!

SHE DOESN'T EVER ASK ME WHAT I WANT.

Diane talked nonstop. I couldn't keep up with her.

UM... YEAH.

I gave up and just nodded and smiled at whatever she said.

By the end of the night, Diane just talked to herself in a monologue.

...

As we walked back to Diane's house, we fell into an awkward silence. My lack of English was building a wall between us.

I AM NOT IGNORING YOU. I JUST CAN'T UNDERSTAND YOU!

By the time we got back to Diane's house, I was exhausted.

DID YOU GUYS HAVE FUN?

LOOK, MOM! WE GOT SO MUCH CANDY!

I felt bad for Diane being stuck with a boring girl like me on Halloween.

When my mom came to pick me up, I was relieved.

HOW WAS IT?

IT WAS OKAY.

Chapter 7

The Cage

November 1995

My first semester was drawing to an end.

My stepdad had gone to LA in October, and since then, the atmosphere at home grew tenser each day.

YOU SHOULD COME BACK HOME!

WHAT KIND OF MARRIAGE IS THIS? THEY DON'T LIVE TOGETHER AND THEY FIGHT ON THE PHONE EVERY DAY.

I asked Mom once why she had decided to marry him.

Mom told me they had met each other through a mutual friend while he was visiting Korea for work.

He had fallen hard for her but had to go back to Alabama.

From there, he called Mom every day until she finally decided to visit him.

Whatever my stepdad felt for Mom didn't extend to me. He was intimidated by my close relationship with her. We pretty much stayed out of each other's way.

My stepdad had been in the seafood import and export business when he lived in Korea.

When he moved to Alabama, he opened his own fish market.

WE ARE THROWING AWAY MORE FISH THAN WE ARE SELLING. HOW LONG ARE WE GOING TO TAKE THIS LOSS?

THE BUSINESS WILL PICK UP SOON.

Mom wondered if Mr. Kim was savvy enough to run his own business.

DAUGHTER-IN-LAW, IT'S NOT A WIFE'S PLACE TO CRITICIZE HER HUSBAND. HER DUTY IS TO SUPPORT HIM.

Mr. Kim's family was very traditional even though they had been living in America for almost two decades.

I COULD PROBABLY MAKE MORE INCOME CUTTING HAIR THAN DOING THIS.

Mom knew arguing with her in-laws would only create bad blood between them.

Despite Mom and Mr. Kim's efforts, the store went out of business by October.

CHUNA AND I JUST GOT HERE. WHY DON'T WE LOOK FOR NEW WORK HERE?

NO, ALABAMA IS TOO SMALL A POND FOR ME.

Mr. Kim left for LA to seek better opportunities.

After Mr. Kim left, the stepfamily visited us daily to check on how we were doing.

I NOTICED CHUNA GOT A NEW JACKET? DIDN'T SHE HAVE SOMETHING SIMILAR ALREADY?

HOW NOSY SHE IS!

DAUGHTER-IN-LAW, THIS SOUP IS TOO SALTY.

I LEFT KOREA SO I WOULDN'T HAVE TO DEAL WITH THIS KIND OF CRAP!

What really drove Mom nuts was how docile my stepaunt was.

HONEY, I NEED THAT SHIRT IRONED BY TOMORROW.

MY SON IS LOOKING A BIT PALE, WHY DON'T YOU MAKE HIM A SPECIAL HERBAL TEA?

She just came home from working ten hours at her deli.

YES, MOTHER-IN-LAW. I WILL GET ON IT RIGHT AWAY.

LEE'S Hair Salon

OPEN
HIRING!

I NEED TO GET AWAY FROM MY IN-LAWS!

Soon, Mom found a job at a local hair salon.

She bought me a piano with her first paycheck and signed me up for private lessons.

WHAT AN EXPENSIVE PURCHASE! ARE YOU SURE YOUR DAUGHTER REALLY NEEDS THIS?

YES, SHE DOES. I BOUGHT THIS WITH MY OWN HARD-EARNED MONEY, SO BACK OFF!

Mom wanted to learn to play the piano when she was little, but her family didn't approve.

DON'T BE SILLY. WE DON'T HAVE THE MONEY TO SEND A GIRL TO PIANO LESSONS.

WHEN I HAVE A DAUGHTER, I WILL NEVER DENY HER ANYTHING!

Mom as a young girl

When I turned seven, Mom bought me a piano and started sending me to lessons.

My piano teacher

I DON'T THINK SHE IS A NATURAL TALENT.

Unfortunately, I didn't have much talent or the desire to play the piano.

Mom woke me up at seven a.m. and made me practice the piano for an hour before going to school every day, hoping I would improve.

AGAIN!

UGH, I WISH THIS PIANO WOULD BREAK SO I WOULDN'T HAVE TO PRACTICE ANYMORE!

Her persistence paid off. By the time I got to seventh grade, I actually began to like the piano.

OH, I LOVE THIS PART.

WHY CAN'T YOU PLAY BEAUTIFULLY LIKE SO-AND-SO'S DAUGHTER?

Even then, I only liked to play the piano alone, without anyone to judge me.

When we left for America, starting piano lessons again was the last thing on my mind.

LOOK WHAT I GOT YOU!

But to Mom, continuing my piano lessons was the proof she needed that she hadn't failed me by leaving Korea.

Even though it wasn't something I asked for, I did enjoy playing the piano.

HEY, THAT SOUNDS GREAT. CHUNA! PLAY FOR YOUR AUNT FROM THE BEGINNING.

Mom asked Miss Jung to send me my old sheet music from Korea. When I played the familiar melodies, I felt at peace.

Mom would drag me out to perform in front of the stepfamily whenever possible.

MOM, I DON'T WANT TO PLAY IN FRONT OF PEOPLE.

DON'T BE SO SHY! SIT AND PLAY.

I absolutely hated playing in front of the stepfamily.

I would get so nervous and make a lot more mistakes than usual.

WHY CAN'T YOU JUST PLAY THE WAY YOU WERE PLAYING BEFORE?

I would often end up in tears.

UGH, SHE IS SO THIN-SKINNED!

The day of the competition snuck up on me in no time.

THE NEXT CONTESTANT IS ...

ROBIN HA.

Even though I'd practiced a lot for it, I didn't feel ready.

The judges terrified me.

But what terrified me even more was my mom, who was watching me intently.

GOOD LUCK, MY DAUGHTER!

Sigh

My piece was Chopin's Fantaisie-Impromptu. It was a hard piece to play, but I loved the score.

WOW....

Before I knew it, it was over.

OH MY GOD, I DID IT!

And I hadn't made a single mistake.

GREAT JOB. CONGRATULATIONS!

I won third place, beating both of my stepcousins.

I hoped this would put an end to Mom dragging me out in front of the stepfamily to play the piano.

But my mom wasn't done with me yet.

MOM, PLEASE, I REALLY DON'T WANT TO.

CHUNA, PLAY THAT PIECE YOU PLAYED IN THE COMPETITION FOR YOUR STEP-GRANDMOTHER!

DON'T BE RUDE TO YOUR GRANDMA. SIT AND PLAY THE SONG NOW!

STOP SIGHING LIKE SOMEONE JUST DIED.

WHAT'S WRONG? YOU PLAYED SO WELL AT THE COMPETITION.

DON'T PLAY LIKE A WOODEN DOLL. PUT MORE EMOTION INTO IT.

WHY DON'T YOU PLAY IT THEN?

WHAT A DISRESPECTFUL BRAT!

I TOLD YOU I DIDN'T WANT TO PLAY IN FRONT OF PEOPLE!

Chapter 8

The Leap of Faith

My mom had always been confident in her decisions. But in Alabama, doubts started to set in.

She thought she had run far away from her past.

Now she realized she was doomed to repeat it.

HOW DID IT COME TO THIS?

My mom's life seemed destined to be a turbulent one. Both of her parents had passed away when she was a teenager.

She met my biological father in her mid-twenties. My father was more than ten years older than her and already divorced twice with kids.

But they fell in love quickly.

Mom and my father were both adventurous. They traveled together from coast to coast. They seemed perfect for each other.

Then about three years later...

I AM PREGNANT.

It's considered scandalous to have a baby without being married in Korea.

DON'T WORRY, HONEY. LET'S GET MARRIED!

Mom loved my father enough to want to have a baby with him.

WHY DON'T WE HAVE THE BABY FIRST AND THEN PLAN THE WEDDING?

But something made her hesitate about getting married.

My father was handsome, full of swagger, and the life of the party.

He was a great boyfriend.

But Mom wondered how great he would be as a father and a husband.

As Mom's belly got bigger, my father came home late more often.

Two weeks earlier than Mom's expected due date . . .

OH NO, ALREADY!

140

My father wasn't there when I was born.

Mom's best friend was there instead.

Two weeks later...

MS. SHIN, YOU CAN'T COME IN HERE ALL THE TIME. WE'RE TAKING GOOD CARE OF YOUR BABY.

CLICK

I was put in an incubator because I was underweight, and she was frightened that I was too fragile for her to handle.

Mom had borrowed my father's camera to take hundreds of photos of me, not to miss a moment.

I JUST CAN'T STOP LOOKING AT HER.

KRRIK

OH, THE FILM RAN OUT.

HI, MISS PARK, IT'S ME. CAN I SPEAK TO MR. HA?

...DO YOU KNOW WHERE HE'S GONE?

...WHEN WILL HE BE BACK?...

...COULD YOU TELL HIM TO BRING ME SOME FRUIT AND FILM FOR THE CAMERA?...

...THANKS. BYE.

WHERE IS HE? HE MUST BE OFF WORK BY NOW.

FORGET IT!

SLAM

WAA—!

OH NO!

Next morning...

Mom went to pick up the photos that she had dropped off the week before.

AWW~

1986, Jeju Island

HORSEY!

A few years after my parents split, Mom met Mr. An and they dated for about ten years. I have more memories of Mr. An than of my father.

Although he didn't live with us, Mr. An, Mom, and I went on many weekend trips together.

CHUNA, BE CAREFUL.

He loved me like his own daughter. We seemed like a perfect family.

DO YOU WANT TO RIDE WITH YOUR DAD?

But I was my mom's daughter and no one else's.

HE'S NOT MY DAD. I'LL RIDE WITH MY MOM.

147

That night...

HONEY, YOU DONE IN THE BATHROOM?

YES, GO AHEAD.

CHUNA, LISTEN. YOU SHOULD CALL MR. AN DADDY WHEN WE'RE TOGETHER.

WHY?

DON'T ASK ME WHY. JUST DO AS I SAY.

OKAY. MOM, I REALLY WANT A HORSE.

WHEN YOU GROW UP AND MOVE TO THE COUNTRYSIDE, YOU CAN HAVE A HORSE.

WHY NOT NOW?

BECAUSE WE LIVE IN SEOUL, WE DON'T HAVE THE SPACE FOR A HORSE.

MY GIRL REALLY LOVED THE HORSE RIDE, DIDN'T YOU? NEXT TIME, RIDE WITH ME, OKAY?

I had no idea how Korean society viewed people like us when I was little.

OKAY, MR. AN... DADDY.

But it didn't take long before I figured it out.

Once I opened my eyes, I saw the judgment and prejudice everywhere.

YOU SHAMED US ALL BY HAVING AN ILLEGITIMATE CHILD. WHAT A DISGRACE!

HOW COULD YOU DO THIS TO OUR FAMILY?

HE SAID HE WAS GOING TO MARRY ME.

TAKE THAT ABOMINATION AND GET OUT!

PLEASE HAVE MERCY! HE'S YOUR GRANDSON. WE HAVE NOWHERE ELSE TO GO!

WAA!

I DIDN'T RAISE A SLUT! YOU ARE NO CHILD OF MINE....

BEEP!

I especially couldn't stand how single mothers were portrayed in the media.

They were always either evil mistresses or helpless victims—

nothing like my mom.

In Korea, it is common for single mothers to be disowned by their family.

YOU'RE A BAD EXAMPLE TO MY CHILDREN.

My mom didn't keep in touch with most of her relatives.

Single mothers also have a hard time finding jobs because they are thought to be untrustworthy.

Mom had to be incredibly strong and savvy to have her own business, because our survival depended on it.

But no matter how hard Mom worked, she couldn't change how society viewed her.

CONGRATULATIONS ON OPENING YOUR SALON!

WE WISH YOU PROSPERITY!

HOW DID SHE GET THE MONEY FOR ALL THIS?

THERE'S NO WAY SHE COULD'VE DONE ALL THIS BY HERSELF.

SHE MUST BE SOME RICH GUY'S MISTRESS.

1990, the first parent-teacher meeting of third grade.

WHERE'S CHUNA'S DAD?

HE IS WORKING OVERSEAS, SO HE COULDN'T MAKE IT TO THIS MEETING.

I SEE.

HOW'S CHUNA DOING IN CLASS?

SHE'S VERY BRIGHT, ALTHOUGH...

WHAT IS IT?

IT SEEMS LIKE SHE DOESN'T GO TO CHURCH?

I DIDN'T WANT TO FORCE HER TO GO.

GIRLS AT HER AGE ABSOLUTELY NEED TO GO TO CHURCH TO LEARN RIGHT FROM WRONG.

OKAY, I WILL ASK HER IF SHE WANTS TO GO. SO EVERYTHING ELSE IS FINE?

YES.

THANKS FOR YOUR TIME. IT WAS NICE MEETING YOU.

AHEM ... MS. SHIN, AREN'T YOU FORGETTING SOMETHING?

I'M SORRY?

YOU REALLY DON'T KNOW WHAT I AM TALKING ABOUT?

ALL THE OTHER PARENTS ARE SMART ENOUGH TO BRING A TOKEN OF GRATITUDE FOR THEIR KID'S TEACHERS. YOU DIDN'T BRING ANYTHING?

NO, I DIDN'T BRING ANYTHING.

REMEMBER TO PREPARE BETTER FOR OUR NEXT MEETING IF YOU CARE ABOUT YOUR DAUGHTER'S EDUCATION.

EXCUSE ME.

HOW DISRESPECTFUL!

I HAVE NEVER BROUGHT AN ENVELOPE TO ANY OF CHUNA'S PREVIOUS TEACHERS AND I NEVER WILL, SO DON'T HOLD YOUR BREATH.

No one openly talked about this bribery tradition in Korea, but many teachers expected and accepted bribes from parents.

After that, my teacher made it her mission to make my life miserable to teach Mom a lesson.

WHAT'S WRONG?

MOM, MY STOMACH HURTS.

MY TEACHER HATES ME AND I DON'T KNOW WHY!

It boiled my mom's blood to see me suffer.

Mom thought about reporting my teacher to the school board, but she knew already that it would be futile because everyone turned a blind eye to the bribery.

153

But she still refused to bring the envelope to my teacher.

In the early nineties, Hollywood's greatest hits were the movies about the American dream.

In these movies, Mom saw a glimpse of the life she wanted to have.

American people seemed to be free to follow their hearts.

FORREST!

JENNY!

And they were judged by what they did rather than where they came from.

WELCOME TO *GOOD MORNING ENGLISH!*

Mom started to take English lessons.

And where there was a will, there was a way.

When Mom decided to move to America, she couldn't bring me with her as my legal guardian.

ARE YOU SURE ABOUT THIS? YOU AND CHUNA DON'T EVEN SPEAK ENGLISH.

When a child is born, it is a Korean custom to register the child under the father's family.

But there is no law for child support in Korea. My father didn't help Mom at all financially and he rarely visited.

I'VE ALREADY MADE UP MY MIND. SO DON'T WASTE YOUR TIME AND JUST SIGN THE PAPER.

Yet he held more custody rights than my mother did.

So my mom had to ask my father to let her "adopt" me under her sole guardianship.

Ugh!

YOU DON'T KNOW WHAT AMERICA IS LIKE! YOU MIGHT BE PUTTING OUR DAUGHTER IN DANGER BY BRINGING HER TO A FOREIGN COUNTRY!

WHAT DO YOU KNOW ABOUT WHAT'S BEST FOR OUR DAUGHTER? IF WE STAY HERE, ARE YOU GOING TO START SUPPORTING HER?

WHATEVER AMERICA IS LIKE, IT'LL BE BETTER THAN RAISING HER HERE. LET US GO.

Chapter 9

Comics to the Rescue!

After our fight, Mom and I hadn't spoken in over a week.

IT'S ALREADY 7:30?!

MOM DOESN'T EVEN WAKE ME UP ANYMORE.

Buung~

I thought she'd given up on me.

Even reading my beloved comics didn't cheer me up anymore.

One of my favorite parts of *Queen's Quest* was when Eshika has been banished from her kingdom.

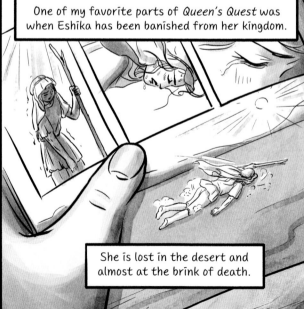

She is lost in the desert and almost at the brink of death.

살아있군!

마쩌...

Then suddenly she gets rescued by a handsome nomad boy who later becomes her love interest.

THINGS LIKE THIS NEVER HAPPEN IN REAL LIFE. NOBODY IS COMING TO RESCUE ME!

BULLSHIT!

I wished I would die.

Then one day...

KNOCK KNOCK

GET UP, I WANT TO TAKE YOU SOMEWHERE.

...WHERE?

JUST GET DRESSED. YOU'LL SEE.

IS SHE TRYING TO GET RID OF ME?

We drove for about an hour.

WHERE ARE WE?

We arrived at a strip mall in the middle of nowhere.

WAIT... COMICS? NO WAY!

I had never seen a comic book store in Alabama before. I didn't think such a thing existed.

In my excitement I had forgotten how mad I was at my mom.

OH MY GOD, MOM, HOW DID YOU FIND THIS PLACE?!

I WAS DRIVING BY AND SAW IT.

The store was full of American superhero comics. Then I saw something I hadn't excepted to see.

IS THIS WHAT I THINK IT IS?!

I found Japanese comics that I used to read in Korea.

YES!

The nineteen nineties were the beginning of the manga* boom in America.

HEY, CHUNA. COME OVER HERE.

LOOK, THEY HAVE COMICS CLASSES FOR KIDS.

IT'S STARTING IN A FEW MINUTES.

DO YOU WANT TO GO?

I had never taken a comic book class before.

GULP

The prospect of meeting these fellow aspiring cartoonists was both exciting and intimidating.

YES!

The comics teacher introduced me to the class.

No one spoke to me other than a quick hello.

HERE'S SOME PAPER AND A PENCIL. DRAW ANYTHING YOU LIKE FOR TEN MINUTES.

THANK YOU.

I CAN'T THINK OF ANYTHING TO DRAW... I GUESS I WILL JUST DRAW ESHIKA UNTIL SOMETHING COMES UP.

EVERYONE LOOKS SO SERIOUS!

It seemed like all the students knew each other already.

I was dying to meet these kids, but I didn't know how to start a conversation with them.

OKAY, EVERYONE, PENCILS DOWN. LET'S SEE YOUR WORK. WHO WANTS TO GO FIRST?

Ready To Show off!

I had always been the kid who drew the best in class.

Then...

I'LL GO.

One by one the students showed their work.

I was in for a rude awakening.

HA HA HA HA

EVERYONE IS SO TALENTED HERE!

These kids were already creating full comics with their own original characters and stories.

I'VE FINISHED THE SECOND *ones* AND *other* IT OUT.

WE SELL STUDENTS' COMICS AT THE STORE. IF YOU FINISH *comer,* WE'LL SELL IT AND YOU MAKE MONEY!

THAT'S COOL!

I'VE NEVER SOLD MY COMICS BEFORE. THESE KIDS ARE PROFESSIONALS!

HE'S EVEN GOOD AT DRAWING BUILDINGS AND CARS. I CAN ONLY DRAW PEOPLE.

ROBIN, DO YOU WANT TO SHOW US YOUR WORK?

Up until then, I'd only concentrated on drawing characters, never comic strips.

UM ... THIS IS A CHARACTER FROM MY FAVORITE COMIC BOOK.

MY DOODLES LOOK SO AMATEURISH COMPARED TO THEIRS.

Silence

I CAN'T TELL IF THEY LIKE IT OR HATE IT.

THANKS, ROBIN. TODAY WE ARE GOING TO LEARN ABOUT . . .

The teacher showed us various comics and talked about panel sizes and other things that I couldn't quite understand.

Then he gave us an assignment to work on.

AH . . . HI! I LIKE YOUR COMICS.

MAYBE HE DOESN'T LIKE ME FOR SOME REASON.

. . . THANKS.

HEY!

For the first time in months, I had something to look forward to.

I was fired up to improve my comics skills after seeing how good the other kids were.

CHUNA, DINNER'S READY!

COMING!

HOW WAS IT?

IT WAS AWESOME! I CAN'T WAIT TILL THE NEXT CLASS!

CHUNA, THE FOOD IS GETTING COLD.

OKAY, OKAY!

Ten minutes later...

GOTTA FINISH DRAWING THAT BUILDING!

Three hours later...

I'VE ONLY FINISHED HALF A PAGE AND IT'S ALREADY MIDNIGHT!

A month later...

The students had warmed to me and I was no longer scared to talk to them.

And I made my first American best friend.

Jessica was half-Japanese, and she was two years older than me. She spoke fluent Japanese and was a fan of many of the Japanese comics I used to read back in Korea.

We had so many things to talk about, from comics, art, and music, to swapping tips on new drawing tools. It was much easier to talk to Jessica because of our mutual interests.

HAVE YOU READ THIS?

OH, YES! IT'S VERY POPULAR IN KOREA. I REALLY LIKE IT.

THIS ARTIST DRAWS ANOTHER COMIC, *RG VEDA**...

YES, THEY MADE IT INTO ANIME*! I'M GONNA ASK MY GRANDPA TO SEND IT TO ME.

An hour of class never seemed like enough for us.

OKAY, GIRLS, CLASS IS OVER.

ALREADY?

DO YOU WANT TO COME OVER TO MY HOUSE ON SATURDAY AND WATCH ANIME?

That Saturday...

MOM, THIS IS ROBIN.

WELCOME, ROBIN. I'M MITSUKO.

HELLO.

WOW, SHE SOUNDS SO ELEGANT!

OH MY GOD, THAT'S SO COOL!

YEAH, THE NEXT EPISODE IS EVEN BETTER.

It was much more fun drawing comics with Jessica than by myself.

We drew fan art of each other's characters.

Jessica's character, Nars—drawn by me.

My character, Ariel—drawn by Jessica.

When I was with Jessica, I felt like myself.

YAY! I FINISHED THE LAST PAGE!

CAST #One AHEMEE

I spent many weekends from winter to spring at Jessica's house. And my English improved tremendously.

ROBIN, YOUR MOM'S HERE TO PICK YOU UP.

AWW, ALREADY?

SEE YOU AT CLASS, ROBIN.

I MISS YOU ALREADY, JESSICA!

My friendship with Jessica gave me so much confidence in myself...

HI, SARAH.

CAN I SIT WITH YOU?

... that I was finally able to do what I'd never had the courage to do before.

SURE, ROBIN.

GUYS, THIS IS ROBIN. SHE'S IN MY ALGEBRA CLASS. SHE'S FROM KOREA.

HI, ROBIN. I'M TARA.

HI, TARA.

HI. I'M CHRIS. NICE TO MEET YOU.

CHITTER CHATTER

NICE TO MEET YOU TOO, CHRIS.

Chapter 10

Time to Say goodbye

While I was busy drawing comics and hanging out with Jessica ...

I TOLD YOU I DON'T WANT TO MOVE TO LA!

...the rift between Mom and the stepfamily was getting deeper.

Stepdad called Mom every day.

CHUNA IS FINALLY GETTING USED TO LIVING HERE.

The pressure from the stepfamily grew unbearable.

HOW COULD YOU LEAVE YOUR HUSBAND ALL BY HIMSELF ACROSS THE COUNTRY?

YOU NEED TO GO HELP HIM NOW.

LEAVE CHUNA AND LENA TO ME. I'LL TAKE GOOD CARE OF THEM WHILE YOU'RE GONE.

... BUT LA IS TOO DANGEROUS A PLACE TO RAISE TWO TEENAGE GIRLS.

The 1992 LA riots had been covered by the Korean media extensively and the images of violence were still fresh in Mom's mind.

Mom was skeptical, but she couldn't continue to refuse.

I NEED TO SEE FOR MYSELF IF LA IS A GOOD PLACE FOR US.

WHAT, AGAIN?! I AM FINALLY GETTING USED TO ALABAMA....

NOTHING IS SET IN STONE. WE'LL DISCUSS IT WHEN I GET BACK.

In March of 1996, Mom left for LA.

DON'T WORRY. EVERYTHING WILL BE OKAY.

I had never been without Mom before. The longest I had been apart from her was for a few days on school field trips in elementary school.

RAAAH!

HAHA

KYAH!

I HOPE MOM WON'T STAY THERE FOR TOO LONG.

I felt anxious about being left alone in this strange place.

My stepaunt took good care of Lena and me while Mom was gone.

She packed our lunches and fixed us dinners. She drove us to all our after-school activities.

Lena and I spent a lot of time at the aunt's house.

HE TOTALLY LIKES YOU!

YEAH, TOTALLY.

I could understand the stepkids' conversations much better now.

TODLY... I KEEP HEARING THIS WORD.

YOU SHOULD TOTALLY GO OUT WITH HIM!

WHAT'S "TODLY"?

YOU MEAN TOTALLY?

YEAH, COULD YOU SPELL IT FOR ME?

T-O-T-A-L-L-Y.

OHHHH, TOTALLY!! I GET IT NOW.

SHE'S BEEN *eaves drop* ON US.

SO? IT DOESN'T MATTER.

But I still felt like I would never be as close to Lena and the stepcousins as they were to each other.

197

If Lena was worried about our family problems, she didn't show it.

HE SENT ME HIS PHOTO, AND HE LOOKS EVEN TALLER THAN I REMEMBER.

MAYBE HE GREW SINCE YOU LEFT.

She seemed occupied with a budding romance with a boy who she knew back in Korea.

He called her every night and they talked on the phone for hours.

HA HA HA
OPPA~♡

I GOT YOU THE SUMMER SHOES YOU ASKED FOR.

OH, BUT I WANTED THEM IN BLACK.

GRANDMA, WHERE'S MINE?

Grandma never bought me anything.

I wished I didn't have to compare myself to Lena all the time.

HOW DID I BECOME SUCH A JEALOUS PERSON? I HATE BEING LIKE THIS!

I took refuge in Barry's company.

BARRY, IT'S GETTING WARM! YOU LOOK LIKE YOU NEED A BATH!

BARK!

Slurp.

MOM'S GONNA BE BACK SOON, RIGHT?

...OR IS SHE? WHAT IF SHE NEVER COMES BACK?

After a week without Mom, I realized...

WHEREVER MOM DECIDES TO GO, I NEED TO BE WITH HER.

Meanwhile in LA...

Mr. Kim was ready to show Mom how great life in LA could be.

He hoped to dazzle her with all the glitz that the city had to offer.

Mom was impressed at first.

But it didn't take long for her to see the reality.

Mr. Kim was living in a poor neighborhood in a rented room.

HOW ARE WE GOING TO RAISE TWO GIRLS HERE?

WE CAN LOOK FOR A NEW HOUSE TOGETHER.

THE RENT FOR THIS TINY PLACE IS THREE TIMES AS MUCH AS FOR OUR APARTMENT IN ALABAMA.

WHAT ABOUT THIS APARTMENT?

THERE ARE NO GOOD PUBLIC SCHOOLS AROUND HERE.

MAYBE WE CAN OPEN A DELI HERE.

WHY CAN'T WE DO THAT IN ALABAMA?

PLEASE, LET'S GO BACK. THERE'S NOTHING FOR US HERE.

I AM NOT GOING BACK TO ALABAMA. GIVE ME SOME TIME, I CAN MAKE IT HERE.

Mom didn't see hope in Mr. Kim's eyes. She only saw how desperate and lost he was.

I DON'T KNOW WHAT YOU THINK YOU'RE CHASING HERE, BUT YOU'RE ONLY RUNNING AWAY FROM REALITY.

Two weeks later, Mom flew back to Alabama.

181

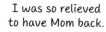

I was so relieved to have Mom back.

But the stepfamily wasn't happy.

WHY DID YOU COME BACK SO SOON?

BECAUSE HE HAS NO FUTURE IN LA. HE'S ONLY DIGGING HIMSELF DEEPER INTO DEBT.

A MAN CAN ACHIEVE WONDERS WITH THE HELP OF HIS NURTURING WIFE.

WE CAN TAKE CARE OF THE GIRLS HERE. YOU SHOULD GO BACK AND BE WITH YOUR HUSBAND.

DON'T EXPECT ME TO LEAVE MY DAUGHTER BEHIND. I AM HER MOTHER.

I LET HIM MARRY YOU EVEN THOUGH YOU WERE A SINGLE MOTHER BECAUSE YOU'VE DONE SO WELL FOR YOURSELF IN KOREA. WHY CAN'T YOU HELP MY SON LIKE THAT?

BUHUUH

YOU'RE GONNA PAY FOR THE PAIN YOU'VE CAUSE MY SON AND OUR FAMILY!

THIS IS CRAZY. THERE'S NO WAY TO REASON WITH THEM.

WE'RE RUNNING OUT OF PATIENCE WITH YOU.

I NEED TO TALK TO MY DAUGHTER AND HAVE SOME TIME TO THINK.

A few days after Mom got back, Mom and I watched a full moon eclipse for the first time.

LOOK, IT'S STARTING!

Shhh.....

WOW, THAT'S AMAZING!

MOM, WHAT'S GOING TO HAPPEN TO US? ARE WE MOVING TO LA?

Shh...

NO, THIS MARRIAGE IS OVER.

WHAT? THEN... ARE WE GOING BACK TO KOREA?

CAN I AT LEAST TELL JESSICA? AND A FEW FRIENDS IN SCHOOL...?

YOU CAN TELL JESSICA, BUT WE MUST BE DISCREET.

I didn't like the fact that we were leaving in secret but I knew Mom wouldn't change her mind.

I wondered, what was Virginia like?

I WAS JUST STARTING TO GET TO KNOW THESE KIDS.

I'd been having lunch with Sarah, Tara, and Chris for a couple of months now.

And I had developed a crush on Chris.

HOW'S YOUR DAY GOING, ROBIN?

I would blush and stutter so much when he spoke to me...

I... IT WAS... IT'S OKAY.

...that I'd avoid eye contact so I wouldn't have to talk to him for long.

I often daydreamed about telling him some clever joke and making him laugh...

...the way Sarah made him laugh with her jokes.

It was clear that Chris and Sarah were more than just friends. I knew there would've been no chance for me even if I spoke perfect English.

Still, I would miss my new friends.

I wished I had more time with them.

UM...I HAVE SOMETHING TO TELL YOU GUYS.

I told them that I'd be moving to LA just in case word got out to the stepcousins.

I just wanted to have a chance to say goodbye to them properly.

But I told Jessica the truth. I really didn't want to lose our friendship.

Suddenly, Virginia seemed like a much more exciting place.

I wondered if I would miss the stepfamily.

IF I STAYED HERE, I'D BE GOING TO THE SAME HIGH SCHOOL AS GRACE AND LENA.

Grace seemed to have a good head on her shoulders. Maybe I would have become closer to her.

BUT LENA AND ASHLEY? PROBABLY NOT.

HEY, BARRY!

THAT'S WEIRD. HE USUALLY GETS SO EXCITED WHEN I COME OUT.

BARRY, ARE YOU SLEEPING?

Barry died of unknown causes.

I THINK HE HAD A HEART ATTACK.

MY GOODNESS, HE'S HEAVY.

POOR BARRY.

HE PROBABLY DIED OF LONELINESS.

WE'LL MISS YOU, BARRY.

YOU GUYS NEVER PLAYED WITH HIM WHEN HE WAS ALIVE.

I LOVE YOU, BARRY.

I was more relieved than sad for him.

REST IN PEACE, BARRY. YOU'RE FREE NOW.

Last day of school...

I learned a new American tradition.

Many other kids' yearbooks came and went. I signed about a dozen yearbooks by the end of the day.

Hey, Robin! I am sorry that you have to move. I have moved 7 times before and I know how hard it is. Good luck in LA. Meet some movie stars too. It was great knowing you. I will miss you next year!

Chris

Robin,

I am so glad that we became friends this year. We had fun together! I wish you didn't have to leave because I will miss you a whole lot! I just hope you make a bunch of special friends where you move to — just please don't forget me. You have improved so much in your English and I'm very, very proud of you. Write to me!

Love ya lots, Sarah

Robin,

It has been a joy to have you in my class. I know this year has been both wonderful and terrible for you. You are so full of life and have so much talent — and you have a kind sweet personality — and you always make me laugh. I wish you much success in life — please keep in touch.

Yours, Mrs. Halls

Only a few months ago, I would have done anything to leave this place.

192

Chapter 11

The Purge

Shortly after the end of school, Lena left for LA to see her mother.

Lena's mother had been begging Lena to come live with her in LA all year.

We never shared a proper goodbye.

But it seemed like she had moved to LA and wouldn't be coming back to Alabama.

Now that only my mom and I were left, we started packing up our things...

... and hiding them in my room in case the stepfamily visited us unexpectedly.

MOM, IS THIS REALLY NECESSARY? NO ONE'S GONNA FIND OUT THAT WE ARE MOVING.

SHHHH!

I KNOW THE IN-LAWS WILL TRY TO STOP US. THE LESS WE HAVE TO DEAL WITH THEM, THE BETTER!

YOU'RE SO PARANOID!

You would think she was planning an escape from a high-security prison.

D day: June 21, 1996

Mom came home with two movers and a U-Haul truck.

HURRY, PLEASE.

Except for the piano, we barely had anything to fill even half the truck.

COME ON, LET'S GO!

I'LL PROBABLY NEVER COME BACK HERE.

BUT I WON'T MISS THIS PLACE ONE BIT.

Mom didn't want anyone seeing our U-Haul truck.

So she drove the truck to her coworker's house in another town.

The plan was to stay there for the night and leave at dawn the next morning.

Although I understood Mom's anxiety, I was mad at her for putting me through this.

THANKS SO MUCH FOR LETTING US STAY HERE.

THIS IS MY DAUGHTER, CHUNA.

COME ON IN!

WHY DO WE HAVE TO HIDE HERE LIKE CRIMINALS?

I HAVE WORKED SO HARD TO GET HERE —I CAN'T GO BACK TO KOREA LIKE THIS!

I WISH THINGS WEREN'T THIS WAY. BUT THEY ARE GIVING ME NO CHOICE.

NO.

THINGS ARE THIS WAY BECAUSE **YOU** MADE THEM THIS WAY!

I WAS JUST REBUILDING MY LIFE IN ALABAMA AND YOU TOOK IT AWAY FROM ME AGAIN.

WHY CAN'T WE JUST LIVE LIKE NORMAL PEOPLE?

I...

I AM SORRY, CHUNA.

This was probably the first time Mom had apologized to me in my entire life.

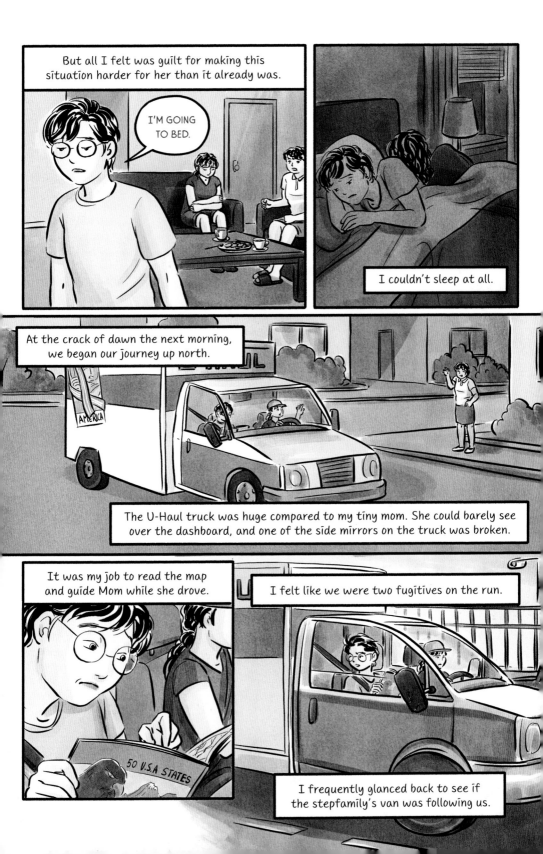

OH NO!

WE KNEW WHAT YOU WERE UP TO ALL ALONG!

YOU THOUGHT YOU COULD JUST RUN AWAY RIGHT UNDER OUR NOSES?

Wee Wee

THIS IS THE POLICE. STOP YOUR TRUCK AND SHOW YOUR ID.

U HAUL

AMERICA

MOM, WHAT ARE YOU DOING? SLOW DOWN!!

VRRRRR

AHHH

CHUNA, WAKE UP. WE'VE JUST PASSED THE BORDER OF GEORGIA.

THANK GOD THAT WAS JUST A DREAM.

Mom didn't show even a hint of fear or weakness, venturing out in this giant country on her own.

I NEED YOU TO LOOK UP THE NEXT TURN ON THE MAP.

I realized it was time for me to stop acting like a selfish child.

OKAY, HOLD ON.

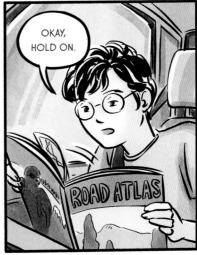

ROAD ATLAS

I wanted to be strong for her.

WE HAVE TO TURN LEFT ONTO GA-140 E.

OKAY. TEN MORE HOURS TO GO!

No matter how we ended up on this road, I was proud to have a mother like her.

We were together and finally free to pursue our own American dream.

Chapter 12
Sweet Home Virginia

MOM,
WE MADE IT!

We moved into a two-bedroom apartment
next to our new city's Koreatown.

Mom found a job at a Korean hair salon that
agreed to sponsor her to get a green card.

I stayed home most of the
summer lying around...

... and writing letters to Jessica.

I'll come visit you
next month and
we can go to the
anime convention
together....

...Yes! You can
stay with me as
long as you want!

Jessica finally came for a visit and we went to our first anime convention. Everywhere I looked there were comics and people who loved comics. It was like heaven for us.

I felt right at home.

JESSICA, WE NEED TO COME HERE EVERY YEAR!

I'M RIGHT THERE WITH YOU!

I had no idea that so many people in America liked the same comics as I did.

After the convention, Jessica went back to Alabama.

I was sad to see her go, but I knew we would continue to be friends, no matter how far apart we lived.

Soon, summer was over. It was time for me to start high school in McLean, Virginia.

The difference between my middle school in Alabama and this high school was noticeable at first glance.

EVERYONE'S SO GROWN-UP AND STYLISH.

The school was full of international students because it was near Washington, DC, and many embassy families lived in McLean.

Nobody looked at me funny for being Asian.

I DON'T STICK OUT HERE.

HI, EVERYONE. MY NAME IS DR. ZHENG. I'M YOUR MATH TEACHER.

I even had a few Asian teachers.

I was placed in the regular ninth-grade classes, including band and art.

And I took a placement test for ESL and was enrolled in a level-two class.

It was amazing to see a class of only foreign students.

Back in Alabama, I had been the only one in the entire school.

EVERYONE, PLEASE INTRODUCE YOURSELVES AND TELL US WHERE YOU'RE FROM.

MY NAME IS MEIFEUNG. I AM FROM BEIJING, CHINA.

HI. I AM MUHAMMAD. I AM FROM SAUDI ARABIA.

I AM FATIMA, FROM EGYPT.

HI. MY NAME IS JOSÉ. I AM FROM COLOMBIA.

HI. I'M YUMI, FROM JAPAN.

MY NAME IS AMADI. I'M FROM ETHIOPIA.

WOW, EVERYONE HAS DIFFERENT ACCENTS!

HI. MY NAME IS CHUNA, BUT YOU CAN CALL ME ROBIN. I AM FROM KOREA.

I felt like a mutant teenager from X-Men who had finally found Xavier's School for Gifted Youngsters.

I BELONG HERE.

I NEVER MET ANYONE FROM EGYPT BEFORE. HOW DO YOU SAY "HI" IN EGYPTIAN?

AHLAN. HOW DO YOU SAY IT IN KOREAN?

ANNYEONG.

ANNYEONG! ARE YOU FROM NORTH OR SOUTH KOREA?

I AM FROM SEOUL, SOUTH KOREA.

Meeting these kids was my first experience with different cultures from all around the world.

Despite our broken English, we somehow became fast friends.

We were in the same boat, trying to learn English and getting used to living in this strange land.

짠식, 연락하라고 했잖아*.

IS THAT KOREAN THAT I'M HEARING?!

Northern Virginia had the second largest Korean immigrant community on the East Coast.

오빠도 참~*.

There seemed to be at least several dozen Korean immigrant kids in McLean High School.

They usually hung out in big groups at the library.

It shocked me to see how different they were from the Korean kids back home.

Every Korean girl seemed to be dressed up in the latest fashion from Korea.

I LOOK LIKE A COUNTRY BUMPKIN COMPARED TO THEM.

Even some of the boys had dyed hair and wore earrings, which wasn't allowed in Korea.

I felt even more intimidated by them than by the American kids in school.

*I told you to call me.
*Oh Brother—

210

And they never seemed to notice me.

THEY PROBABLY THINK I'M NOT COOL ENOUGH TO HANG OUT WITH THEM.

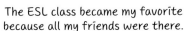
The ESL class became my favorite because all my friends were there.

HI, ROBIN.

HEY, YUMI! HERE'S YOUR *AMURO NAMIE** CD BACK.

And we loved to swap music and videos from each other's countries.

ROBIN, DO YOU KNOW ANY NEW KOREAN DRAMAS TO WATCH?

I DON'T REALLY KNOW KOREAN DRAMAS, BUT I CAN LEND YOU KOREAN COMICS!

CHI...

CHATTER-CHATT...

I WROTE DAVID A LETTER AND PUT IT IN HIS LOCKER, BUT HE IS STILL IGNORING ME.

MEIFEUNG, I HEARD HE IS A PLAYER. FORGET ABOUT HIM.

We ate lunch together every day.

The memories of eating lunch alone seemed like a lifetime away.

WHO'S YOUR CRUSH, ROBIN?

AH ... I DON'T HAVE ONE.

COME ON, TELL US!

HA HA HA

I really wanted to make Korean friends, but I didn't know how to approach them.

SHHH!

WHAT'S HER PROBLEM?

WHATEVER.

Despite feeling embarrassed, I eavesdropped on them sometimes.

It was like every Korean kid knew each other.

YOU KNOW JIWON FROM OAKTON? SHE'S DATING DAVID NOW.

NO WAY! SHE GOES TO MY CHURCH!

HOW DID THEY MEET? DIDN'T DAVID JUST BREAK UP WITH SARAH KANG?

YOU KNOW HIM—HE'S A PLAYER.

And their lives seemed much more exciting than mine.

YOUNGMIN'S HAVING A BIRTHDAY PARTY AT CAFE NOIR TONIGHT, YOU COMING?

I DON'T KNOW, MY MOM'S BEEN SO STRICT SINCE SHE FOUND OUT THAT I AM GOING OUT WITH PETER.

COME ON, YOU CAN TELL HER YOU'RE STUDYING WITH ME.

Then one day...

Brrrr~!

FIRE DRILL?

EVERYONE LINE UP AGAINST THE WALL AND WAIT FOR FURTHER INSTRUCTIONS.

DO YOU KNOW IF THIS IS JUST A DRILL OR WHAT?

IT'S ONE OF THE KOREAN GIRLS!

WHY IS SHE SPEAKING TO ME IN ENGLISH? DON'T I LOOK KOREAN?

잘 모르겠는데*.

OH, YOU'RE KOREAN? I'VE SEEN YOU AROUND AND THOUGHT YOU WERE JAPANESE OR CHINESE!

REALLY? WHY?

I DON'T KNOW. MAYBE BECAUSE OF THE WAY YOU DRESS? HEY, SOYOUNG, SHE'S KOREAN!

NO WAY! HOW COME YOU NEVER HANG OUT WITH KOREANS?

I JUST NEVER GOT A CHANCE TO TALK TO ANY OF YOU GUYS.

WHAT MIDDLE SCHOOL DID YOU GO TO?

I DIDN'T GO TO MIDDLE SCHOOL HERE. I JUST MOVED FROM ALABAMA.

ALABAMA! HOW DID YOU END UP THERE?

*I don't know.

213

AH... IT'S A LONG STORY.

I AM MINJI, BY THE WAY.

I AM SOYOUNG.

I AM ROBIN. NICE TO MEET YOU.

ROBIN? WHAT'S YOUR KOREAN NAME?

AH...

Suddenly all the bad childhood memories of my Korean name came flooding back to me.

FALSE ALARM, GUYS. GO BACK TO YOUR CLASSROOM.

COME TO THE LIBRARY DURING BREAK, I'LL INTRODUCE YOU TO EVERYONE.

YEAH, EVERYONE THOUGHT YOU WERE NOT KOREAN.

HA HA, REALLY? OKAY.

WOW, THOSE GIRLS ARE SO MUCH NICER THAN I THOUGHT!

SEE YA!

SEE YOU SOON!

Through Soyoung and Minji, I got to know most of the Korean kids in my high school.

DID YOU WATCH H.O.T.'S* NEW MUSIC VIDEO?

YES! OH MY GOD, KANGTA* LOOKS SO COOL!

WHO'S H.O.T.?

WHAT?! YOU DON'T KNOW H.O.T.? ARE YOU REALLY KOREAN?

I wished some of them would be into Korean comics, but they were mostly into K-pop and drama, which I wasn't interested in.

A lot had changed in Korean pop culture since I had been living in Alabama.

I HAVE THE LAST EPISODE OF *KAYO TOP TEN*. COME OVER TO MY HOUSE LATER. I'LL SHOW YOU.

THANKS, JENNY *EONNI!*

I started hanging out with many Korean kids, but I still liked Soyoung and Minji the best.

WE SHOULD GO TO KARAOKE SOMETIME WHEN YOU'VE MASTERED THE K-POP CHART!

Soyoung was in my year, and she had moved to Virginia the same time I moved to Alabama.

Minji was a year below Soyoung and me, and she'd grown up in the States since she was a little girl. She spoke perfect Korean and English.

EONNI, YOU'VE GOT SOME MOVES!

Soyoung and Minji were both goofy and down-to-earth, and we always made each other laugh.

216

Epilogue:

Motherland Vs. Homeland

In June of 2002, I visited Korea with Minji and Soyoung. It was my first time visiting since I left Korea.

THANKS FOR LETTING ME STAY WITH YOU.

OF COURSE! YOU'RE LIKE A DAUGHTER TO US!

I was a sophomore in college. I stayed with Soyoung's family in Gangnam*.

The first thing we did after arriving in Seoul was go for Korean BBQ.

It was one of the best meals of my life.

Every day, Soyoung, Minji, and I explored the city together.

WHAT A PRETTY STREET! I LOVE THESE OLD HOUSES!

I visited the neighborhood I grew up in.

서울도시 학원

금산 ⑩ 서적

I FEEL LIKE A TOURIST IN MY OWN NEIGHBORHOOD.

All of my favorite corner stores and street vendors were gone, and fancy malls and high-rise apartments lined the streets.

I met up with my old friends from middle school who I had kept in touch with.

CHUNA!

JAEHYUN! SUNHEE, JEONGWON, MINKYUNG, IS THAT YOU?

The city wasn't the only thing that had changed.

WOW, LOOK AT US, ALL GROWN UP!

BUT WE ALL STILL ACT THE SAME!

HA HA HA

IT'S SO GOOD TO SEE YOU GUYS!

GUNBAE!

THIS IS MY FAVORITE MAKGEOLLI!* JOINT.

WHAT ARE YOU GUYS MAJORING IN IN COLLEGE?

ACCOUNTING.

EDUCATION.

MEDICINE. WHAT ABOUT YOU?

ART.

I KNEW IT!

WHAT DO YOU THINK OUR LIVES ARE GONNA BE LIKE IN ANOTHER SEVEN YEARS?

YEAH, ME TOO.

I'LL PROBABLY WORK FOR A COUPLE YEARS, THEN GET MARRIED AND HAVE BABIES.

REALLY? DO YOU WANT TO GET MARRIED THAT EARLY?

TWENTY-EIGHT ISN'T THAT YOUNG. IF YOU'RE OVER THIRTY AND NOT MARRIED, PEOPLE PITY YOU.

NO GUY WOULD DATE A WOMAN OVER THIRTY. THEY ASSUME SOMETHING IS WRONG WITH YOU.

Sigh

YET GUYS OVER THIRTY HAVE NO PROBLEM GETTING A GIRL.

THERE ARE SO MANY OTHER THINGS I WANT TO DO RATHER THAN RAISING CHILDREN BEFORE I AM THIRTY.

YOU HAVE THAT LUXURY 'CAUSE YOU LIVE IN AMERICA.

Soon I realized my old friends and I didn't have much in common anymore.

I WILL PROBABLY HAVE TO MARRY A DOCTOR SINCE MY DAD IS A DOCTOR. HE WOULDN'T ACCEPT ANYONE ELSE.

And I could tell that our lives would only become more different in the future.

Korea was hosting the 2002 World Cup, and the entire country was in a festive mood.

ROBIN, MINJI, SOYOUNG! THIS IS LIKE A HIGH SCHOOL REUNION!

JENNY EONNI!

Many of our other high school Korean friends from Virginia were also visiting Korea. We all met up to watch the soccer game together.

The World Cup game was broadcast on several building-sized televisions in the middle of Seoul.

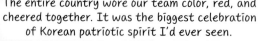

Our team played so well. We went all the way to the semifinals.

The entire country wore our team color, red, and cheered together. It was the biggest celebration of Korean patriotic spirit I'd ever seen.

I AM SO PROUD TO BE KOREAN!

ME TOO!

I had never been a sports fan, but the passion everyone felt for our team and country was infectious.

The nightlife in Seoul dazzled me. I had never experienced this side of Seoul before.

I met a lot of new Korean people by going to bars to watch the game.

YOU'RE FROM AMERICA, AREN'T YOU?

ME? YES, HOW DID YOU KNOW?

I had no accent when I spoke Korean.

I COULD TELL BY HOW WILD YOU ARE.

WILD! WHAT DO YOU MEAN?

Then I noticed that most Korean girls would act demure in front of guys, especially older guys.

Even the Korean girls I knew from the States would fit themselves into this mold when they were in Korea.

JENNY, MY GLASS IS EMPTY.

YES, OPPA*.

WHAT THE HECK!

I'd known about these unspoken gender rules when I was growing up in Korea.

ROBIN, MY GLASS IS EMPTY....

YOU'VE GOT HANDS. POUR IT YOURSELF.

I began to see why my mom had wanted to leave Korea.

A month flew by.

DING DONG

OUCH, EXCUSE YOU!

The World Cup had ended and the nightlife started to lose its charm.

I was also bothered by the emphasis on physical beauty and conformity in Korean society.

I WONDER HOW MANY PEOPLE HERE HAVE HAD PLASTIC SURGERY.

I was an American art student after all. I had been taught to value individuality.

SHE IS IN PROGRESS....

SHE'S PROBABLY DONE HER EYES, MAYBE THE NOSE TOO.

HER JAW IS TOO NARROW, THAT CAN'T BE NATURAL.

OH, HE'S DEFINITELY HAD HIS NOSE DONE.

DOES ANYONE HAVE THEIR ORIGINAL FACE ANYMORE?

SOYOUNG, I'M HOME....

WHAT HAPPENED?

I GOT MY NOSE DONE. I CAN'T GO OUT FOR A WEEK.

225

Glossary

Amuro Namie: Japanese pop star from the 1990s. Think the Britney Spears of Japan.

Anime: Japanese animated TV series and films

Bungeoppang (붕어빵): Korean street snack of waffles filled with sweet red-bean paste. It is shaped like a fish, which is where its name comes from: Bungeo (fish) ppang (bread).

Eonni (언니): Term for a female to call her older female relatives or older female friends

Gangnam (강남): A district in Seoul. Yes, the same one from popular K-pop song "Gangnam Style," by Psy.

Gomujul (고무줄): Korean version of jumping rope

Hagwon (학원): Cram school in South Korea. These for-profit institutes can provide supplementary education outside of regular school education. They can also specialize in sports, music, and art for extracurricular activities.

H.O.T.: A Korean boy band from the mid 1990s. Think NSYNC of Korea.

Hotteok (호떡): Korean street food of fried yeasty bread with various fillings. Most common fillings are brown sugar with crushed nuts or sweet potato noodles.

Kangta (강타): The most popular member of H.O.T.

Kayo Top Ten (가요톱10): The most influential K-pop chart-ranking show from the 1980s through the '90s

Kimchi (김치): Korean fermented vegetable side dish. Most common vegetables used are napa cabbage and daikon radish.

Makgeolli (막걸리): Traditional Korean rice wine

Manga: Japanese comics

Motnani Doeji (못난이돼지): Means "ugly pig." It was the name of our favorite restaurant, which specialized in grilled pork belly.

Oppa (오빠): A term for a female to call her older male relatives or older male friends

Patbingsu (팥빙수): Korean summer treat of shaved ice topped with sweet red beans, rice cake, fruits, and condensed milk

RG Veda: A fantasy comic series by CLAMP, an all-female Japanese cartoonists' group. It was first published in Japan in 1989 as CLAMP's debut. The plot is based on Vedic mythology contained in the Rigveda.

Sailor Moon: A popular Japanese comic series by Naoko Takeuchi. It was later adapted into an animated TV series and became one of the first Japanese comics to break into the American market, in the mid-1990s.

Tteokbokki (떡볶이): Korean street food made with rice cake, fish cake, and boiled egg, cooked in Korean red pepper sauce

Tteokkochi (떡꼬치): Fried rice cake skewers

Twigim (튀김): Korean street food that is battered and fried. Most commonly made with squid legs, assorted vegetables, or potato.

Acknowledgments

For most of my life, I never truly understood why Mom had uprooted our lives in Korea and caused us so much pain by moving to America. Our lives in Korea didn't seem that bad at all. Mom was a successful business owner and I was doing well in school. Whenever I asked Mom why, she would give me the most nonchalant answers like: "America is a better country than Korea." Or, "There are so many golf courses in America that I want to play on." Mom is an avid golfer, to the point that she wants her ashes to be spread on her favorite golf courses all over the world. But still, these answers just didn't cut it for me. If I pressed her further, she'd clam up and say, "We are doing well in America now, so what's the matter? You're making me tired. Leave me alone!"

So, you can only imagine how thrilled Mom was when I finally told her I had been working on this memoir for over a year and found a publisher for it. After realizing there was no turning back on this project, Mom insisted that I at least leave her out of my story completely. I told her that would be impossible. She was the driving force behind it. If she hadn't wanted me to write this story, she shouldn't have brought me to America in the first place. Mom was so upset with me that she avoided me for months.

My desire to make this book overpowered my guilt about causing Mom anxiety. I pushed on, chasing her down to talk to me. Exasperated, Mom asked, "Why this story? Couldn't you just make up some story to draw comics?"

I told her this was my way of understanding why things happened the way they did. What happened when I was fourteen changed my life forever, and I wanted to write about it. I wanted people to read it and feel understood if they were experiencing the depression and isolation I did when I moved to Alabama. And if Mom wanted to have a say in how she was portrayed in it, she'd better start answering my questions seriously. (These weren't really fighting words. Only the truth.)

Mom stopped insisting I take her out of my story, but she still would give me only glib answers when I asked her about the past. Through numerous painful conversations, I convinced her that I was not going to portray her in any kind of demonizing, hurtful ways. And I promised to show her the manuscript before it was published.

Finally, Mom started telling me great stories about her past—things I didn't know about or didn't remember much about. The more I talked to her, the clearer it became to me that Mom is a much more interesting character than I am. To borrow from Mary Karr, one of my favorite memoirists, why would I make up a story when my own family is already so interesting?

To write a truthful memoir, I knew I had to write about things that Mom would be uncomfortable with. I feared it might damage my relationship with her and wondered if my effort in writing this memoir was even worth it. But whenever I tried to retreat from it, this project would come back to haunt me. I just had to see it through. When I finished inking and lettering all the pages, I gave a copy of the manuscript to Mom. A few days later, she gave it back to me with a note that began with "Great Job!" followed by a couple of minor factual edits. Like the stoic Korean mother she is, she didn't say much else, but I knew she was proud of it.

I am so grateful that she loves me enough to overcome her fear of being exposed. Writing a memoir is like wearing your heart on your sleeve for the whole world to see. And in my case, I was dangling my mom's heart along with my own. Writing this memoir was the hardest thing I've done in my life, apart from moving to America when I was fourteen. I can't say I'd do it again, but it healed me and made me understand and respect my mother a lot more. And I hope Mom finds more peace with her past by reading it, too. For that, I am glad to have done it.

This book wouldn't have been possible without the help of three great women: I thank Cassie, my mom; Samantha, my agent; and Alessandra, my editor, for giving me the chance to deliver this book to the real world.

I would also like to thank my comics community—including the members of DrawBridge and Hypothetical Island in Gowanus, Brooklyn, and the artists at Atlantic Center for the Arts residency #155 and #163—for encouraging me to continue on this project whenever I faltered.